Sue Johnson is a published poet, short story writer and novelist. Her first novel 'Fable's Fortune' was published by Indigo Dreams Publishing in 2011. She is a Writers' News Home Study Tutor and also offers her own brand of writing classes.

Sue has also published a collection of booklets and two non-fiction books on writing. Further details can be found on her website – www.writers-toolkit.co.uk

THE YELLOW SILK DRESS

SUE JOHNSON

Indigo Dreams Publishing

First Edition: The Yellow Silk Dress

First published in Great Britain in 2015 by:
Indigo Dreams Publishing Ltd
24 Forest Houses
Cookworthy Moor
Halwill
Beaworthy
EX21 5UU
UK
www.indigodreams.co.uk

Sue Johnson has asserted her right under the Copyright, Designs and Patents Act 1988 to be identified as the author of this work.
©2015 Sue Johnson

ISBN 978-1-909357-39-6

A CIP record for this book is available from the British Library.
All rights reserved. No part of this publication may be reproduced, stored in a retrieval system, or transmitted at any time or by any means, electronic, mechanical, photocopying, recording or otherwise without the prior permission of the copyright holder.

This book is a work of fiction and, except in the case of historical fact, any resemblance to actual persons, living or dead, is purely coincidental.

Designed and typeset in Minion Pro by Indigo Dreams.
Cover design by Ronnie Goodyer at Indigo Dreams
Printed and bound in Great Britain by 4edge Ltd
www.4edge.co.uk
Papers used by Indigo Dreams are recyclable products made from wood grown in sustainable forests following the guidance of the Forest Stewardship Council

For Roger Bloss and Diana Challen –
the best brother and sister-in-law on the planet.

With thanks to Ronnie Goodyer and Dawn Bauling for their continued support and encouragement.

Also to the Literary Ladies Wot Lunch group, my Number 8 students and to Lynda Dunwell, Lesley Eames and Val Andrews for keeping me focused and providing loads of inspiration, as well as wine, tea and chocolate.

Special thanks to my partner Bob Woodroofe for just being there.

THE YELLOW SILK DRESS

ONE

London 2000

It all started on a sweltering Monday in early July. Rod Milligan, one of the producers, stumbled on some archive material about the early seventies and the news headlines about a beautiful actress using a stolen identity. Masquerading as Mitzi Shapiro, she'd caused a scene in the Café Royal after being auditioned for the leading role in a Hollywood blockbuster called 'Dragonflies'. She got the part and 'Dragonflies' was a raging success but afterwards the mysterious actress never made another appearance on screen.

"She was some lady," said Rod pushing his sunglasses onto his forehead and wincing as he took a gulp of black coffee. Judging by the redness of his eyes, he'd had a heavy night. "It kind of got me thinking about where is she now? She wasn't that old then – seventeen – eighteen maybe. So what happened to her? She's not the sort of person you'd imagine fading into the background and playing Scrabble or knitting sweaters for the rest of her life."

We sat round the table waiting while he drank his coffee, wondering where the axe was going to fall, watching as he finished his last few mouthfuls and then flung the Styrofoam cup towards the waste bin in the corner of the room. It missed, spattering the cream wall with coffee grounds, but nobody went to pick it up, least of all Rod. He was a 'move on, never admit you've made a mistake' kind of guy.

The air conditioning in what was called the 'training room' wasn't working and the stuffy air could've been cut with a knife. I glanced enviously out of the window at the girls walking past in butterfly-bright summer clothes, oblivious of us trapped behind the one-way glass.

Rod leaned forward and looked around the table. I felt uneasy and started doodling on my notepad. It was always *dangerous to make eye contact in these situations. I wouldn't have sat opposite him intentionally, but I was late as usual and it was the only free seat.*

"It's got me thinking about making another of those 'where are they now' programmes," he said. His finger moved slowly like a roulette wheel at the end of its circuit and ended up pointing at me. "You – Sabrina – bring me some ideas and a storyboard by three o'clock Friday."

'Bastard,' I thought, 'he knows I'm going away for the weekend because he signed my holiday form.'

Everyone else melted away like early morning mist, no doubt heaving sighs of relief that he hadn't picked on them, leaving the two of us alone in the room with its overpowering smells of stale perspiration and bitter coffee left bubbling too long.

I sat there staring at the flower doodles on my pad thinking 'why me'? Was it just because, at nearly forty-three, I was the oldest member of the team and I sensed he was looking for any excuse to get rid of me? Rod must've sensed my frustration because I heard him rummaging through a folder.

"You can have these. They might give you a start." He sounded smug, as if he knew he'd given me an impossible task, and like an angler reeling in a large fish, all he had to do was wait until I flopped into his landing net.

I took the faded brown envelope from him and stuffed it into my patchwork leather bag with my notebook and mobile phone. I felt as if I was wearing lead boots as I walked slowly to the door. I knew without turning round that his eyes were on me all the way.

I went back to my office, glad that it was lunchtime and everyone else had gone out into the sunshine so I could open the envelope in private without everyone asking a load of questions as to why I'd been chosen for the job. In any case, if I was going to achieve anything by Friday I'd have to get my skates on.

I opened the envelope and laid the photos on my desk. As

I did so, the old feelings of inferiority, of being second best, flooded my mind. The black and white stills were of a young girl with a rippling waterfall of hair spilling over her bare shoulders. In the first few, she was storming through a gaggle of reporters, scattering microphones and notebooks, flinging items of her clothing to right and left as she went – a fringed shawl, a tiara and a jewelled bag.

There was one close up shot of her with luminous eyes full of tears. Looking at that picture aroused feelings of jealousy and frustration that had festered below the surface of my life for thirty years.

She'd changed her name, of course, but then so had I – a pathetic attempt on my part to reinvent myself. I'd not realised you see, that the process needs to be done from the inside out. It's the same for people who have cosmetic surgery. No matter how you dress up the outside, no matter what label you put on yourself, the change needs to go right through like the lettering on a stick of rock. I wondered what new disguise 'Mitzi' had adopted in later years, and if she was happy with the life she'd chosen. Did she ever look back at these same photos and wonder 'what if...?'

I cast my mind back wondering how I'd managed to miss this incident when it happened. After all, it had obviously made headline news. Then the years rolled back and I remembered what had happened and why I'd missed the news reports.

At the time of the Café Royal incident, I was on a whirlwind romance with Georges in Paris with all the drama of an unplanned pregnancy that followed the glitter and the magic.

I looked at the photos again, resisting the urge to tear them into tiny pieces and stamp on them. Once upon a time we were at school together. She was plain Kelly Smith then – Smelly Kelly from the rough side of town. I remembered how my friends and I had nudged each other and tittered when she'd turned up for the auditions for 'Romeo and Juliet', feeling certain that she never stood a chance.

"Can't see her as Juliet can you?" asked my friend Anne as

we tidied our hair in the girls' toilets before the auditions. She spat on her tablet of mascara. "You'll walk it, Susan. And guess who's already been picked for Romeo? Couldn't be better, could it?"

I'd been in love with Jamie Collins for the last two terms. I'd tried bending over in short skirts and undoing more buttons on my school blouse than was decent, but so far he hadn't responded. I was confident things would change when I heard he was going to play Romeo. After all, when I was playing Juliet, I could suggest extra rehearsals, just the two of us. I had it all planned. In no time at all, he'd be mine.

But I didn't get the part. I'd never felt so humiliated in my life when Kelly got it instead of me. The headmaster, Mr Taylor, had as good as told my Dad who was Chairman of the School Governors that the part was mine. Dad complained big time when I didn't get it and Mr Taylor called a meeting, but that cow Mrs Wilson got her way. She said either Kelly played Juliet or someone else could organise the play. Since there was nobody else prepared to do that, Mr Taylor had to back down.

That was when my life started going wrong - and it was all Kelly's fault.

TWO

Thursday 5th July 1973

Kelly awoke with a thrill of excitement that started as a warm feeling in her stomach and radiated outwards making her fingers and toes tingle. It was the performance of the play tonight. She didn't allow herself to think about what happened after the curtain went down on 'Romeo and Juliet', that today could be the beginning and end of her career as an actress.

Kelly's Gran, Ivy, had always told her she'd be an actress because she'd been born on 2nd February – the same day as Nell Gwyn. Ivy had grown up in London and told Kelly endless stories about the theatres she'd worked in and the plays she'd watched. Kelly also liked the stories about Nell Gwyn, almost feeling that she could smell oranges and spices as Gran was talking.

As Kelly had believed in Ivy, Ivy had believed in Kelly.

"You'll do it, Kelly. You'll be a great actress one day. Now put on that green shawl – the one I wore in 'Pygmalion' and pretend you're a rich woman fallen on hard times asking for a favour …"

And Gran would criticise and show Kelly how to do it better and then they'd have tea together – bacon sandwiches or toasted crumpets and chocolate éclairs before Kelly walked home, her head spiralling with dreams for the future.

They talked about taking a trip to London together and visiting all the special places they'd talked about like St Martin-in-the-Fields and the Theatre Royal in Drury Lane that was said to be the most haunted theatre in the world.

That trip had never materialised because Ivy died just before Kelly's eleventh birthday. Even seeing her grandmother looking small and frail in the hospital bed, surrounded by the antiseptic smell she'd always hated, her face as white as the pillows, Kelly never imagined that she'd go home that night and never see her again.

"I love you Kelly. Don't forget your dream," Ivy said. "Remember me when you're a famous actress."

"You'll be there watching me, Gran," said Kelly, but Ivy had got tearful and turned her face to the pale green wall.

Later that night, the ward sister telephoned to say that Ivy had passed away just after midnight.

Kelly had loved Ivy's stories about her early life in London – the museums and galleries she'd visited, the people she'd met and the parts she'd played when she'd been an actress. The one thing she hadn't talked about was why she'd given up that life and moved to North Cornwall.

Even Kelly's Mum wasn't prepared to talk about her childhood and the reasons why they'd left London. "We all have skeletons in the cupboard," she'd told Kelly. "What's done is done. She's gone now, so just forget about it, it doesn't matter."

"Did you ever go to the theatre with her?" Kelly wanted to know. "You know, when she was an actress?"

Viv had given a harsh laugh and dragged on her ever-present cigarette. "That's all pie in the sky, Kelly. You don't want to believe everything people tell you – not even your Gran. As far as I know, the nearest she got to treading the boards was doing the cleaning at the local flea pit when we were kids."

But Kelly had gone on believing the stories she'd been told. After all, if you were just a cleaner in a cinema, you wouldn't know how to recite whole chunks of Shakespeare with the sort of feeling that made whoever listened believe the story and be drawn into the magic.

As she woke up and stretched that July morning, Kelly felt the familiar shaft of sadness when she remembered that Gran wouldn't be there to watch her first proper performance as an actress

The happy feeling evaporated completely when the smell of burnt toast drifted up the stairs accompanied by the sound of her Mum and Mick arguing about whose turn it was to pay for the shopping, and then the sound of Mick, no doubt clad in his usual low-slung pyjama bottoms and string vest, clumping back up the narrow staircase in a temper and the creak of the springs as he settled back into bed for the morning.

Kelly got out of bed, her bare feet feeling for the matted sheepskin rug as she pulled on her pink towelling dressing gown. Even in summer, her room, which overlooked the overgrown postage-stamp front garden, was cold. The clothes in her wardrobe felt damp and she'd taken to leaving the doors open to stop mildew forming.

'*When I'm a famous actress,*' Kelly thought as she went along the narrow landing to the bathroom, '*I'll have a house that feels warm. I'll have a bathroom with a heated towel rail and a proper mirror, and no more cheap shampoo and watery bubble bath from the corner shop.*' She turned on the hot tap and a trickle of tepid water oozed into the grubby white basin. A stray hair – one of Mick's greasy black ones - lay across a fragment of cracked pink soap. The threadbare green towel had been left on the side of the bath and felt damp.

She squinted at her reflection in Mick's greasy shaving mirror, deciding that she'd wait until she got to school before she put on her make-up. The light was better in the girls' toilets and it was best not to give her Mum anything else to moan about before she left this morning. She washed quickly, wincing at the feel of the damp towel and sprayed on deodorant and Gingham perfume.

Back in her bedroom, she put on her school uniform – white blouse, grey skirt, striped green and black tie. She brushed her waist length auburn hair and deftly plaited it without needing to look in the mirror, so that it hung like an arrow straight down her back, securing the end with a piece of yellow ribbon – her favourite colour.

She packed the little black china cat her Gran once gave

her for luck into the bottom of her school bag. She'd already decided that she wouldn't come home between the end of school and the start of the performance. After all, it wasn't as if her Mum was going to be there to watch her. She'd already made known what she thought about Kelly's 'arty-farty' ideas. Kelly felt a twinge of sadness that she'd be the only member of the cast who hadn't got a parent there to watch her.

Another reason for not coming home was so that her Mum couldn't arrange something for her to do without asking her like looking after her sister Miranda's kids or babysitting for one of the neighbours.

Viv, wearing blue denim jeans and a purple v-necked jumper was chain-smoking as she read yesterday's 'Daily Sketch' – passed on by the lady next door. Her bleached blonde hair was short and spiky and her eyelashes so heavy with mascara Kelly sometimes wondered how she kept her eyes open.

She grunted as Kelly came into the kitchen, slopped a dash of milk into a pink mug and topped it up with strong tea from the chipped brown teapot. She pushed the mug across the sticky plastic cloth to Kelly who was eyeing two charred pieces of toast on a plate next to the tub of margarine and the dregs of a jar of marmalade.

"Eat your breakfast," said Viv, not lifting her eyes from an article about a new miracle diet.

Kelly pulled a face. Burnt toast was one thing she couldn't stand. Why was it that their house always smelled of it? Other people's houses smelled of nice things like soap powder and cakes cooking. Hers always smelled of bleach and burnt toast.

"Just give it a scrape - fussy cow!"

Kelly ignored her and went across to the pantry. There was the usual faint smell of gas when she opened the door. There was a box of Cornflakes standing next to a tin of beans, a tin of peaches and a packet of oxtail soup.

Kelly didn't particularly like Cornflakes either, but they'd be better than burnt toast – if there was any milk left.

"It's empty. Mick finished them last night." Viv's voice was muffled because she was putting on her lipstick.

"What's the point in leaving an empty box in the cupboard?"

"Come and eat this toast. That's all there is. You can pick up some shopping after school. I've made a list."

"Mu-um," Kelly dragged the word out, "it's the play tonight. I told you – I'm playing Juliet. I'm staying at school to help Mrs Wilson, remember?"

The last bit wasn't true, but Kelly knew her Mum wouldn't bother to check up.

"Don't expect me to remember crap like that." Viv was zipping up her white leather handbag and sorting out her keys. "I suppose I'll have to get the bloody shopping then – as usual."

She stormed out, slamming the back door, not bothering to wish Kelly good luck for the performance.

After she'd gone, Kelly searched the rest of the cupboards for something edible, wondering why it was that their shopping was done on such a hand-to-mouth basis. She'd listen, fascinated to the girls at school talking about how their mums bottled fruit or made cakes and biscuits. She couldn't remember Viv ever making anything apart from chips.

Her search yielded a few soggy Ryvitas stuffed behind the tea caddy, left over from when Viv was last on a diet, and a packet of ready salted crisps crammed behind the bread bin that were probably part of Mick's secret stash.

Kelly put the crisps in her bag and the Ryvitas in the bin just as Mick lumbered into the kitchen. He glared at Kelly, bleary eyed, his body in its string vest and pyjama bottoms reminding her of a slab of lard in a net shopping bag.

"Encha got the kettle on, girl?"

Kelly sighed and lit the gas under the kettle. It was easier to just do it rather than argue.

"What was all the shouting between you and yer Mum just now?" he asked. "Yer woke me up makin' that bleedin' racket."

If that wasn't the pot calling the kettle black, thought Kelly, heading towards the door before he could get too close or pretend to give her some 'fatherly advice.' She wasn't in the mood for his so-called friendly gestures this morning. She hated the way he squeezed her arm as if testing bread for freshness, his fingers a little closer to her bust than was comfortable. She'd tried suggesting to Viv that he keep his distance, but this had only resulted in another row, with Viv calling Kelly a liar and a trouble-maker.

Mick peered at the burnt toast.

"Cor, yer've burnt this 'aven't you Kelly? I wouldn't give that to a dog."

"Mum did it," said Kelly, edging her way towards the door just as Mick opened the pantry door and found the empty Cornflake box.

"Fancy puttin' an empty box back," he said, flinging it down on the floor. "Yer better get some on the way home from school."

Kelly always found it infuriating that it was never suggested that Mick should go and restock the pantry. He'd never had a job as far as Kelly could remember unless you counted a couple of hours collecting glasses in 'The Three Tuns' – the sleazy pub on the main road – on a Friday and Saturday night. Most of his days were spent lying in bed or watching the telly. He never cleaned, tidied or washed anything or attempted to do anything with the garden. Kelly was certain that the Cornflake box would still be there when she got home after the performance – unless Viv could be bothered to pick it up.

"Sorry. Got to go," said Kelly grabbing her school bag, wrenching open the back door and stepping out, the soles of the leather thong sandals they weren't supposed to wear at school slapping on the concrete slabs. She turned her grey skirt over at the top as she walked until it reached halfway down her thighs. She was wary of doing this before she left the house in case Mick thought she was giving him a "come on" signal.

She hurried along the shared passageway between their house and Mrs Harrison's, careful not to catch her clothes on the rampant wild roses and brambles on their side. Their back garden was the only one in the row of eight that didn't have a neat tidy vegetable patch. A small area of the scrubby lawn had been cleared of brambles so that Viv could sunbathe. It was surrounded by convolvulus and smelled of cats but Viv didn't seem to bother as she lay on a blanket in her black mock-leather bikini and sunglasses.

Mrs Harrison kept giving them bags of runner beans and cabbage that Viv had no interest in cooking and that Mick wouldn't eat if she did. They stayed in the bottom of the vegetable basket until they went yellow and dry and were eventually thrown away.

Kelly turned left out of their road and into the narrow lane that led to the crossroads where many years ago a gibbet stood and criminals were hanged and their bodies left suspended for crows to peck.

As always, Kelly was drawn to the sunken lane straight ahead that led to Tredannoc Bay with its single street of small shops and cafes, shingle beach and tiny fishing harbour. The sunken lane was rumoured to be haunted by a young man dressed in old-fashioned clothes who was said to have been captured for stealing a sheep and hanged at the crossroads.

Kelly and her friends had gone ghost hunting on many occasions but had never seen anything more than a fox or a badger. Jane Cooper in her class claimed to have seen a ghostly shadow when she'd been walking there one dark winter's night. This had led to a chorus of questions as to what she was doing there – and who was she with.

This morning, all thoughts of ghosts were banished by the brightness of the sun filtering through the trees. The drystone walls were covered with foxgloves and pink campion. Kelly wished she could head for her favourite place on the cliffs overlooking the bay and sit and sketch until it was time for the performance. The only thing that kept her heading towards school was the thought of not wanting to let Mrs Wilson down – especially after all she'd done to make sure Kelly got the part of Juliet.

With a sigh, Kelly turned left and headed towards Tredannoc High School, passing the turning towards the Blue Anchor Business Park where Viv put in regular shifts at the biscuit factory that had replaced the fish processing works as the main employer in Tredannoc. The single storey brick building down on the quayside that was once the fish canning factory was now a craft centre where a man and his wife made sculptures and decorated mirrors from junk washed up on the beach and painted pictures of mermaids.

Kelly didn't want to think about the biscuit factory. Opportunities for school leavers in Tredannoc were few and far between. Some of the lads would be helping their Dads on their fishing boats or taking tourists on boat trips round the headland to see the seals. Most of the girls, like Kelly, were destined to end up working in the biscuit factory or the pickle factory – also on the Business Park - where you came home every day reeking of onions and vinegar.

For the last six months, Viv had talked about little else but Kelly starting work and bringing some money into the house. She'd not bothered to turn up for the last parents' evening and hadn't answered the letter Mrs Wilson had sent home suggesting that Kelly could go a long way with art and drama and that she should think seriously about doing a course at the college in Launceston.

"You can forget those airy-fairy ideas, we can't afford for you to go swanning about like Lady Muck." Viv had tossed the letter into the bin with the remains of their fish and chips, shutting the door on Kelly's hopes for the future.

Early morning traffic heading towards Penzance and the south streamed past Kelly. She wondered what it would be like to work somewhere like Penzance or Truro. Some kids from her class – like Susan Baker and Jamie Collins – had apprenticeships waiting for them in London when they left school and Kelly's heart twisted with envy.

Tredannoc High School was a purpose-built school, with big glass windows that made it difficult to sneak out when you weren't supposed to.

A gaggle of girls were chatting on the far side of the playground and Kelly could see Susan Baker at the centre of them holding court.

"She's turned up," said one of Susan's friends loudly, gesturing towards Kelly, as if they'd been taking bets as to whether she would or not.

"Take no notice," said Kelly's friend Jess falling into step beside her. "They're not worth it." She looked at Kelly, her dark eyes just visible under her long straight fringe. "Are you nervous?"

"A bit," said Kelly.

"They say it's a good thing," said Jess, who'd been involved in painting the scenery. She offered Kelly a sherbet lemon as they went towards the coat pegs. "I still say it's a real shame your Mum won't think about drama school for you."

"Can't afford it," said Kelly.

"Hasn't she seen you act?"

Kelly shook her head.

"She'll have a surprise tonight then."

Kelly didn't say anything.

"Kelly... she is coming isn't she?"

"She's working," said Kelly shortly. "But don't tell anyone..." She bit her lip, thinking to herself that Viv could've come if she'd really put herself out. If Miranda needed her kids looking after then Viv would've been there like a shot.

"'Course not," said Jess as they headed toward their classroom for registration.

Jane Wilson, the Head of English, had spent a restless night with images of Romeo and Juliet replaying endlessly inside her head every time she closed her eyes. She was relieved to see Kelly arrive at school this morning. She'd had nightmares that Kelly's dreadful mother was going to find some excuse to keep her at home today and that she'd have to eat humble pie and ask Susan Baker to act as understudy.

"You never know with a mother like Kelly's," she'd said to her husband. "The fact that Kelly's got a leading part in the play means nothing to her. She's just as likely to insist that Kelly stays at home to look after her sister Miranda's kids."

Having witnessed Kelly's safe arrival, Jane Wilson went to the staff room and made herself a cup of tea. She sat sipping it slowly, remembering the interview she'd had with Mr Taylor the head teacher just after she'd done the auditions for the play.

She'd sat in his study with its smell of beeswax polish, feeling defensive. He'd been the one who'd suggested that they do some sort of production to mark the school's tenth anniversary. Now she'd started work on it, he seemed intent on controlling every aspect of the proceedings and overturning every decision she made.

"What's the problem?" she asked.

Mr Taylor appeared to be obsessed with a point on the floor just in front of Mrs Wilson's feet. "I'd like you to reconsider the casting of Juliet," he'd said. "It would make my life – easier."

"But Kelly's got real talent," she'd insisted. "She was by

far the best candidate at the auditions. I just wish there was more opportunity for her to do further training when she leaves here – that I could get her mother to see sense..."

"You can't help every lame duck," said Mr Taylor softly. "No doubt, despite all your efforts she'll be in the family way just like her sister before too long."

Kelly's sister, Miranda, had left school three years ago without taking any exams, pregnant with her first child. Jane Wilson had seen her in Launceston a year later, pushing a grubby looking pram, her blonde hair looking lank and greasy and the bump of a second pregnancy already visible under her crumpled dress. She looked as if she'd already given up on life.

Jane felt that Kelly deserved a chance, even though warning bells in her brain told her she was in danger of getting too involved with a pupil again. It had happened once before, at her last school. A boy had shown great talent as a writer and Jane had invested a lot of her free time encouraging him to complete the novel he was writing and suggesting ways of improving it in the hope that it would draw him away from an undesirable group of friends. However, despite all her efforts, he'd died from a drugs overdose at a party that got out of control and it had taken her a long time to recover her willingness to help another pupil beyond the terms of her contract.

"Kelly's not like that," she told herself – and besides, she'd promised Kelly's grandmother before she died that she'd do all she could to help her beloved granddaughter achieve her ambitions.

She switched her thoughts back to the present, thinking how she'd chosen the dress for Juliet (borrowed from a local drama group) with Kelly in mind. It was buttercup yellow silk and would look perfect with Kelly's auburn hair and creamy skin. It would do nothing at all for Susan Baker's sallow complexion. Jane was under no doubts as to who had complained about the casting. John Baker had a reputation for throwing his weight about and had no doubt agreed to become Chairman of the Governors because he could make sure his children came out on top whether they deserved to or not. Susan had apparently been offered a trainee reporter job in London when she left school and Jane wondered why it was that some kids had success handed to them on a plate while others had no luck at all.

"I'd like Kelly to play the part of Juliet, Mr Taylor," she'd said firmly. "If you'd prefer someone else, then maybe you should look for another director for this production."

She'd walked out of Mr Taylor's office, knowing she'd won. Nobody else wanted the job of rehearsing and directing the play. However, a nagging doubt had persisted that something might go wrong at the end – that Kelly might be ill or not turn up and that Susan would end up playing the part after all.

The day passed more slowly than usual for Kelly and contained all the lessons she hated most – like maths and science. In the maths lesson Mr Ringwood did his usual trick of scribbling a problem on the board and working through the solution so quickly that Kelly couldn't follow it. Then, having written down an answer and underlined it, he'd then scratched his head, waved his short arms around and said briskly, "No, that's not right is it?" and proceeded to scrub the calculation out with the board rubber and begin again.

Kelly, who'd given up on the idea of being any good at maths several years ago, started daydreaming about the play. She knew some of the other girls were envious because they wanted to get close to Jamie Collins. Even girls that Kelly hadn't spoken to before would come up to her in the playground and ask if she'd tell Jamie that they fancied him.

"For all they know, you and Jamie might have something going together," said Jess as they sat out on the school field at lunchtime. The grass was cool against Kelly's bare legs as she sat gazing up at the clear blue sky, waiting for one o'clock when she had to go to the hall for a final pep talk with the other members of the cast.

"The problem is everyone thinks I'm like my sister," said Kelly, chewing on a blade of grass, "and I'm not. We've got different fathers for a start."

"Are you going home first?" asked Jess.

"Are you kidding? My Mum might not let me out again." Kelly tried to make a joke of it, but there was a lump of anxiety at the back of her throat.

"Come back to my house for tea, then," offered Jess. "Mum won't mind."

Jess's Mum was in a state of excitement when they got home.

"The confirmation's come, Jess. They've said we can go."

"Go where?" said Kelly.

Jess looked embarrassed and scuffed at the carpet with the toe of her sandal. "I didn't say anything in case it didn't happen. Mum, Dad and I have applied to go to Australia to join my two brothers. It looks like they've said yes."

"I'll miss you," said Kelly, her throat feeling tight.

"We'll still be friends," said Jess as they sat in her purple and gold bedroom trying on different nail polish. "And maybe when you don't need your Mum's permission any more, you'll be able to come out and visit us."

She looked sympathetically at Kelly. "Don't be sad, Kelly. Just think – when you're a famous actress and I'm a famous artist we'll be able to go where we like."

"Yeah," said Kelly, flopping down on Jess's purple velvet bedspread, "that's really gonna happen. I sometimes feel I'm kidding myself with the acting. Yes, it's the one thing I love doing and I know I can do it, but I've just got a nasty feeling that as sure as England won the World Cup in 1966, I'll end up in that biscuit factory."

They played through Jess's collection of singles, jigging around and dancing, until her Mum called them down for tea. Kelly didn't have a record player – just a second-hand transistor radio she'd bought in the local junk shop on which she listened to Radio Luxembourg under the bed-clothes at night.

"It's funny," said Kelly, when they'd finished eating fish-fingers, beans and chips, "how life's really exciting when you're a kid and it feels like when you grow up you can do anything. And then it starts shrinking right in front of your eyes – like one of those horror films where the sides of the room start coming in…"

"Come on," said Jess. "You're playing Juliet, remember? This is the start of your journey to fame."

By the time Kelly arrived in the history classroom that was designated as the girls' changing room, everyone else had almost finished putting on their make up and costumes.

"Mrs Wilson told me to get made up. She didn't know if you'd turn up," said Susan Baker.

"You'd have to find yourself another costume then," said Kelly, turning her back and sorting through her tubes of make up. "This one won't fit you"

"Make the most of the way you look," said Susan. "If you're anything like your sister, it won't last." She moved to the far side of the room to join her friends, her make up looking unnaturally bright in the shaft of evening sunlight coming through the classroom window.

Kelly began to get changed, feeling as uncomfortable as she usually did in communal changing rooms, as if everyone was looking at her, which in this case they probably were. She wished she'd remembered to wear her other bra – the one that wasn't the colour of chewing gum from being washed so many times at the local Launderette and held together by a small gold safety pin because she couldn't be bothered to find a needle and cotton.

Kelly knew the other girls were talking about her as she eased herself into the close-fitting buttercup yellow silk dress, wondering what she'd do about the line of silk-covered buttons down the back. It was all very well for Mrs Wilson to assume that everyone would help each other. Kelly wouldn't give these girls the satisfaction of saying 'no' to her if she asked for their help. If necessary she'd go to the boys' changing room next door and ask Jamie.

She placed the lucky black cat her Gran had given her next to the card with the yellow roses on it that Mrs Wilson had given her at lunchtime to wish her luck. As Kelly was leaving the hall, she'd slipped a small package into her hands. When Kelly tore off the paper in the privacy of the girls' toilets, she found a necklace of glittering amber stones.

She didn't tell anybody about the unexpected gift. The other girls already saw her as teacher's pet, there was no point making things any worse. Rumours had gone flying round as to how Kelly got the part in the first place, varying from an amount of money changing hands to Kelly being an illegitimate child that Mrs Wilson had given away years before.

Mrs Wilson came in and swept the room with an appraising glance. She was wearing a blue dress and jacket and looked as if she'd just left the hairdressers. "Is everybody nearly ready? I thought I told you not to bother putting make-up on Susan? Turn round, Kelly, let me button your dress."

Susan's round face was sulky after Mrs Wilson left the classroom. "The cow said that maybe I could write a report for the local paper," she grumbled to her friend Cathy who was playing Juliet's Nurse, "as if I'd want to write about her!" She glared spitefully towards where Kelly was brushing her long auburn hair.

Mrs Wilson came back at that point – almost as if she'd been listening outside the door. "Why aren't you in the prompt box, Susan?" she asked.

As Susan left the room, Kelly heard Mrs Wilson say: "You'll find in the newspaper business that you'll be asked to write about a lot of people you don't like, and have to portray them in a positive light. You may as well get some practise in now."

There was a poster on the classroom wall about the Great Fire of London and Kelly focused on it, trying to imagine what it would've been like to be an actress in one of the old play houses. What would Nell Gwyn do in this situation? Kelly closed her eyes, thinking. She had a good idea that Nell would go out there and knock the audience dead. She certainly wouldn't waste time worrying about someone like Susan Baker.

Kelly tried to concentrate, to believe she was Juliet. She remembered what Mrs Wilson said about how the great actresses worked – building the character of the person they were playing from the inside, really making the audience believe in them. How would someone like Juliet feel when she woke up in the morning? What would she eat? Certainly not burnt toast like Kelly was offered day after day...

"I've stuck my neck out for you, Kelly. Don't let me down," said Mrs Wilson when she returned to the classroom. "Don't worry, I know you won't," she said softly, thinking what a wonderful picture Kelly made in her buttercup yellow silk dress with all that stunning auburn hair rippling loose over her shoulders.

She wished that at least one member of Kelly's family had bothered to buy a ticket for the performance. The poor kid was the only one in the whole cast who hadn't got somebody out there in the hall watching her. That was the real reason that she'd sent her a card – although she'd made a point of sending one to Jamie as well, just so it didn't look like she was singling Kelly out. The necklace was another matter – something that had been entrusted to her safe keeping until Kelly was eighteen. However, Mrs Wilson decided that now was the right time to give it to her – although the letter that accompanied it could wait.

She led Kelly down to the wings, past where Susan Baker was sitting sullenly in the prompt box, her round face a picture of martyrdom.

As soon as Kelly looked out at the audience, her nervous feeling subsided. She thought of Nell Gwyn again, imagining her standing beside her like a best friend, urging her on to give a good performance. She was concentrating so hard she could almost smell the faint scent of oranges mixed with old roses. She was Juliet Capulet, living in Verona. Instead of dusty floorboards, the ground under her feet was cool marble.

Kelly heard her cue and stepped onto the stage, her voice clear and true as she answered with "How now! Who calls?"

The play progressed faultlessly towards the interval where glasses of wine and orange juice were served to the parents in the grandly named 'vestibule.'

"You were good," said Jamie gruffly to Kelly as they left the stage, earning himself a sour look from Susan who was emerging from the prompt box. It was obviously warm in there, because her make up had run, giving her the look of a pantomime dame.

"Thanks," whispered Kelly, sensing the magic between them tonight as if Jamie really believed that he was Romeo. Once or twice during the first act, she'd noticed him looking at her in the sort of way that made her stomach flip over.

She took her glass of orange juice having first put an old shirt over her dress to make sure nothing was spilled on it. The door from the corridor that led to one of the quadrangles was open so that the cast could get some fresh air. Kelly stepped outside, gazing up at the stars forming in the darkening sky. She sipped her drink slowly, breathing in the smell of freshly mown grass.

Jamie came and stood beside her, making Kelly's skin tingle. She was glad she'd accepted a splash of Jess's Mum's Chanel perfume. That was another thing she'd buy when she was famous - expensive perfume and sexy underwear. No more bras held together with safety pins.

"Amazing aren't they – the stars I mean," Jamie said. "And you as well," he said huskily, just as Mrs Wilson called them back in to get ready for the next act. His hand grazed hers as he passed - the touch warm and electrifying, making her jump.

At the end of the play they earned a standing ovation from the audience and effusive thanks from Mr Taylor and Mrs Wilson. Someone from the local paper spent a long time interviewing them and taking their photographs.

Mrs Wilson helped Kelly take off her make up and costume. Most of the cast had gone, including Jamie, swallowed up by his proud parents. Everyone had someone to collect them except Kelly.

"Let me give you a lift as far as the crossroads," said Mrs Wilson.

A slim crescent moon had risen above the horizon, surrounded by a scattering of stars. Kelly sat in the passenger seat of Mrs Wilson's blue mini, not speaking, going over in her mind the excitement of her first press interview.

"Star quality" the reporter said and he'd looked at Kelly with respect, asking if this was to be her chosen career. Kelly's lips framed the word 'yes' and it was down on the page before she'd had time to think

She stood at the corner of the road after Mrs Wilson dropped her off, gazing at the crescent moon and making her wishes for the future. Some day - she didn't know how - she would have her own dressing room with a big silver star on the door.

Kelly reluctantly headed home, not wanting the bubble

of magic to be burst too soon. Viv had probably forgotten about the performance by now, anyway. The back door was open and Kelly crept in quietly. The kitchen smelled of meat and potato pie and burnt chips. Viv and Mick were in the front room arguing against the noise of a game show on the telly as to whose turn it was to put the rubbish out.

Kelly hurried upstairs and got ready for bed, hanging her school uniform on the wardrobe door. She lay with her curtains open so that she could see the moon and stars, trying to retain the evening's magic.

THREE

That same night, over 250 miles away in Chelsea, poet Jed Matthews noticed the moon as he stepped outside David Martin's bookshop for a breath of air. He caught sight of himself mirrored in the shop window – tousled black hair curling over the collar of the dark blue linen shirt that the sales girl said matched the colour of his eyes.

Gazing at the crescent moon against a backdrop of indigo sky sprinkled with stars calmed Jed a little. It looked – peaceful – against the neon-lit mayhem of the city, reminding him of that nursery rhyme book his mother, Gloria, used to read from when he was little, tucked up in his pyjamas, teeth cleaned, safe. He wondered what had happened to the book. Knowing his mother, she'd probably have squirreled it away somewhere amongst her drawers and cupboards, like she did with the oddest things to do with his earlier life. First teeth and locks of hair were secreted in jewellery boxes, his first little babygros and cot quilt were packed carefully away in a box in the loft together with every splodgy picture he'd done at nursery school and every birthday and Christmas card he'd ever given her.

He wished she could've been here tonight. He imagined her dressed in the grey skirt and jacket she wore for important occasions, her hair freshly shampooed and set, clutching a warm glass of wine and clinging to the shadows, a bewildered expression on her plump face.

Jed hadn't made too much of a thing about his book launch, knowing how difficult it would be for her to get away, especially if his father was at home. There was certainly no way that Eric Matthews would allow Gloria to attend. He'd made it crystal clear he considered writing a waste of time – especially poetry - and that his only son had given up a promising career and was now in the process of throwing his life away.

Jed sighed and made his way back into the crowded

bookshop. His father was right in some ways. What Jed had done would be seen by some people to be suicidal – to throw up a good steady job with a pension in the vain hope of making it as a writer. The publication of 'Changing Tides' whilst boosting his confidence, hadn't made much difference to his financial situation.

Even though a gratifying number of people had bought copies of the book this evening, they'd soon forget him unless he got something else published soon. Sometimes it was hard to stay motivated. He had a dead end job working in a late night supermarket, stacking shelves, clearing away rubbish and cleaning floors or anything else the Asian owners wanted him to do. Jed had the feeling that Ali, the older man, enjoyed the reversal of roles. In his youth in India, the white man had been king, the Indian his slave.

David's bookshop was swelteringly hot and the cocktail of expensive perfumes was making Jed's head spin. People were crammed in close together, balancing glasses of wine and the sort of canapés and snacks that would've cost Jed a whole week's food bill. Luckily the publisher was picking up the tab for that.

Jed would've preferred a pint of Guinness and a packet of cheese and onion crisps to the fiddly little vol-au-vents and cheese straws that were being circulated with the sparkling wine by two young girls in short black dresses and frilly white aprons employed as waitresses. All that stuff did was to give him wind and remind him of how long it was since he'd had a proper meal.

Jed gave himself a mental shake. This was his first book signing for Christ's sake. He'd made it, against all the odds, against all the opposition from his father and the discouraging remarks by so-called friends.

He'd lost touch with most of those friends now and hadn't yet built a circle of fellow writers. He hadn't mentioned the book signing to anyone at the supermarket. He'd learned his lesson with that one. When he'd first started there, he'd got on well with one of the checkout girls and mentioned that he liked reading.

"I love books," she'd said enthusiastically, but her eyes had glazed over when he'd mentioned a few of his favourite novels.

"I've not heard of those," she'd said. "Which paper shop do you go to?"

When he'd asked more about the sort of things she read, it turned out that by 'books' she meant women's magazines – the more gossipy the better.

Jed had given up any attempt at friendliness with girls after that, despite the fact that he knew most of them were attracted by his Heathcliffe-like rugged good looks. He was finding it hard enough to cover his monthly expenses without taking on a girlfriend.

He wondered how most of these expensively dressed people who were making such a fuss of him would react if he told them where he was going after he left here – changing his smart trousers and shirt for faded jeans and a black polo shirt with the red supermarket logo on. It was the Cinderella story again. Dressed like that they probably wouldn't look twice at him, like the posh woman last year who'd spent ages talking to him at a poetry reading he'd taken part in for a local charity and had hinted at further opportunities for him. Then when he'd seen her on his way to work the following day and had spoken to her she'd looked him up and down in his work clothes pretending she didn't recognise him, hurrying along the street away from him as if she suspected he had leprosy.

The supermarket was OK really. Mostly he was left alone to do his work and he could take regular breaks if the manager went home early as he usually did. There was a staff canteen upstairs that did free mugs of strong tea and they usually left out stale buns and cakes for the staff to eat that would otherwise be thrown away.

Most of his poems had been written there in the notebook that went everywhere with him. He'd sit by the radiator, looking out of the window towards the neon lit city skyline.

Sometimes he wondered if the sacrifice had been worth it – he'd not had a girlfriend for ages now – couldn't afford to take anyone out. He lived in a damp bed-sit near Clapham Junction and earned only just enough to cover his bills. His father had disowned him. His mother met up with him occasionally during the day and she'd sneak him small amounts of money, no doubt squeezed from the housekeeping, or some pies and cakes that she'd made but she wouldn't openly defy his father.

"I wish you could get this writing fad out of your system and make friends with your father again," she'd said the last time they'd met for lunch.

"It's not a fad, it's my dream," Jed said, wishing he could make her understand.

"Dreams aren't real life," she'd said sadly as she kissed his cheek when they said goodbye.

Since Jed had arrived at David's bookshop and begun signing copies of 'Changing Tides', hands feeling sweaty on the new pen he'd bought for the occasion, an American girl had latched onto him. Judging by the well-groomed look and the expensive smell of her, she was high maintenance and therefore not for him. He knew the type. They spent all their free time in the hairdressers or the beauty parlour and never once considered the cost. He'd signed a copy of the book for her – *to Mirabelle with best wishes from Jed Matthews* and she'd handed him the money. Her soft hand had lingered on his for a fraction too long. The nails were almond shaped, painted sugar pink to match her lipstick.

"Gee, I've never met a real life author before," she cooed,

flicking back her glossy raven's wing waterfall of hair and smiling at him. She smelled of rose bath oil and expensive perfume and she wore a figure-hugging red lace dress that probably cost more than Jed earned in a year.

He didn't expect the attraction to last beyond the next hour and was surprised to find her waiting for him outside the bookshop. "You wanna come to a wine bar with us?" She gestured towards a group of friends disappearing in the direction of a place with amber lights twinkling outside.

Lust fought with common sense. It was nearly nine o'clock and he needed to be at work by ten. If he didn't turn up at work then his boss, Mr Alzanki was just as likely to give him the sack. In any case, he'd got no money spare till Friday. *'Don't start something you can't carry on with,'* he told himself. *'She's American and probably thinks all writers are loaded. If she knew how dirt poor you really were she'd drop you like a hot potato.'*

"Sorry, not tonight," he mumbled. "I've got somewhere I need to be."

"Okay sweetie," she drawled, "but I'm real disappointed. Catch you sometime soon."

Jed watched her go, cursing himself for a fool. She probably thought he'd got a wife and six kids at home waiting for him.

He sat on the tube watching the faces reflected in the dark windows, feeling suddenly exhausted. Eight hours work loomed in front of him and all he wanted to do was sleep. The memory of Mirabelle's voice and the feel of her soft hand lingering on his had a disturbing effect on the lower half of his anatomy.

'Forget her,' he told himself as he reached the supermarket cloakroom and changed into his work clothes. *'She's out of your league.'*

FOUR

Kelly walked slowly up the narrow cliff path between clumps of pink sea thrift and coconut scented yellow gorse. The sea, murmuring and splashing far below, was a patchwork of blue – turquoise deepening to indigo near the rocks. A clear blue cloudless sky arched above her head, patterned by gulls looking like a collage of grey paper shapes.

The peacefulness of the landscape was at odds with the tumult going on inside Kelly. The row she'd just had with Viv echoed round in her head and she wondered why it was that some mothers wanted the best for their kids whereas hers didn't seem to care.

Kelly had come home from school feeling excited about the job she'd just been offered. It had all happened at lunchtime, when she'd received a message that Mrs Wilson wanted to speak to her urgently.

"I wonder what she's done," Kelly heard Susan Baker whisper to her friend Cathy as she stood waiting outside Mrs Wilson's classroom.

At that moment, Mrs Wilson arrived carrying a pile of exercise books. "There you are, Kelly," she said. "Come on in."

She shut the door and motioned Kelly to sit in the chair opposite her desk as she dumped the pile of books in a box by the window.

"Have a piece of chocolate?" She offered Kelly half a bar of Cadbury's fruit and nut.

Kelly accepted, feeling sure that Mrs Wilson hadn't asked to see her just to offer her chocolate.

"I expect you're wondering why I wanted to speak to you."

Kelly nodded.

"I just wondered what your plans were when you leave here."

"Working at the biscuit factory, Miss," said Kelly, knowing her face gave away how she felt about it.

"It doesn't sound very exciting to me. How would you feel about working in a museum?"

"What sort of museum?"

"It doesn't pay as much as the factory and it may only be for a year – but after then, who knows? There may be other opportunities if you do a good job. The curator Miss Bates will see you this afternoon if you're interested."

So Kelly had gone into Tredannoc Bay that afternoon and had an interview with Miss Bates at the Museum of Local Life (who turned out to be Mrs Wilson's aunt). She looked about ninety, wore a high-necked white blouse and smelled of mothballs and peppermints. The building was old, chilly and smelled of mice but anything was better than the biscuit factory and, as Mrs Wilson said, you never knew what might happen in a year. Kelly had found herself smiling and accepting the job in a new mood of optimism.

She'd walked home slowly, wondering how she'd broach the subject with her mother – to find that her sister Miranda was there with the two children. The tatty grey double pushchair was hidden amongst the weeds in the front garden and she could hear Miranda bawling at the kids.

"You're late," said Miranda accusingly when Kelly pushed open the kitchen door. She was sat at the kitchen table blowing smoke rings at the ceiling while Viv banged and clattered around cooking egg and chips for Miranda and the kids with as much drama as if she was concocting a royal banquet.

"I've had an interview," said Kelly, deciding there was safety in numbers. "Don't do that Lisa," she said sharply to her two-year-old niece. The local paper with Kelly's photo on the front page had been tossed onto the floor and Lisa was busy watering it with orange squash from her trainer cup.

Kelly snatched up the paper, smoothing the creases out

of the photograph.

"For Christ's sake, Kelly, it's not that big a deal," said Miranda, settling her fat backside further back onto the wooden chair. "Anyone would think you'd done something really special, not just pranced around in dressing up clothes for the evening."

"It was special," said Kelly, wondering why it was that her Mum and sister always managed to take the shine off anything good that happened to her.

"It's time you got real Kelly," went on Miranda taking another drag at her cigarette. "Life's not all glamour and it's not about kids' games."

"She'll soon find out," said Viv dumping a plate of egg and chips on the table in front of Miranda. "Miranda, you'll have to sit the kids in their pushchair. And I've only done them chips – I'm not having them making any more mess than they have already."

She glared at Kelly. "What d'you mean you've been for an interview? You've already got a job at the factory. I really stuck my neck out to get that for you."

"I'm not going to the factory. I've been offered something at the museum."

"Ooh listen to her," said Miranda, "a museum! Let me tell you, Kelly, you may think you're a cut above the rest of us, but the same shit comes out of your arse and whatever you think you're no better than the rest of us."

"You'll do as you're told and take the job I got for you." Viv turned the kitchen taps on full and slammed dirty crockery into the sink.

Liam and Lisa, imprisoned in their pushchair and alarmed by the shouting, started squalling. Their faces were smeared with tomato ketchup and thick yellow snot.

"Shut up," yelled Mick from the front room. "Or I'll take a stick to the lot of yer"

Viv turned to Kelly. "See what you've done with your

stupid ideas?" She dried her hands on the grubby kitchen towel, ripped a cigarette from the packet on the table, flared the lighter and lit it with trembling fingers.

"Why can't you ever be pleased for me for once? Why can't you be like other people's mothers?" Kelly picked up her bag and walked out of the back door, swallowing the lump in her throat that threatened to spill over into tears.

She could hear Viv shouting: "Come back and do this bloody washing up."

Kelly ignored the curious glances of neighbours as she strode away from the house. She knew there was no way she'd turn down the offer of this job. Her mother could either like it or lump it. She should've known this was a bad time to mention it. Viv was always more stressed when Miranda and the kids turned up

As she walked, Kelly focused on her dreams for the future. When she reached the cliff-top she flopped down on the springy grass near the ruins of the haunted house. Not many people came here, which was why it was Kelly's favourite spot. A local legend said that the ghost of a woman walked after dark, looking for the lover who was taken from her and murdered there on the cliff-top.

All that was left of the rough stone house was the chimney breast and the foundations showing the outline of what were once two rooms with a washhouse or privy at the back. It was overgrown, the edges softened by yellow lichen and pink thrift, but an echo of past times remained.

The local boys dared each other to spend an hour up on the cliffs alone after dark looking for the White Lady. The headmaster had given warnings in assembly about severe accidents as a result of boys falling over in the dark in their haste to get to the bottom of the pathway.

Being near the house filled Kelly with a deep sense of peace – as if she'd come home. The smell of salt and heather on the soft breeze and feeling of welcome she always had was so different from the experiences of some of the boys who had reported seeing an eerie white mist rising from the stones and a feeling that something evil wanted to drive them over the cliff onto the jagged rocks below.

Kelly half closed her eyes as she began a sketch of what she imagined the cottage would've looked like on that stormy night when the murder happened. She drew ominous banks of grey cloud above a boiling charcoal sea and was so engrossed in her task she forgot everything.

"Do you often come here?" asked Jamie flopping down beside her, clearly not bothered about getting grass stains on his white school shirt. He smelled of apple shampoo and was carrying a newspaper-wrapped portion of chips.

Kelly's mouth watered at the smell of salt and vinegar. She didn't especially like chips – they had oven chips at home nearly every night - but chip shop ones were different.

Kelly's hand shot out and grabbed a fat chip before she'd thought about it.

"Are you hungry or something?" Jamie looked amused.

Kelly looked at the light in his eyes, like the sun on a turquoise sea, and her stomach did a back-flip remembering their stage kiss at the end of the play that had gone on for far longer than most stage kisses.

"You're some actress," said Jamie. "Is that what you're going to do when you leave school?"

"No," said Kelly through a mouthful of chips. "I'd like to but I can't."

Somehow, the newspaper package was between them and they were sharing the chips, each of them reacting when their fingers accidentally brushed together.

"I wish I wasn't going to London," said Jamie, "at least, not to learn engineering. Drama school or Art College would be a whole lot different."

"Don't go then," said Kelly. "It's not compulsory."

"You don't know my Dad."

"I wish my Mum was more like your Dad. I'd love to go to London."

"It's not London I object to exactly," Jamie wrinkled his forehead. "It's that I'm not going to be doing what I want when I get there…"

"If my Mum has her way I'll be working at the biscuit factory on the business park."

"You'd do all right for free samples," said Jamie.

"Big deal," said Kelly eating the last chip. "Anyway, I'm not going to."

"So what are you going to do?"

"I'm going to be the assistant at the Museum of Local Life down there in Main Street. So much for my dreams of getting away from here - but at least it's one better than the biscuit factory."

"That's probably the only good thing about going to London – getting away," agreed Jamie.

They sat for a few minutes, not saying much.

"You've got a sister haven't you?" asked Jamie.

Kelly nodded, not really wanting to talk about Miranda who'd got pregnant at sixteen and left school without taking any exams. Kelly was thirteen at the time and could still remember the temper Viv had flown into and the way she'd yelled at Miranda, sitting white-faced at the kitchen table. The registry office wedding had been arranged quickly, with Miranda in a blue dress and matching hat clutching a bouquet of white roses. Viv's attitude had changed completely when baby Liam was born, followed just over a year later by Lisa.

"Are you studying me for an exam or something?" she asked, knowing that her face and neck were getting hot under Jamie's steady gaze.

"Have I told you you're very pretty?" he asked.

Kelly swallowed hard. He'd already mentioned Miranda. The condition she'd left school in was no secret, but what if Jamie thought she was easy like Miranda? If he decided he wanted her, here and now on this cliff-top, there'd be nothing she could do about it. That would certainly finish her dreams of ever becoming an actress.

"I've got to go," she said, shoving her sketch-book into her bag and hurrying down the cliff path, her feet slipping on the rough stones.

Jamie watched her go, her green and white striped school dress billowing up when the breeze caught it, kicking himself for not even getting to first base with her. He didn't dare admit to the other lads that he hadn't even managed to kiss Randy Miranda's sister or feel her tits.

Yesterday in the boys' toilets, dark haired Rocky Rawcliffe had pushed him up against the wall. His entourage stood just behind him, three weedy-looking henchmen with sawn off ties, trying to look hard.

"'Ere Collins, you're always goin' on about how great you are with women – well now's your chance to prove it."

They dragged him to the door just as Kelly was walking across the playground, her black schoolbag on her shoulder and her dress riding up slightly on that side revealing an expanse of slim brown thigh.

"We'll give you two weeks – then we want proof you've got into her knickers. Or else…"

"Do me a favour." Jamie tried not to show how nervous he felt. He should've been mouthy back – asked Rocky what was in it for him when he came back with the proof – and what sort of proof did they want. Maybe Rocky could show him first? In reality, it was all he could do to stop shivering. Rocky's breath was hot and sour on his cheek and his meaty fingers were crushing Jamie's collar-bones.

"From what you've said about that bird you pulled on holiday, you'll be doin' Smelly Kelly a favour. And as a little incentive to keep you on the job - no success after four weeks - you owe us twenty quid. Think about that one. We'll be watching you." Giving Jamie a final shove against the wall, Rocky and his henchmen sloped off.

Jamie felt sick. Twenty quid was as much as his cousin earned in a week. How was Jamie going to get his hands on twenty quid to pay Rocky off if he didn't succeed with Kelly? He knew without being told that if he hadn't got the money or the proof, then Rocky and Co. would do him over. It had happened last year when that kid Sam Spence had supposedly 'fallen' on the cliffs. Despite the incident being said to be an accident, most of the fifth year knew how Sam had acquired his injuries. He was likely to walk with a limp for the rest of his life.

Jamie sat by the harbour wall, tossing stones into the deep indigo water. It was his own fault for bragging about what he'd done with that girl on holiday. Not only had he bragged about staying in a posh hotel in the South of France, when they'd really only gone down to a chalet on The Lizard, he'd compounded the error by boasting about having sex with a girl he'd met on the beach.

Jamie felt sick, remembering how he'd been goaded into making these boasts by one of the other boys talking about the brilliant time he'd had white water rafting. He'd had a sly dig at Jamie saying he'd probably spent the summer playing with buckets and spades on some boring beach.

Jamie suspected that the nearest the other boy had come to white water rafting was playing in a dinghy in a rock pool, but the lies about the exotic hotel in Nice, the marble floors, the food they'd eaten and the wine he'd been allowed to drink had slipped out. Following close behind were the tales of the girl with long blonde hair who he'd shagged in a beach hut on the long hot afternoons.

What really happened was that Jamie and his Mum and Dad had arrived at their chalet on The Lizard on the Saturday lunchtime. Jamie's Dad was fed up with traffic jams and was complaining about being hungry. Jamie was already bored. It wouldn't have been so bad if he could've taken a friend, but his Mum said that this time they just wanted time to just be a family and not have to worry about anyone else's child – especially after last year when Jamie's friend Alex had brought a bottle of whisky pinched from his Dad's drinks cabinet and the two boys had been up all night being sick, having drunk half the bottle between them.

This time, Jamie's Mum and Dad had gone for a lie down after lunch and he'd wandered round the site feeling bored. There was nothing to do. No clubhouse, no amusement arcade within miles – just a shop that sold groceries, plastic buckets and spades and dog-eared postcards.

A narrow lane bordered by high stone walls, gorse and pink campion led to the beach. Jamie wandered down there, thinking that his Mum and Dad probably wouldn't care if a freak wave washed him away. The beach was deserted, apart from a family on the far side. The parents were sitting on striped deck chairs and two tiny blonde girls were digging a sandcastle with red plastic spades. Jamie explored the rock pools listlessly and then wandered back to the chalet.

His Mum and Dad were still asleep when he let himself back in – he could hear his Dad snoring, the sound building up to a crescendo. Jamie explored the living room. It was a dull oxtail soup colour – walls, carpet, sofa and chairs. There were two prints on the walls of sailing boats, a square pine dining table and four matching chairs and a vase of yellow plastic chrysanthemums. Jamie looked through the cupboard labelled 'games' – feeling depressed because the most exciting thing in there was snakes and ladders.

The magazine rack, however, yielded something more

interesting. Someone had left a girly magazine there. There was a photo of a busty brunette leaning out of a low-cut bra on the front cover, but it was the blonde on page twenty-seven that sent Jamie's senses reeling. Hearing someone stir in the bedroom, he shoved the magazine under his t-shirt and hurried into his bedroom with it, hiding it at the back of his wardrobe where his Mum wouldn't see it.

That night, he couldn't wait for bedtime. His Mum looked surprise when he went to bed early. "Are you feeling all right, Jamie?"

"Fine," he said, deliberately turning his mouth up at the corners. He couldn't wait to be re-acquainted with the blonde.

His Mum and Dad were busy chatting about when they'd honeymooned at this cove. Jamie was hard-put to find out what was special about it and how they'd occupy themselves for a week, but after a few glances at the blonde on page twenty-seven, he began to think that a week wouldn't be long enough.

He cheered up considerably on the second day. His Mum and Dad had left him to make a brief trip into Penzance to buy each other an anniversary present. Walking in a different direction along the beach, Jamie found a beach hut. It was well above the strand-line and made of old fishing crates tied together with orange and blue nylon string. There was a purple and blue striped blanket on the sandy floor and a few driftwood shelves built into one corner. Someone had spent the night here recently. Jamie noticed a pack of condoms stashed behind a driftwood mirror with the remains of a bar of plain chocolate.

He hurried back to the chalet for the magazine. Back at the beach, he was relieved to see that, apart from the family he'd seen earlier on the far side of it, there was nobody else about.

Jamie settled himself on the rug, wondering what it would be like to spend the night here with a girl. There were gaps in the structure of the make-shift hut so you'd see the stars as you lay there on the floor. Through the bead-curtained doorway, he could see the sea in the distance, tiny waves rippling across the damp yellow sand.

He opened the magazine at page twenty-seven, gazing at the double page spread of the blonde in the black lace underwear and high heels. Her mouth was set in a sulky pout and Jamie wanted to kiss away the frosted lipstick and touch the full breasts straining at the thin fabric.

His trousers were becoming impossibly tight, his erection throbbing against his jeans. Jamie felt the familiar flood of shame as he unzipped his jeans and took hold of his throbbing penis. He'd always been wary of masturbating at home in case his mother came into his bedroom without knocking as she often did, or in case he left a stain on something or the room smelled different. His mother was always alert for any changes in him, any hint that he might be with the wrong crowd.

The blonde stared disdainfully back as Jamie grew harder. His eyes half closed in ecstasy as his hand worked up and down, then there was the wonderful moment of release, like a champagne cork bursting out of a bottle and his seed spilled onto the powdery sand at the edge of the rug. He let go of himself, shoving his penis back inside his jeans and zipping them up again. He felt exhausted, settling down on the rug as if he hadn't slept for a week, the magazine rolled up and shielded under his body from any possible prying eyes.

When he woke up, it was nearly lunchtime and he knew his Mum and Dad would be back from Penzance by now. They'd talked about a pub lunch and then a visit to Mullion Cove for the afternoon. Earlier this morning, Jamie thought this sounded the most boring thing out. Now, his energy released, he thought that sounded fine. He might even get round to doing a few sketches, even though he'd probably earn a few comments from his Dad about time-wasting.

"You'll have to put those daft ideas out of your head when you get to London, lad," he'd said. "An engineering apprenticeship will be more use to you than painting pretty pictures. One day you'll have a wife and kids to support – you won't do that on fresh air I can tell you."

Jamie always felt his Dad was secretly comparing him to his older brother Danny. Danny did brilliantly with his 'O' and 'A' Levels. Danny got a place at Exeter University to read Chemistry. Danny had a glittering future ahead of him and was always smiling. Danny shared Dad's interest in football. Danny died in a car accident on an exchange visit to America. You couldn't argue with a ghost…

FIVE

The letters arrived on the day Jed's boss at the supermarket had called a staff meeting and had talked about a cut in working hours. He'd decided not to keep the store open so late at night in order to deter the gangs of youths who came in, often the worse for drink, making a nuisance of themselves and causing damage.

Jed was already wondering how he was going to make ends meet. There had been a lot of interest in *'Changing Tides'*, the glamour of the launch party and some good reviews, but he knew the book wouldn't make his fortune. This cut in working hours would put him under even more pressure. He was working on another collection of poems and the outline for a novel, but the constant hand to mouth worry over money was siphoning his creative energy and it felt as if the ideas were sticking inside his head.

He returned home feeling dejected clutching a bag containing a stale jam doughnut that would comprise his breakfast to find that a scrappy looking note had been pushed under the door of his bed-sit. It was from his landlord saying that as from the end of next month he was raising the rent.

Jed sat on his bed, negative thoughts spiralling round in his head. Maybe his father was right – he shouldn't have given up a promising career to chase his dreams. He felt stiff, cold and hungry. The last thing he'd eaten was a slice of cheese on toast at lunchtime. It wasn't until he got up to put the kettle on to make himself a mug of tea that he noticed the thick cream envelope that had been pushed to one side when the landlord delivered his note. The address of his publishers was written on it in loopy black letters. This had been crossed out with blue biro and Jed's address written underneath.

Jed opened it, his heart racing when he realised it was from Mirabelle. It was written in black ink on thick cream paper – the letters dramatic and swooping across the page like birds blown by the wind.

"I'd so love to see you again," she'd written. "I'll be mighty disappointed if I don't. How about we meet at De Vito's on the Kings Road for coffee at eleven next Thursday - my treat."

Jed didn't intend to go. Then the words 'my treat' leapt up at him.

On the night of the book signing he'd known she was out of his league. She reeked of wealth and privileged background. So why was she chasing after an impoverished poet? Did she want to take him on as her latest 'bit of rough'? The thought had an unsettling effect on his anatomy as he remembered the touch of her hand on his.

His first instinct was to ignore the note, but he sensed that she was the sort of person who'd keep writing until she got a response. He knew he should write back with a polite refusal. After all, there was no way he could reciprocate – he couldn't exactly take her to Mike's greasy spoon café round the corner.

He made a mug of tea and sipped it as he munched the stale doughnut.

Why not, he thought, reaching for a sheet of paper. He'd got nothing to lose. He'd have a coffee with her, explain his circumstances, and she'd drop him like a hot potato.

Even so, on the Thursday morning he was surprised at how nervous he felt. He'd taken ages to decide which shirt to wear and had probably put on too much Brut aftershave. He didn't particularly like the smell – someone had bought it for him last Christmas - but it was the only bottle he owned so it would have to do.

Mirabelle looked pleased to see him when he arrived. She was sitting at a table outside, her sunglasses on top of her rich dark hair, wearing a short white dress that emphasised her long slim legs and olive skin.

She got up, kissed him on the cheek and drew him down

onto the chair opposite hers. When the waitress came she ordered coffee for them both and a Danish pastry for him as big as a dinner plate.

"What about you?" he asked.

"I'll have a small piece of yours," she said, making a funny intimate face at him. "A girl has to think of her figure."

He'd meant to keep her at arm's length. One coffee he told himself and no more. Judging by the chrome and glass look of the place and the way the waitresses were dressed, a coffee here would set him back his whole week's food money.

He was touched that Mirabelle had her copy of his book in her bag and that she'd marked the poems she'd particularly liked with slips of paper between the pages.

"What does this mean?" she'd asked, fishing the book out of her bag and reading out sections of the poems. "And this...?"

And he'd found himself telling her about his frustrations with his work and how he'd argued with his father and refused to follow the career path mapped out for him. He'd spoken of his regret that his mother hadn't attended the book signing.

"She'd never openly go against the old man, whatever he does," he said bitterly.

"So what's your next project - more poems? A novel?" she asked - her head on one side like an inquisitive blackbird.

He told her about his current struggle to put words on the page because of the constant battle to make enough money. He hoped he wasn't sounding like a whinger, but he needed to make her see that he wasn't the man for her, despite the fact that the longer he sat near her inhaling her perfume and talking to her, the harder it would be to tear himself away.

This girl is high maintenance, he told himself. She'd think nothing of spending five pounds on a pot of face cream or blowing more money than he earned in a year on a dress.

She told him that her father was in the oil business in

Texas. When her Momma died last year, they decided to move to London for a while.

"Daddy and I thought it would help to be away from the house and all the memories – but the funny thing is they follow you. You never escape…"

Her eyes filled with tears, and Jed covered her hand with his, aware that he was already getting in far deeper than he'd intended.

"My real ambition from when I was a little girl is to act in a movie," said Mirabelle. "Daddy says he knows people who can make the movie. All we need is a good story." She looked searchingly at Jed as if waiting for him to take the bait. "All I need is someone like you to write one for me. You could, couldn't you – something romantic?" She licked her lips seductively and a pulse beat in her throat. "Promise me you'll think about it?"

The late July sunshine was warm. Girls in brightly coloured summer dresses were going past. Jed could hear the tinny sound of a transistor radio playing Mungo Jerry's *'In the Summertime.'*

He thought about Mirabelle's idea. It was typical of how some people were about writing. They assumed because you could write a book of poems that you could produce a movie script in a couple of weeks. The sooner he cut loose out of here, the better.

"I should go," he said, feeling reluctant to leave her.

"Must you?"

Jed wasn't used to being paid for and it was an uncomfortable experience. Mirabelle didn't notice his discomfort as she wrapped her arms round him, enveloping him in a tide of Chanel No. 5. The feel of her body through the thin fabric of her dress had an unsettling effect on Jed and he almost stumbled as she released him.

"Come for dinner with me and my Daddy on Sunday evening so we can talk about this more," she said as she readjusted her sunglasses. "I'd really like to have you write something for me. And Daddy wants to meet you. I've kept on about your poems so much. Come at seven and you can have a beer together. This is the address." She flipped through her pink leather bag and handed him a gold-edged card.

She held him again and kissed his cheek before spinning away from him and disappearing into the lunchtime crowd.

Again Jed spent the time between Thursday lunchtime and Sunday afternoon kidding himself that he'd phone and make some excuse as to why he couldn't go. Again, he looked at the clothes in his wardrobe, fretting about what to wear.

He wondered what Mirabelle's father would be like. All he knew was that he was from Texas and in the oil business, which conjured up visions of six-guns and ten-gallon hats. What if he wanted to know what Jed's intentions were with regard to his daughter? What if he thought Jed was a gold-digger? No, it was probably safest to phone and make his apologies.

In the finish, it was sheer frustration with his writing that made him decide that he would go. He'd written two poems for his next collection and torn them both up. The space inside his head felt like soggy cotton wool, he was permanently hungry and he despaired of ever writing anything publishable again.

He was down to his last two pounds before he got paid next Friday. A search in his fridge yielded a mouldy piece of cheese and the dry heel of a loaf of bread and his stomach churned with hunger. Glancing from his window, he'd noticed a tramp conducting a search of a rubbish bin, and Jed felt desperate enough to go down and join him.

At least at Mirabelle's place he'd get a decent meal. The only worm of doubt was that her father might decide they should go out to a posh restaurant and then Jed would feel bad because he couldn't pay his way. He felt bad enough anyway accepting Mirabelle's hospitality twice. He'd have to really try and make her

– and her father – understand that they were out of his league and that Mirabelle should look elsewhere for whatever it was she wanted.

Armed with a bunch of marigolds filched from the borders of a little park he walked through on the way and a box of Black Magic that was on the reduced counter in a corner shop that he passed, Jed made his way to Chelsea.

He'd expected the house to be posh, but even so, he almost turned back when he saw the imposing Greek columns and the shiny liquorice black door with its big brass knocker.

Mirabelle accepted the marigolds and chocolates graciously. "Gee are these from your garden?"

Jed felt himself growing hot with embarrassment. "Not exactly - I borrowed them."

"C'mon Mirrie, let the guy in and give him a bottle of beer." Mirabelle's father was just as Jed had imagined – minus the pistols and ten-gallon hat - casually dressed in blue jeans and red and white checked open-necked shirt.

Jed stepped over the threshold into a hallway flooded with a shaft of light from a glass dome in the roof far above them. Lozenges of colour danced on the black and white marble floor from the stained glass in the long windows either side of the door.

Huge paintings of Regency beauties in gilt frames that looked as if they'd come from a stately home stared down at him from the walls. Jed's footsteps echoed as he walked slowly past them.

"Mirrie's got a thing about English history," said her father indulgently, "but I 'spec she's told you that already."

Jed shook his head and allowed himself to be led into a sitting room with a cream carpet that he almost sank into up to his ankles.

"Should I take my shoes off...?"

"Nah – Jenny, our cleaning lady comes in every day –

she's only too glad to have something to do."

This was so typical of the majority of supermarket customers who thought nothing of tossing a plastic bag or an unwanted piece of cardboard onto the floor and watching him pick it up that Jed felt a flash of sympathy for Jenny.

He sat on a brown leather sofa next to Mirabelle. Even though it was July, a log fire burned in the grate.

"It's these high ceilings," explained Mirabelle's father, pointing upwards to what looked like the elaborate icing on a wedding cake, "this room doesn't get much sun and Mirrie feels the cold after Texas."

The curtains were red brocade with red and gold tie-backs and a chandelier hung down from the white encrusted ceiling, a breeze from somewhere making the glass crystals tinkle.

Jed hoped dinner wouldn't be long. Mouth-watering smells came from somewhere along one of the corridors, reminding him of how hungry he was. Besides, the beer was strong, he hadn't eaten all day, and he was beginning to feel light-headed.

They talked about the house which had once been lived in by Lady Georgiana somebody and Mirabelle drank a small glass of dry sherry. Then she left the room in a flurry of short pink dress and long brown legs. Mitch Jordan eased himself back in his chair, stretched out his legs and took another pull at his ice cold beer.

"Mirrie tells me you're a writer."

Jed nodded.

"So whatcha doin' working in a damned supermarket?"

Jed – in the process of pouring more beer into his glass almost dropped the bottle with shock. "What's that to you? I've never pretended to be anything I'm not." He was aware of how defensive he sounded. If he hadn't felt so light-headed he'd have walked out there and then.

"I wasn't checkin' up on ya sonny," said Mitch putting

down his beer glass and looking Jed in the eye. "It's just a way of mine. If you'd been in the oil business as long as I have you'd know ya need to check credentials. There have been too many guys in the past just after my little girl's money."

Jed put his beer glass down on a crocheted mat on the polished table beside him.

"For your information," he said slowly, hoping he wasn't slurring his words, "it was Mirabelle who chased me, not the other way round. As you so rightly point out, I know when someone's out of my price range. I've not tried to hide anything – as Mirabelle will tell you. But if you think I'm totally undesirable, maybe you'd rather I left now."

He could hear the clip-clip of Mirabelle's heels on the marble floor outside and could smell the exotic fragrance of frying meat and onions. His stomach curled with hunger, and to leave was the last thing he wanted to do.

Mitch spread his hands wide. "There's obviously a lot of this story I haven't been told, but if that's the way of it, and if she's made up her mind, then I may as well try and stop a runaway train. Her mother was just the same."

"You guys OK?" asked Mirabelle coming back into the room to announce that dinner was ready. Her face looked flushed from the oven.

"Sure am."

"We're fine."

Mirabelle cut them both a sharp look as they followed her along the passageway to the primrose yellow dining room with its large round table decorated with candles and Jed's offering of marigolds.

The cutlery was silver and there were crisp white linen napkins. Mirabelle poured herself a generous glass of red wine and brought more bottles of beer for Jed and Mitch. Huge gold-edged oval plates were filled with steak and chips and all the trimmings.

"Daddy always says you can't beat a good piece of steak," said Mirabelle taking a sip of her wine. "Cheers you two guys and when we've eaten you can tell me what you've been talking about. Did I detect some hostility between you just now?"

Neither Mitch nor Jed said anything.

"You've done a great job with this Mirrie," said Mitch, belching appreciatively.

"Hear, hear," said Jed, feeling a bit more sober now he'd got some solid food inside him.

Mirabelle smiled graciously and told Jed another story about Lady Georgiana who'd once lived in the house. She touched his ankle with her foot while they were eating dinner, the touch of her bare skin against his leg creating an electric spark.

Once again, even as he savoured the taste of peppered steak with onions and mushrooms and fat chips, Jed told himself that this was the last time he'd be drawn into Mirabelle's web. No matter how hard life was, it was up to him to sort things for himself. There was no way anyone was going to accuse him of being a gold digger.

SIX

It was two days before school ended for the summer and time was running out for Jamie. If he didn't take Rocky and his gang proof of some sort that he'd slept with a girl, or twenty pounds, then he may not even get to London.

He'd moped around the house desperately thinking of how to get out of the mess he was in. His Mum, who'd found him sitting at the bottom of the stairs, had commented on how moody he was and what she wouldn't have given for the opportunity he'd got when she was his age.

"You look like a wet weekend on a dry Sunday," she said, applying lavender polish to the already shiny hall table, "anyone would think you'd got the cares of the world on your shoulders."

Jamie almost burst into tears and told her everything, like he would've done when he was a little boy and had kicked a football through someone's greenhouse. But this was grown up stuff and he had to deal with it himself. Images of the boy who'd been permanently injured on the cliffs floated into his mind. He almost wondered if he should write a letter and leave it somewhere, just in case something like that happened to him...

"You don't know what its like," he'd growled at his mother.

Ignoring the hurt look she gave him, he slammed out of the front door, not really knowing where he was heading. He didn't feel like calling for any of his friends, and either way, they were bound to make the same comments as his Mum. He shoved his fists in his pockets and kept walking, head down, towards Tredannac Bay.

Once there, he wished he'd stayed indoors. He felt wary, as if Rocky and his henchmen were lurking in every alleyway and the space between his shoulder blades prickled with tension.

He'd almost made up his mind to just let them have the twenty pounds - after all he had got a savings book. His parents and grandparents had paid in money for him every birthday and Christmas and he'd also been encouraged to save some of his pocket money. The problem was his father had the book for safe-keeping, and there was likely to be an inquest if Jamie wanted to draw money out. His father was likely to insist on going with him to the Post Office and then go with him to buy whatever it was he said he wanted.

Jamie wandered by the harbour, mulling over the problem. The tide was in and fishing boats and dinghies rode the oily water. No – he couldn't solve the problem that way.

He was wondering what to do next when he saw Kelly. She was carrying her black wet-look bag and her copper coloured hair was loose and fell almost to her waist. She wore a yellow cotton dress that reminded him of the play and the passions that had been aroused.

She smiled when she saw Jamie.

"Hi," he said, falling into step beside her. "Is your Mum any happier about your new career?"

She rolled her eyes in comic-dramatic fashion, but seemed pleased that he'd asked.

"D'you fancy hanging about for a bit?" he asked. "We could get some more chips if you like."

"O.K. then," she said with a smile.

As they walked towards the fish and chip shop, Jamie's mind was whirling, trying to think how he'd persuade Kelly to do what he wanted.

She was carrying on about her sister Miranda and her two snotty kids and how her mother thought the sun shone out of Miranda's backside and she could do no wrong. Jamie hoped she'd stop talking once they'd finished the chips, otherwise how was he supposed to even manage to kiss her, let along get into her knickers if she didn't shut up?

He wasn't even quite sure what he was supposed to do anyway. He'd skulked in the library a few days ago, looking through the 'facts of life' books, frustrated because he couldn't find anything that told him how he was supposed to feel and which bits you were supposed to touch and how did he know if he was doing it right?

Armed with the warm newspaper-wrapped package and two ice-cold bottles of coke, they made their way towards the cliffs. The late afternoon sun glittered on the sea and the air smelled of coconut and salt. Kelly's hair blew in the soft breeze, its softness grazing Jamie's bare arm and making him want to bury his face in it.

As they'd left the fish and chip shop, one of Rocky's henchmen was just going in. His eyes bulged in surprise when he noticed the pair of them, but as Jamie suspected, he wouldn't take any action on his own. He stopped feeling anxious. Everything would work out.

Kelly had hesitated momentarily before accepting Jamie's offer. She'd regretted rushing off so suddenly last time. She remembered how Miss Franks the Biology teacher had done that talk on the facts of life and how it was up to the girl to decide how fast a relationship went.

"Not very if she's anything to do with it," Clare Connor had giggled. "I couldn't imagine any man getting excited about buck teeth and bottle-bottom glasses."

"Just remember girls, it's up to you to say 'no.'" Miss Franks had said. "Don't do anything you don't want to do."

Kelly had been dodging Mick's advances for so long, Jamie would be easy. She wondered why he was looking so down – especially as he'd be off to London in a couple of weeks. The thought flitted through her head that if the job at the museum didn't work out, she could move to London to be with him – except that she remembered he was going to be staying with an uncle and aunt.

They walked on up the narrow path, and Kelly nearly

tripped on an uneven bit of ground. Jamie put his arm out to steady her – and kept his arm round her waist as they moved on up the path towards Kelly's favourite spot by the ruined house. They sat down on the soft grass and undid the chips. Kelly hadn't realised how hungry she was.

"Why do they always taste better out of newspaper?" she asked.

Jamie shrugged. "Dunno, but they do don't they?"

He scrunched the empty paper into a ball and threw it at a passing gull. Then he leaned across and kissed her gently on the lips.

"You're very special, Kelly," he said."

Kelly felt as if she was melting inside as she kissed him back.

They were sitting in a sheltered spot with the kitchen wall of the ruined house behind them, protected from the sea breeze and the prying eyes of anyone walking along the path because they were in the little gap between the kitchen and some sort of outbuilding.

The grass was soft and Jamie laid his sweater on the ground so Kelly could rest her head on it. He lay down beside her and took her in his arms. The kisses got deeper and Kelly's feelings spiralled into a rainbow of colours. She pulled back slightly when she felt his hand on her breast, tentative at first, then getting more confident. She was not like Miranda, she wouldn't let this go too far.

"Shh, it's all right. I love you, Kelly. I'm not going to hurt you."

Jamie's voice was reassuring. Kelly heard the magic words 'I love you' and relaxed as his hand bunched up her dress and touched her body gently, skin to skin, his fingers grazing the waist-band of her knickers. They were lying so close she could feel the hardness of his erection through his jeans.

Kelly's knickers felt damp as Jamie's fingers explored

further, turning her skin to fire. The colours intensified and she could hear someone screaming.

"Shh, Kelly, don't …I'm not hurting you am I?

He was pulling at her knickers, trying to take them off. He wasn't going to take them off. Kelly wasn't like Miranda.

The world span wildly as Kelly opened her eyes, feeling as if she'd just got off a fairground waltzer. She took in their dishevelled clothing and Jamie's flushed face.

She heard voices and a stampede of feet on the cliff path. Kelly sat up, smoothing her crumpled dress over her hips and plaiting her tangled hair, rescuing her sandals from where she'd carelessly kicked them off.

Rocky was at the head of the group, carrying a camera.

"It doesn't look like you've even got to first base, Collins! I'd have thought a tart like her would've had your trousers off by now. You may as well give us the money."

Kelly leapt to her feet. "I don't know what sort of nasty game you're playing, Jamie, but you can find some other girl to play it with."

She pushed her way through the gang of lads and hurried down the cliff path, sobs tearing at her throat. She felt cheap and sordid, as if she wanted to get in the bath and scrub herself for a week. Was that what Jamie was up to – staging some sort of sex show for Rocky and his mates? And she'd been chosen because of her sister's reputation for being easy.

She hurried home, tears streaming down her face. She wanted to get away from Tredannac Bay – and she didn't want anything else to do with Jamie Collins for as long as she lived. The house was empty when she got home. Mick was at the pub and Viv was working an extra shift. Kelly had a bath, scrubbing herself with a flannel until she was raw. Then she got into bed and pulled the covers over her head. She fell into a disturbed sleep, punctuated by dreams about Jamie and the brilliant colours their love-making had aroused, now faded to ashes.

Jamie was at the front door before eight o'clock the next morning, bearing a wilting bunch of pink roses.

Viv, who was busy putting on her make up and getting ready for work, shouted up the stairs to Kelly. In doing so, she woke Mick who stumbled to the top of the stairs calling out: "What's the bleedin' racket about, can't a bloke get any sleep?"

"Kelly," Viv shouted, "get down here now."

"Might've known it'd be some lover's tiff," grumbled Mick, heading back to bed.

"What is it?" asked Kelly, after Viv had shouted her for the second time.

"Jamie's here for you."

"I don't want to see him."

"Come down and tell him yourself then."

"Don't bother," said Jamie, "I'm going." He dumped the roses on the sticky kitchen table amongst the remains of Viv's breakfast and left the house, slamming the door behind him.

Viv squeezed her mascara and lipstick into her purple make-up bag and shoved it into her white leather handbag. Then she went upstairs and pushed open Kelly's bedroom door.

Kelly was lying in bed, eyes open, staring at the ceiling. She looked as if she'd been crying.

"What's going on, Kelly? What was he doing round here at this time in the morning?"

"It's none of your business," said Kelly.

"I think it might be if you're pregnant."

"Well I'm not. OK?" Kelly stared defiantly back at Viv.

"You should know." Viv's face softened slightly as she turned to go back downstairs. "They're not worth getting upset about, love. And anyway, he's not our type."

SEVEN

Jed had every intention of staying independent but Mirabelle had other ideas. He'd returned home from a shift at the supermarket feeling tired, dirty and in need of a bath

One of his jobs had been to clear away a pile of rotting fish from the back of the warehouse. He'd gagged on the smell and everything he'd eaten since, even though he'd scrubbed his hands, seemed to be tainted with it.

The hot water taps in the grimy bathroom at the end of the landing that he shared with two other bed-sits never produced more than a trickle of lukewarm water, no matter how many coins were put in the meter, so he had to make the best of a strip-wash.

The last thing he'd expected to find pushed under his door when he returned from the bathroom was a note from his landlord thanking him for his letter terminating his rental agreement. His flat would be re-let to someone else as from the beginning of next month. His bond money would be returned provided that Jed had kept the bed-sit in good condition. Jed lay on his bed holding the scruffy piece of paper, staring out at the night sky wondering how such a misunderstanding had occurred.

At eight thirty the next morning he pounded up the dusty wooden stairs above the betting shop where the letting agent's office was. The desk was littered with paperwork, yellowing newspapers and half-empty coffee cups that looked like they were growing penicillin. Niall Kennedy, a big man in a crumpled beige suit, sat with his feet up on the desk talking to someone on the phone.

"Yes, Mona darling, anything you say." His Irish brogue got more pronounced the longer the conversation went on.

Jed fidgeted in the doorway. The only other seat in the room was taken up by Niall Kennedy's Yorkshire terrier, Violet, who with tiny paws buried in a tattered red silk cushion, was yapping and growling and all set to repel the intruder, the pink bow in her topknot moving with each yap.

"I'll call you back later, Mona darling. Violet needs to go out."

Jed could hear the luckless Mona shouting, "and make sure you do this time," as Niall replaced the receiver.

Niall Kennedy stood up, reached across the desk and picked Violet up. "Sit down. What can I do for you?"

Jed held out the piece of paper. "What's this about?"

"Your lady friend's arranged it all. Going up in the world aren't you, sir? Talk about the luck of the Irish!"

"What d'you mean?" Jed's lips felt stiff and dry.

Niall rummaged in the pile of paperwork nearest to him and pulled out a piece of thick cream paper. Jed recognised the swooping black writing.

"'Course, you've done me a favour in a way – me nephew's coming over from Galway for three months and I was wondering where to put him."

"This wasn't my idea," said Jed. "Can't you find me something else?"

Niall spread his hands wide. "Like I said, my properties are fully booked – and I couldn't offer you anything as flash as Chelsea. Now if ye'll excuse me, Violet needs her morning walk."

Mirabelle didn't look at all surprised to see Jed when he knocked on her door an hour later. He was so mad he'd gone straight there from the letting agent's.

She wrinkled her nose. "You smell like you've just been to a fish market." They were standing in the hallway, bathed in white light from the cupola above them, like actors on a stage.

"I want to know what gives you the right to meddle in my life."

She looked at him, eyes wide with innocence. "I was only trying to help."

Mitch came out of one of the downstairs rooms. "At least have a cup of coffee with us and let's talk about things properly."

Jed reluctantly agreed. He was light-headed from lack of food and he'd wasted a lot of energy complaining to Niall Kennedy and then getting to Mirabelle's house.

"Look sonny, what's ya problem?" asked Mitch, clapping him on the shoulder after they'd finished the tray of coffee and blueberry muffins. "Mirrie's got money – you haven't. Call it a sharing of wealth if it makes you feel better. She wants to act in the movies. She needs a script to work from. You've already proved you can write. Mirrie likes and trusts you. She wants to bankroll you until you've got the level of success you deserve. What's the matter with that?"

"I was managing on my own," growled Jed. "I don't need charity."

"Sonny, that squat you were in was a hell-hole. Sooner or later you'd have gotten sick and then what? Why d'ya have to be so stiff-necked about this? Look – if it makes you feel better, look on it as an advance... At least go and look at the place Mirrie's made ready for you before you say no."

Jed followed Mirabelle up the sweeping curve of the stairs, imagining the women in flowing ball-gowns who must have come down them. Portraits of snooty looking men in wigs hung on the lemon sorbet coloured walls next to women in low-cut diaphanous dresses. They went along a carpeted corridor that had several closed doors leading onto it. The paintwork was white and shiny.

Mirabelle flung open the door at the end of the corridor. There were three inter-connecting rooms like a private hotel suite. "This used to be Lady Georgiana's bedroom, dressing room and withdrawing room," said Mirabelle, "and I just love this view of the walled garden."

The bedroom had a king-size bed – so different from the

single divan Jed had slept on since he'd lived at the bed-sit. The peach and cream décor was a bit too feminine for him, but who was he to quibble. The en-suite bathroom boasted a big bath, a walk in shower and a shelf full of toiletries to rival anything in Boots, but it was the study that really inspired him.

Sitting at the conker shiny desk, he could see the rose garden and a fascinating collection of rooftops beyond. His feet sank almost to his ankles in soft grey carpet and the room was warm, not damp and chilly like his bed-sit.

On the desk was a new electric IBM Golf-ball typewriter of the sort he'd only just read about. Wooden shelves were neatly stacked with paper and envelopes and the room smelled of freshly ironed linen and beeswax polish.

"What d'ya say?" asked Mirabelle.

She was standing so close to him, he could feel the heat from her body and smell the rose and jasmine scent of her shampoo.

Jed nodded slowly. "It's wonderful," he said, spinning round on the chair behind the desk.

"So does that mean yes?"

He could feel her warm breath on his cheek.

"It still doesn't seem right. I'd feel like a kept man."

Mirabelle ran a manicured hand through her waterfall of dark hair. "So you'd let your stupid pride stand in the way of success? I don't believe you, Jed. I thought you wanted to be a top author."

"I do."

Mirabelle knelt on the floor in front of him. "Then let me help you. We'll draw it all up properly if you want – and if you feel real bad about it you can pay me back when you make the big time."

Jed nodded slowly. "In that case – I don't see how I can refuse."

Suddenly his arms were full of Mirabelle and her lips

were fused to his.

It was some time before they separated. "Gee, my father will be wondering what we've been doing," said Mirabelle as she led the way back downstairs, "especially as I stink of fish now." She made her funny intimate face at him.

"I was looking out the champagne glasses," Mitch called. "I guessed there might be something to celebrate."

As he sipped his champagne, Jed wondered if he'd done the right thing by taking the easy option. He'd noticed how Mirabelle's lips had curled in a triumphant smile as she poured the champagne. He felt guilty, knowing he was attracted to her but didn't love her. He hoped she wasn't expecting more than he could give.

EIGHT

I was Susan then – not Sabrina. It was after that stuff with Jamie – and the way Kelly's shadow always came between us - that made me decide to change my name. The problem was, as any psychiatrist could've told me if I'd bothered to ask enough questions, the inside of me was still seething with hurt and anger. For a change of name to work, you need to be a new person right through – like the lettering on a stick of rock.

Mrs Wilson was the only person who knew my secret ambition was to be a writer. I'd felt that way since I was seven – ever since 'that' lesson in school when our teacher asked us what we wanted to be when we grew up.

I can remember how the rest of the class tittered when I said I wanted to write stories.

The teacher went bright pink and said: "I don't think that's a proper job, do you dear? I think you'd better write about being a nurse instead."

I obviously wrote the story convincingly enough because she put it on the wall for Open Day, but I can remember how cheated I felt because my heart wasn't in it.

There were terrible arguments when I decided I wasn't going to University – something that my father had set his heart on just so he could brag about his two clever girls. Jennifer and I had never got on and there was no way I wanted to be like her with two perfect children and a chinless wonder of a husband.

We always had to be the best – that was why Dad threw his weight around over the Juliet affair.

It was Mrs Wilson who suggested I do a newspaper apprenticeship and become a journalist. Dad pulled a few strings with someone he'd been at school with and I was offered a job. However, going to London didn't change my life in the way I'd hoped. That's why I changed my name when I went to Paris.

On Tuesday morning I was sitting in the cubby hole in my

flat that masquerades as a kitchen, sipping a mug of tea with my ginger cat Max curled up on my lap, looking as if he was dong me a favour.

I didn't have to be in work until nine, but I'd been up since six-thirty drinking mugs of tea and trying to find a fresh angle for my assignment. Since looking at those photos yesterday so many images from the past had raced back towards me. Every time I fell asleep last night I was sixteen years old and back in Tredannac Bay believing I could make Jamie Collins love me, feeling excited that I was on the threshold of a new career in London. I knew I was luckier than most of the girls in my class. Even having to stay with my godmother in Pimlico and be chaperoned by her wasn't that bad when you considered that people like Kelly probably wouldn't get to go any further than Launceston.

How was I to know that she'd have better luck than me?

Max looked surprised to see me up and about when he came in through the kitchen window at seven o'clock. Usually I leapt out of bed with about half an hour to go until I was meant to be at work, had a quick wash, put on some clothes, swallowed a few mouthfuls of cereal, left food and water for Max and hurried out of the flat.

The assignment I'd been given had changed all that. For years, I'd locked Jamie and Kelly in a secure place inside my head and hadn't thought about them. Seeing the photographs of Kelly had smashed this door down and I was in a state of turmoil.

'Think calmly,' I told myself. 'Kelly can't hurt you now. This is your chance to set the record straight - to put your side of the story.'

But I had a feeling that whatever I said would sound like sour grapes – the whingeing of a middle aged woman still trying to get her own back on a much prettier classmate – still envious despite the fact that three decades had passed.

'Stick to the facts,' I told myself. 'You can't go too far

wrong if you do that' I can remember Mrs Wilson saying that to me at school once, when she was giving me some advice on writing articles before I went for my interview in London.

"There will be times when you need to put your own feelings on one side," she said, "a bit like being a lawyer. Just imagine if someone was writing about you – you'd want them to show the situation in a positive light wouldn't you?"

I'd agreed with her, of course, but I knew I'd never forgive Kelly or be able to say anything positive about her.

I knew all about Kelly and her family – the whole class did. I suppose she was pretty in an old-fashioned sort of way. The fashion then was for straight hair – I could remember my Mum telling me off because she caught me trying to iron my hair under a sheet of brown paper – but it was Kelly who drew the glances with her pre-Raphaelite rippling mass of auburn curls.

I changed my hair colour years ago, so I've been blonde for more of my life than I was mouse-brown. 'Bottle blonde' Jamie referred to me as once. I must stop thinking about him – that way madness lies! Was it Hamlet who said that? Why does everything take me back to that time when my life started to go wrong?

I knew I wasn't the right person to play Juliet, however much my father ranted and raved about it. I hadn't wanted him to complain to Mr Taylor. I'd sat in the French lesson with my stomach churning - dreading that when the meeting was over I'd be told I'd got the part after all.

Dad thought I was disappointed because I didn't get it. How could I tell him it wasn't playing Juliet I minded about, I'd just wanted the opportunity to get close to Jamie Collins?

Mrs Wilson said my acting was wooden – and she was right. I learned the lines and I said them, and that was that. I didn't live the part like Kelly did.

I was the sort of child who had a natural talent for eavesdropping – ideal for a reporter – finding out titbits of salacious gossip, dishing the dirt, going through the rubbish bins of life and discovering all manner of guilty secrets. That's why I knew about Jamie's problem with Rocky. I'd overhead the gang talking about what they'd do to him if he didn't deliver.

A slow smile spread across my face when I realised that with a bit of clever talking I could have Jamie Collins exactly where I wanted him. He needed proof he was a man. I was happy to help him supply it.

Somehow it all fell into place – we were both going to London. If I started something now, then there was every chance of finishing it when we got there. I caught up with Jamie down near The Copper Kettle in the main street. He eyed me warily when I said I had a proposition to put to him. Even so, he followed me into the café, stumbling past the old women and their shopping baskets until we reached a table in the corner where we wouldn't be disturbed.

I ordered cokes for us both, and waited till they arrived, complete with slices of lemon in ice-cold glasses before I launched into my speech. The café was stiflingly hot and the air smelled of cinnamon and hot buttered toast.

"You need a favour to get you off the hook with Rocky and his pals," I swallowed down the nervous lump in my throat, "I want to lose my virginity before I go to London. I think you're man enough for the job - how about it?"

My legs were shaking under the white lace tablecloth and I was glad Jamie couldn't see them.

The effect on him was more dramatic. He spluttered on his coke, causing a stain on the white table-cloth and the ladies on the table nearest to us who'd been discussing the church flower rota muttered angrily that children shouldn't be allowed in The Copper Kettle without supervision.

"Where could we go?" asked Jamie when he'd recovered himself.

"Does that mean yes?"
He nodded.

"My house," I said, "now."

My Dad was at work and Mum was out shopping in Launceston and would be home on the six o'clock bus, and I needed to do it before I lost my nerve.

It felt weird walking up the street with Jamie. I had an excuse prepared if anyone saw us go indoors together. He'd come to borrow some Stones records.

We went straight upstairs and into my bedroom, shutting the door behind us. I have to say that what happened next was the biggest anticlimax of my life up till then. We didn't take all our clothes off – at the back of my mind was the nagging thought of what if my Dad came home early?

I took off my knickers and we lay down stiffly on my single bed – I'd put a towel under us because I'd heard there might be blood. Jamie unzipped his trousers and slid them down over his hips. He looked pale with nerves and his hands were cold and clammy.

I was no expert – all I'd done before was the odd fumble with my cousin David when we visited my uncle and aunt in Lincolnshire. David was one year older than me and what we did took place when we were eleven and twelve and probably wouldn't have made a rabbit pregnant.

That was one thing I hadn't thought of – and from the look of him neither had Jamie.

"Have you got anything?" I whispered, still trying to sound passionate.

"What d'you mean?"

"You know – those things blokes wear…"

The penny dropped. He rummaged in his trouser pocket and pulled out a small crumpled packet. I pulled him towards me, smiling to myself as I felt him harden. He seemed to come to life then, his hands going everywhere, until we were both in a state of excitement. I didn't expect it to hurt like it did. He didn't appear to notice, arching above me and pumping away as if he'd had an electric shock.

When it was all over, he flopped down against my shoulder and I heard him groan her name. Kelly.

We sorted the proof he needed for Rocky and his gang. Then he left me. I tidied the crumpled bedspread and sat wrapped in my old pink dressing gown. I thought I'd feel like the Queen of Creation but all I felt was dirty.

It was only later I realised we'd never got round to using the condom. I was off to London to start my new life. What would I do if I turned out to be pregnant?

NINE

Jed was happy at first, although it was strange having a bathroom he didn't have to share with anyone else and to go down the curved staircase to breakfast – a bit like being on holiday. Usually Mirabelle would sit with him, sipping a glass of orange juice while he ate his breakfast.

He found it even stranger to start the day with a full stomach after the long months of having no more than a slice of dry toast and Marmite and a mug of black coffee.

However, Jed soon discovered his wonderful study with its IBM typewriter wasn't the private space his bed-sit had been. When he discovered Mirabelle in there going through his work, he felt irritated. In the bed-sit, he could leave his work all over the bed or the floor if he wanted to with nobody to interfere. He sometimes found it helped to spread the work out and step back from it as if he was painting a picture.

Now here was Mirabelle or Jenny the cleaner tidying his things, wrecking his creative maze, getting in his way. It was hard to suppress his irritation.

"I was watching you from the doorway yesterday," Mirabelle said sulkily. "It's not like you were doing anything then either – just staring out of the window and then back up at the ceiling, so there's no need to be cross."

It was no good trying to explain to her about creative daydreaming – she didn't understand. She took to coming up mid-morning on the pretext of bringing him a cup of coffee. Jed found that he might as well abandon the day's work then. With Mirabelle chattering there was no room in his head for creative ideas.

Jed was glad that at least he'd got a bed to himself. At least the nights were his alone. He could sit up in bed and write undisturbed, gazing through the open muslin curtains at the expanse of midnight blue sky and the jumble of rooftops backlit by the sodium orange lights of London. He was frantically searching the pages of his mind for an idea that would make a good film. So far he'd come up with nothing that inspired him.

One night he was just settling down to sleep when he heard a noise on the landing outside his door. He lay listening, wondering what or who it could be. Mitch's rooms were on the floor below, Mirabelle's were in the other wing on this floor.

Jed had read a brief history of the house written by a previous occupant who stated that some of the rooms were haunted by the ghost of Lady Georgiana. The idea interested him and certainly didn't scare him – he thought he might include her in a future novel. She'd been a feisty woman who'd travelled extensively through Europe collecting works of art and lovers as she went. She'd held regular salons in this house and had died peacefully in her bed at the age of seventy five.

Jed had been thinking about the way some houses vibrated with energy as if the walls held memories. He heard a faint click as his bedroom door opened as if blown by the wind that was making the trees dance in the garden below. He never closed the curtains when he slept, enjoying the views of moon and stars. Through half closed eyes he noticed a white clad figure moving quietly across the floor, the fabric of its thin nightdress billowing in the breeze coming through the open sash window.

Mirabelle slid into bed beside him.

"What's up?" Jed did a convincing display of someone who'd just woken up.

"I couldn't sleep," said Mirabelle, snuggling against his chest, the smell of her shampoo filling his nostrils.

Within two days, she'd moved her things into his room.

"Won't your father object?" asked Jed. He couldn't think of many fathers who'd take kindly to the situation.

"He likes you sweetie," said Mirabelle, wrapping her arms around his shoulders as he sat at his desk and knocking his neatly typed sheets of paper askew. "He's waiting for you to finish the movie script and announce our engagement."

"Our engagement?" Jed felt as if he was on a runaway horse.

"You can't say we're not compatible," she cooed.

Jed grew hot thinking of the passionate embraces they'd shared between the linen sheets.

"After all," she went on, "if you're writing my movie script then I should be your leading lady in every sense of the word."

"It's not right. I should be in a position to look after you if I ask you to marry me." Jed was searching his mind for any excuse to get out of this situation.

"When the movie's produced then you'll be making your own money," she said. "And for now you can have whatever you want. You only have to ask."

She flicked through the papers on his desk – a habit that irritated Jed because she never put things back in the right place. "So how's the movie coming along? When do I get to read some of it?"

"Not till I've finished writing," he said, flipping her nose, wishing he felt as playful as the gesture implied. All he wanted was to get away from here to a place where he could think properly. He wished more than anything that he could come up with an idea for a movie script. If he didn't then all he had could disappear like fairy dust in a strong wind and he'd be back in a crummy bed-sit staring at years of no prospects.

TEN

Kelly was spending a boring morning at the Museum. This was nothing new. Ever since she'd started work there, Miss Bates had looked down her nose at Kelly and had only given her the most menial jobs to do – like going through piles of newspapers searching for cuttings and sticking them in a book and filing bits of yellowing paper that she'd probably not want to find ever again.

Miss Bates did all the tours of the Museum herself – not that there was anything much to tell. Kelly felt she knew the script by heart now and it was all dull facts and figures. She sometimes wondered if she did the right thing turning down the job in the biscuit factory – the work couldn't be any more mind-numbing and at least the pay was better and she'd have had people to talk to. Miss Bates looked like a dried up moth and only spoke to Kelly to issue instructions or to tell her off.

"I'm going to a meeting in Launceston this morning," she'd said. "I'm entrusting you with the responsibility of looking after the Museum and getting on with your work. I shall expect to see those cuttings finished by the time I get back. Please tell any visitors there will be no tours until after lunch."

It was cold in the Museum, even in summer. The walls were thick and the small windows didn't let in much light. Kelly sat at the desk opposite the entrance where a cold draught blew under the heavy wooden door even though the sun was shining outside, glad that she'd remembered to bring a cardigan.

She got on with her work, feeling that a transistor radio would do a lot to lift the dismal atmosphere. It might even persuade some people to come in. A coach load of holiday makers were walking down the street but none of them ventured inside the Museum.

At ten-thirty Kelly made herself a cup of tea. She felt more relaxed with Miss Bates out of the way, releasing her hair from the plait she usually put it in while she was at work. Miss Bates considered that hair, particularly when it was as wild as Kelly's, was frivolous and should be tied back.

She sat at the reception desk, careful not to put the tea anywhere it could spill on the precious cuttings. A shadow fell across her work.

"Any chance of a ticket please, Miss?"

Kelly looked up into a pair of intense blue eyes in the handsomest face she'd seen in a long time. Despite her vow since the business with Jamie to have nothing else to do with men, she felt surge of excitement. It was obvious that the man felt it too, and although they'd never met before, Kelly felt a spark of recognition.

She took the money he offered her and handed him a ticket. "I'm sorry but the official tour isn't available till this afternoon," she said.

The man smiled. "Can you give me an unofficial one? I have a feeling that might be a lot more interesting."

Kelly felt herself blushing. "It depends what you want to know…"

She led the way into the Local History room. "You're not from round here are you?" she asked, wishing she could take back the question as soon as she'd said it. She was conscious of her Cornish burr and felt she must sound like an old-fashioned country yokel.

He wore denim jeans and a black t-shirt and dangled a leather jacket by its chain loop. He'd pushed his sunglasses on top of his head when he came indoors, making his dark hair look casually ruffled.

"I'm from London," he said, "although it was always my ambition to live in Cornwall when I was young. We used to go to Penzance on holiday every year and I can remember how I never wanted to come home."

"My Gran lived in London," said Kelly.

"And she doesn't any more?"

"She died," said Kelly.

The door opened and Miss Bates came in looking flustered.

"I thought I told you to get on with your work, Kelly," she said. She turned to the man. "I do apologise. Kelly hasn't worked at the Museum very long so she has no experience of giving tours. She was instructed to tell you that if you'd like an official tour then they will be available after two o'clock." Her mouth closed in a straight line and Kelly knew she'd be for it when the man left.

"Thank you for your hospitality," he said to Kelly, giving her a mock bow. "I'll try and call back later."

The temperature seemed to drop by about ten degrees after he'd gone. Miss Bates glared at Kelly as if she'd come back to find her in a compromising position on one of the desks, rather than trying to help a valued customer.

"You're on your last warning, Kelly. I knew it was a mistake taking you on. You've been nothing but trouble since you got here. Now go and take your lunch break and make sure you're back on time for once. And when you come back I want those cuttings finished and your hair tied back in the proper manner."

Kelly grabbed her bag and made for the door, feeling warmer as she stepped outside. In the distance, the sea glittered and shimmered from jade to turquoise and she wished she could be up on the cliffs with her sketchbook.

He was waiting for her by the low white wall near the bakery, sunglasses on so she couldn't read the expression in his eyes. His smile was real enough though.

"Kelly isn't it?" I forgot to say, before we were interrupted by the Dragon Lady, my name's Jed. Jed Matthews. I'm from London and I'm a writer."

He fell into step with her. "Is there somewhere nice I

could buy you lunch so you can tell me more about local history?"

Kelly was about to say she was busy, but then the door of The Copper Kettle opened and Jamie came out with Susan Baker. They both had grins on their silly faces and Susan had her arm linked through Jamie's. She knew Susan hadn't seen her, but Jamie had. He looked shocked to see Kelly with someone else, as if he was about to break away from Susan and come after her. She felt a shaft of anger. What did he expect? That she was still in a crumpled heap in her bedroom because of the way he'd treated her?

Kelly's mind was made up. Fate had given her a new opportunity. Not a permanent one probably, but it was enough to make Jamie sit up and take notice.

She turned to Jed. "We could go to the pub down by the harbour. I mustn't take more than an hour though or Miss Bates'll have my guts for garters. I'm already on my last warning."

"That's a London expression if ever I heard one."

"One of my Gran's," said Kelly as they walked down the sloping street towards the harbour, past shops and white painted cottages with their window boxes overflowing with red geraniums, blue lobelia, hot pink petunias and orange marigolds.

Kelly was aware of people looking at them, certain that the story of her being picked up by a fancy man from London would be all round Tredannac Bay by the time she got home. *'Let them think what they like,'* she thought. Getting back at Jamie for treating her so shabbily and then going off with Susan was uppermost in her mind as she and Jed sat down on varnished wooden barrels that served as chairs on the paved terrace outside The Anchor, overlooking the harbour.

The tide was low and small boats lay marooned on the ribbed sand near the shore, while further out, tied to the harbour wall, boats made ready for the next night's fishing, yellow oilskin-clad figures hosing down decks and taking on water and provisions.

"What can I get you?" Jed passed the menu with its anchor logo on it to Kelly.

Kelly ferreted in her bag for her purse, not looking at the menu. "Just a coke and a packet of crisps, please, I haven't got much money."

"This is my treat," he said. "And if anyone asks awkward questions, you're giving me some useful information about my film script."

"Film script?"

"Between you and me I'm trying to come up with an idea," he said conspiratorially. "And I need to be inspired by the time I go home on Friday. How would you fancy a steak sandwich and a glass of wine?"

"It sounds lovely, but it's so expensive," said Kelly.

"It's going on expenses," said Jed. "Do I l take that as a yes?"

He went into the pub to place the order, coming back with two glasses of red wine. Kelly sipped it, trying to look as if this was what she did every day of the week. Her only previous experience of alcohol was at parties she'd gone to with Jess and her other friends that usually involved cans of Party Seven beer for the lads and Cinzano and lemonade for the girls. She hoped the wine wouldn't go to her head – coming back drunk would be all that Miss Bates needed as an excuse to sack her.

"Is that OK?" Jed asked settling back on his barrel.

Kelly nodded. Being with him felt like meeting up with an old friend. She'd read stories in the newspaper about men who preyed on young girls, told them all sorts of stories and then raped or murdered them. She instinctively trusted Jed in a way that she wouldn't trust Jamie or most other men she'd met.

"I've never met a writer before," she said as their steak sandwiches arrived, thick with fried onions, the plates garnished with salad and fat chips glistening with salt. "What do you write?"

Jed took a bite of his sandwich and chewed thoughtfully. "I feel a bit of a fraud calling myself a writer at the moment. I've been suffering from a massive case of writers' block – and now I've got a week to come up with an idea for this film."

"And you think I can help?" Kelly bit into her sandwich, thinking it was the best thing she'd eaten in a long time.

"What's a girl like you doing working in a Museum?"

"It was that or the biscuit factory," said Kelly.

"And what would you like to do?"

"Be an actress," said Kelly. "Or if I'm not good enough, painting the scenery or dealing with the costumes."

"You like the theatre?"

"I've only been a few times," said Kelly, sprinkling more vinegar on her chips. "Gran always promised that when I was older she'd take me to London and we'd go to the places Nell Gwyn would've known."

"What's the fascination with Nell Gwyn?"

"Our birthdays are on the same day – 2nd February. That's always made her feel like a special kind of sister." Kelly realised how daft that must sound, but Jed obviously didn't think so. He was scribbling furiously in a little black book that he'd taken from his jacket pocket.

"Are you writing down what I just said?"

"It's interesting. What else can you tell me? You mentioned drawing – what do you draw?"

Kelly fished her sketchbook out of her bag. She handed it to Jed and got on with finishing her sandwich, savouring every mouthful.

Jed looked through the sketchbook, a frown furrowing his brow. "Where's this? It looks familiar."

"It's a ruined house on the cliffs," said Kelly, trying not to think about the time she was there with Jamie and the feelings he'd aroused. "I've always felt drawn to the place – as if there's a magnet pulling me there. It's said to be haunted by a lady in white waiting for her lost love. The local boys dare each other to go up on the cliffs at night and call for the white lady."

Jed scribbled some more.

The church clock struck two.

"I'm supposed to be back at work," Kelly yelped, leaping up and grabbing her bag and sketchbook. She'd reached the door of the Museum, her full stomach aching after the dash up the street from the harbour, before she realised she hadn't thanked Jed for lunch. She didn't expect to see him again.

ELEVEN

Jed watched her go in a flurry of long legs and flying auburn hair. He went into the pub and got another glass of wine and drank it slowly staring blankly at the boats in the harbour. In all the time he'd been with Mirabelle, he'd never felt that spark of recognition that he'd experienced when he first saw Kelly sitting at the desk in the Museum.

He sat looking at the notes he'd made, feeling relaxed in the salt-scented air, questions he wished he'd asked Kelly about the cottage on the cliffs and what was supposed to have happened there spiralling round in his head.

Why did he think it was their story he was asking about – his and Kelly's from a long time ago? Jed shook himself. He didn't believe in reincarnation or whatever they called it. And he really needed to get on with this script. If Mirabelle found out he'd taken another girl to lunch, he could very well find himself homeless. He'd seen what her temper was like when she didn't get her own way.

He hadn't said anything to Kelly about his personal circumstances and she hadn't asked. Come to that, he hadn't asked her if she'd got a boyfriend. A pretty girl like her was bound to have one stashed away somewhere – more likely some hunky fisherman who would beat him to a pulp if he hung around too long.

He wasn't going to hang around, was he? Or only long enough to do a bit of research. He wished Kelly hadn't had to dash off so quickly – there was so much he wanted to talk about.

"Does Tredannac Bay have a library?" he asked the barman who'd come outside for a smoke and was obviously anxious to shut up shop for a few hours.

The man pointed up the street to a building that looked like a chapel. "Open until four," he said.

Jed checked his watch. It was three o'clock. He'd just

have time to visit the library and see if they'd got any information about the white lady. He didn't think there was any point in asking the old trout at the Museum. He hoped Kelly hadn't got into trouble for being late – and that she'd forgive him for not turning up for the tour this afternoon.

In the library a young woman with short dark hair helped him find a book on local legends. He searched through, looking at stories about ghost ships and phantom horses until he came to the story Kelly had mentioned - about Morwenna and Jethro, the star-crossed lovers. With a surge of excitement he realised he'd found the subject for his movie script.

He sat scribbling down notes, drawing maps and diagrams and jotting down book references. He'd finally tracked down a suitable idea and he knew he should phone Mirabelle and tell her. There was no excuse for not going back to London tomorrow, now he'd got a starting point, but somehow he wasn't ready to leave yet. It was as if that magnet that Kelly talked about was drawing him towards the ruined house on the cliffs as well. He'd heard that the rocks in Cornwall were supposed to have magical properties. Was it possible that the stones could hold a memory for over two hundred years?

They had to throw him out of the library at closing time.

"I'm sorry," said the librarian, "but we're closing in two minutes. We are open from nine o'clock tomorrow morning if we can be of any further help." She had kind brown eyes and a friendly smile that showed crooked teeth.

Jed stood in the sudden glare of the afternoon sun wondering what to do next. He knew he should get in his car and head back to Penzance, finish the outline of his story and head back to London and forget all about Kelly, but somehow his feet wouldn't move.

He thought about going back to the Museum and braving a tour with the dragon lady in the hope of catching another glimpse of Kelly, but he didn't want to get her in any more trouble.

As he hesitated, the Museum door opened and Kelly came out. He hadn't expected her to be finished yet - the 'opening times' bit on the door stated five o'clock. Her hair flew wildly round her shoulders and tears were pouring down her face.

She glared at Jed when she saw him and walked past ignoring his outstretched hand.

TWELVE

Miss Bates had scowled at Kelly when she flopped into her seat at five minutes past two, flushed from her glass of wine and the run up the hill.

"You're five minutes late," she snapped. "What have you got to say for yourself?"

"I'm sorry," said Kelly, "I'll stay later this afternoon."

"You will not," said Miss Bates. "I have a dental appointment and therefore need to leave promptly. I certainly cannot trust you to lock the Museum doors properly."

The milkman bustled in whistling, clanking the bottles in his crate.

Miss Bates winced.

"Hello my beauty," he said to Kelly. "Didn't I just see you down by The Anchor? You must have moved some to get back here before me. Who's the new boyfriend – not seen him round here before…"

He took the money Miss Bates slapped into his outstretched hand and went banging out of the door, still whistling.

Miss Bates glared at Kelly. "What have I told you about being over-familiar with visitors? No doubt it was that young man you were all over when I came back earlier. I will not tolerate such disgraceful behaviour – bringing the Museum into disrepute by hanging around a public house, behaving loosely with all and sundry. And may I remind you that you're too young to drink alcohol?"

"I wasn't drunk," said Kelly, "and I wasn't misbehaving with Jed. I was helping him with some information he wanted. He bought me lunch in return."

Kelly was so angry her hands were shaking. She was trying to finish the newspaper cuttings, but her eyes misted over with hot tears and she mistakenly snipped through the middle of an article.

She was saved another tirade from Miss Bates by the ringing of the phone in the other room.

Miss Bates went to answer it. Kelly could see her opening and closing her mouth but she couldn't hear what she was saying. As the conversation progressed, Miss Bates' face turned from pale and moth-like to an unbecoming purple. She slammed the phone down and came back to face Kelly.

"What precisely was the nature of the 'information' you gave that young man?" her voice was clipped.

"I was telling him the legend of the ruined house on the cliff," said Kelly. "He wrote it down in his book."

"I bet he did," hissed Miss Bates. "You little fool! He's gone straight to the local paper with his story, quoting you as the source of the information. I've just had to dispel some nonsense about a ghost ship that's supposed to appear when someone's about to die... Didn't you think what damage your silly stories could do to the credibility of the Museum? What did he pay you for the information you gave?

"He didn't pay me anything," said Kelly getting to her feet. "And for your information I'm not a fool – only for staying in this godforsaken hole for so long."

She got up, knocking a bottle of milk over in her haste. The bottle smashed and a tide of milk spread across the pile of newspaper cuttings. Ignoring Miss Bates' irate squawks, Kelly snatched up her bag and wrenched open the door, slamming it behind her as she raced out into the glaring afternoon heat.

THIRTEEN

I wanted to get my own back on Kelly. I couldn't forgive Jamie for calling her name at that most intimate moment.

I know that probably sounds illogical, but that's how I felt back then.

After all, I was off to London in a couple of weeks and would probably never see Smelly Kelly again. Whereas Jamie would be all mine and I was sure with time he'd come to feel the same about me as I did about him.

That's why I made that phone call to the local paper – to mess things up for Kelly like she'd fucked up my life.

It was deceptively easy – all it took was a handkerchief over the mouthpiece to disguise my voice – after all I'd done a bit of work experience there courtesy of Daddy pulling a few strings. I knew how things worked, which buttons to press.

How was I to know that Kelly had been talking to that guy from London about the old legends? I didn't think she'd be interested in anything like that.

All I'd intended to do was to make things a bit hot for her. I never expected things to turn out as they did and for her to end up following me to London. Some folk would say it was judgement on me for behaving as I did.

FOURTEEN

Kelly caught sight of Jed as she stormed out of the Museum. She walked past him with her nose in the air, determined he wouldn't see how much his nasty trick had upset her.

He caught up with her at the top of the street. Now Kelly was outside, the bubble of anger she'd felt against Miss Bates was deflating and she didn't know what to do next.

"Hey, who's upset you? What's going on?"

Kelly rounded on him. "You shouldn't need to ask that question. You know perfectly well what you've done. Selling the story I told you to the local paper... Do you realise I've just lost my job."

She stopped talking, knowing that one more word would cause the delicate balance of her emotions to tip and she'd start crying again.

"What are you talking about?" Jed pulled Kelly round to face him. She could tell by the look in his eyes that he didn't have a clue what she was on about.

"That phone call you made to the local paper about the story I told you ..." she began.

"Nothing to do with me," said Jed, "I've been in the Library all afternoon. Go and check with them if you don't believe me."

"That cow Miss Bates just had a right go at me because the local paper rang her to say they'd had a call about someone from the Museum telling stories about ghost ships. She's worried it's going to bring her precious Museum into disrepute and that it will turn into another trashy tourist attraction."

"I'm going to see her," said Jed. "Wait here."

Kelly watched him stride off down the street, sunglasses on and looking as if he meant business.

He returned a short time later, his mouth tight with anger.

"What a bundle of laughs that woman is! She began by accusing me of seducing you – and ended by implying I was a one-man wave of destruction." He paused. "She did let me call the local paper – 'The Echo' is it? And the girl I spoke to said it was a woman who called them with the story. She said the voice was muffled as if she was trying to disguise who she was."

Kelly stared at him, feeling as if her feet had turned to stone. "But who would do something like that?"

"It's probably one of those silly hoax things like kids do when they're let out of school. It's daft of Miss Bates or the paper to take it too seriously. Someone I was at school with once called The Evening Standard with a story about a haunted telephone box in Pinner that was all completely untrue! Within three days another fifty people had called the paper with so called ghostly sightings in the same place."

In spite of herself, Kelly laughed. The laugh changed to a shiver and then before she knew what had happened, tears were pouring down her cheeks.

Jed offered her his handkerchief. "You don't really believe I'd do a thing like that do you?" he said as she dried her eyes.

Kelly shook her head. Jed's handkerchief smelled of his aftershave. All she could think of was how attracted she was to him. It sounded crazy, but she felt as if they belonged together and yet she knew nothing about him or his life in London.

Jed looked at her. Kelly flushed under his scrutiny.

"You look better," he said, "but I can't send you home in that state."

"Home," said Kelly. "Oh my God - home."

"What's up?"

"My mother's going to go barmy when she finds out I've walked out on my job, that's what. She'll have me in that blasted biscuit factory before my feet have a chance to touch the floor. And she'll be all 'I told you so' about it."

"That's not the only job on the planet. There's always an alternative if you look for one."

"Not round here there isn't."

"Tell me about the house on the cliffs again."

Kelly knew Jed was trying to distract her and she was grateful to him. She'd have to face her mother soon enough. "I can show you if you like."

They walked down towards the harbour, retracing their steps from earlier in the day and up the cliff path. The sun came out again, warming Kelly's bare arms and the short grass felt springy under her feet. She wished she could stay here forever with Jed, surrounded by the vanilla scent of the gorse, the crash of the waves against the cliffs far below and the cry of the gulls.

She looked curiously at him. He was pale and trembling and had sunk down with his back against the remains of the front wall of the house.

"You OK?" She crouched down beside him, taking his hand in hers. It felt ice cold, and his face was pale as milk, his breathing shallow.

"Jed," she whispered, "what's the matter?"

He turned deep blue eyes towards her, shaking himself as if just waking from a bad dream. "That was weird. I had the strangest feeling as I was walking up here that I was coming home – except that I wasn't here – now. I was trying to get home but a sea mist had fallen – I could taste the smoky flavour of it and feared with every step that I'd go over the edge of the cliff to my death. It was unnaturally quiet, and I knew that somewhere up here they were waiting for me and I'd never see her – you – again."

Kelly's heart thudded in her chest. "That's so like the dream I get sometimes - where I'm lost in the mist and I can't find my way home. I draw and paint better here than anywhere else, but it's as if I'm waiting for a missing piece of my life to appear."

She didn't add that being here with Jed made her feel different. He'd think she was totally crazy – and besides after today she'd probably never see him again, no matter how drawn to him she felt.

The silence hung between them, feeling centuries old.

Kelly looked at her watch. "I should go. I bet Mum's heard all about what happened by now."

"Can you call her?"

"Yes. Why?"

"Don't go home yet. I'm still trying to make sense of what just happened. Let me take you for a meal first. No strings – no hanky-panky, whatever Miss Bates might think of me."

"And have people talk about me?" said Kelly.

"We can go a few miles away where you won't be recognised."

Kelly called Viv from the phone box near the harbour to say that she'd met up with someone from school and was having tea with them, so not to bother getting anything for her. It sounded as if Viv had got Miranda and the kids there again and was relieved there was one less to cook for.

"She can't know anything – yet. Or she'd have wanted me home. I'm dreading it when she does."

They'd got back to Jed's car – a sleek navy blue Jaguar with matching leather seats.

"People'll talk if they see me riding round in this."

Jed glanced up the street. He'd parked the car near the church. "There's nobody looking."

"Don't you be so sure, the folk round here have got eyes in their bottoms."

Kelly got in the car, snuggling into the soft leather of the seat. Who could've predicted her ending the day like this when she got up this morning? Maybe Jed was right, surprising things did happen. Maybe if he really liked her he'd offer her a part in that film he was writing and take her back to London with him.

FIFTEEN

Jed knew he should've followed his first instincts and left Tredannac Bay immediately after lunch. Better still, he shouldn't have taken Kelly for lunch in the first place. But then if he hadn't met her, she wouldn't have given him that fantastic idea for the movie script.

Jed had been writing long enough to know that when you got that special tingle of excitement you were onto something good. He felt the gloom of writer's block lifting and a sense of hopefulness return. It was also a relief to have a bit of time away from Mirabelle. He knew her heart was in the right place, but the relationship was suffocating him. He couldn't marry her, he was certain of that, but he couldn't find the right words to tell her how he felt.

He felt guilty that he didn't love her enough, especially after all she'd done for him, but love wasn't something you could buy with an American Express card. The least he could do was finish the movie script, pay back what he owed her and move on.

Now, with Kelly beside him in the car, her long bare legs stretched out, he felt a sense of peace. He took in the cheap yellow cotton dress she wore and the scuffed leather sandals. If he were to cast Kelly in the lead role for the film, then yellow would be the colour of the heroine's dress - yellow silk that would show up the smouldering amber of her eyes. It wasn't a colour he could ever remember Mirabelle wearing.

He started the engine. "I passed a nice looking place on the way here – shall we try that?"

Jed realised what it would look like to anyone else – a bloke old enough to know better preying on a young girl. He knew she was only sixteen and had told her he was twenty-three. Why had he lied about his age? What did he think she'd do if he'd admitted to being five years older than he'd said?

They pulled up in the car park in front of a black and white building decked with baskets of scarlet geraniums and dark blue lobelia.

Kelly felt everyone was looking at them as they walked into the restaurant through the iron studded wooden door. She could feel the heat of Jed's hand through the thin cotton of her dress, resting in the small of her back, guiding and protecting her .An appetising smell of garlic and frying meat enveloped them and Kelly's stomach growled with hunger.

The restaurant was arranged in separate little booths, upholstered in wine red velvet. The light was dim after the brightness outside and the flames of dozens of candles were reflected in the polished oak furniture. There were little posies of cinnamon-scented pinks on each table and proper white linen napkins as big as sheets. Kelly looked at the bewildering array of heavy silver cutlery and began to feel anxious about picking up the wrong ones.

"I'm never sure which knife and fork to use," said Jed after he'd given their order to the waiter. "But I don't suppose they'll throw us out if we get it wrong."

Kelly smiled gratefully at him. She looked at his carefully manicured hands and thought distastefully of Mick's big red ones and of Jamie's hands with their ink stains and bitten nails and the hot feel of them against her skin the last time he'd tried to touch her. She pushed the unwanted images away, wanting to make the most of her time with Jed.

Their starter arrived – Parma ham and melon – and she noticed how Jed worked from the outside in with his cutlery and tried to copy what he did. The plates were white with gold edges and Kelly thought of the cracked blue ones they had at home and of her Mum's kitchen with its smell of chip fat and burnt toast – and the way Mick always mashed his dinner up and added half a bottle of cheap brown sauce so that everything he ate probably tasted the same.

A bottle of white wine arrived in a bucket of ice. The starter plates were cleared and replaced with chicken in a garlic and ginger sauce.

"Tell me about your writing," said Kelly. "Have I really helped you with your work?"

"You've saved my life," said Jed. "The book I found in the library mentioned the story you told me. It said that the lady, Morwenna, was originally from a place near here, but was sold in marriage to a titled gentleman and sent many miles away to live in a big house. She left behind the man she loved – an artist – and he promised he would rescue her.

The reason Morwenna was chosen was because she bore a startling resemblance to the gentleman's first wife who'd mysteriously died. There were rumours that she'd been murdered and Morwenna was worried the same thing might happen to her.

When she heard that her husband had arranged for a portrait painter to come, she was certain she didn't have long to live and she was afraid."

"Why would anyone want to kill her?" asked Kelly.

"Nobody really found out. It could've been his possessive mother, or the strange housekeeper or a local doctor who was given to experimentation. Anyway, imagine her relief when the artist arrived and it was her own dear Jethro." Jed paused. "The problem was it didn't take long for the husband to become suspicious. The walls surrounding the house were thick and they both knew it wouldn't be easy to escape. But escape they did and they made for the little house on the cliff Jethro had bought in readiness for when he and Morwenna married."

"How did they escape?" asked Kelly.

Jed frowned. "Haven't quite worked that one out yet, but what I do know is their happiness wasn't set to last. They had a blissful year together, during which time a daughter was born to them, and then the rumours started about men looking for them and questions being asked."

Kelly shivered.

"Are you cold? Would you like my jacket?"

He went and fetched it off the coat stand and put it round her shoulders. The black leather felt soft as butter, the blue silk lining carried the smell of his aftershave.

The waiter cleared their plates and brought crisp white dessert menus. "I know it sounds daft – but sometimes when I'm there on the cliffs it feels…"

"What?" Jed reached out a hand, covering her trembling one. "What does it feel like Kelly?"

"It feels like I'm waiting for somebody to come back to me – and that when I find them, I'll be happy for the rest of my life."

Jed went quiet for several minutes. He hadn't let go of her hand and Kelly sat still, hoping he wouldn't. The energy that pulsed between them was like warm honey and she just wanted to stay there safe and warm.

The waiter came to take their order, breaking the mood.

Jed let go of Kelly's hand as he studied the menu.

"How about chocolate mousse?" he asked.

"I'll be getting fat, eating like this," said Kelly.

"No, you're the sort of girl who'll be slim into old age," he said to Kelly. "Make that two chocolate mousses," he told the waiter.

Kelly sat quietly, nursing the hope that Jed would make some declaration about wanting to take her back to London with him. Despite a few careful questions, he'd said nothing about where he lived or who with – other than it was in Chelsea. He had talked about his argument with his father over his writing and how sorry he felt for his mother.

"Hasn't your father come round, with your book being published and everything?" she'd asked as they finished their chocolate mousses and were waiting for the waiter to bring their coffee.

Jed shook his head. "I didn't even bother to invite him to the book signing – and I know my mother never mentioned it. I don't think he'll ever admit he was wrong about my writing, even if I get really famous."

"When," said Kelly, "you have to think when. That's what my Gran always told me. That you have to believe you'll do something, no matter how impossible it seems – that you have to keep building pictures in your mind."

"Pictures in your mind," said Jed thoughtfully. "I like that. And what pictures do you have in your mind, Kelly?"

"Being a famous stage actress, with a theatre named after me." Kelly looked at her watch. "It's half past ten! I'm supposed to be in by ten, not that Mum will probably be there to notice anyway – unless she's found out what happened by now, that is."

She went to the Ladies while Jed settled the bill. Jed's jacket was still round her shoulders and she knew she'd miss its comforting warmth. The stars were out and the sky was velvet-dark when they walked outside.

Kelly asked Jed to drop her by the crossroads, wishing the journey there could last forever.

When they got there he stopped the engine, leaned across and kissed her cheek. "Thank you," he said, "for the ideas you've given me. Like I said, you've saved my life."

He got out and opened the door for her, as if she was a VIP. She left his jacket on the passenger seat as she got out, giving him a quick hug before racing up the road towards her house so he wouldn't see her cry. Behind her, she heard him re-start the engine. She didn't turn to watch him go. Gran always said it was unlucky.

SIXTEEN

Jed watched Kelly run up the road, her long legs pale in the moonlight. He wished he'd given in to the temptation to just drive away with her – just the two of them and start a new life somewhere far from London where nobody knew them. He wondered what she'd have said if he'd suggested it.

"*Don't be a fool,*" he told himself. '*You're just on the verge of making it as a writer. You've landed on your feet, got a woman in London who is oceans deep in love with you and now you want to screw things up by messing about with a teenage girl.*'

Mirabelle had probably phoned the hotel dozens of times by now, demanding to speak to him. If he didn't get in touch with her pretty soon, she'd be down here wanting to know what he was doing. He didn't like to imagine what she'd say if she found out about Kelly.

He checked his watch. Mirabelle didn't go to bed till late. He could stop at a call box on his way back to Penzance and give her the good news about his breakthrough. The thought of talking to Mirabelle didn't excite him as it would've done a few months ago. He wondered what was wrong with him.

He'd begun today with a clear idea of where he was with his life. Now, since meeting Kelly, he felt as if he was in the middle of a kaleidoscope and someone had turned it and jumbled the picture. He told himself the best thing to do was pretend that today had never happened. But as he drove into the long empty night, he knew that was easier said than done. He couldn't stop thinking about Kelly.

SEVENTEEN

Kelly woke the next morning with an aching sense of loss. She didn't know how she'd cope with not seeing Jed in the next ten minutes, let alone the rest of her life. She wished there was some way she could've made him take her away with him last night.

The sickening smell of burnt toast drifted up the stairs together with Viv's grumpy voice yelling: "Kelly, you out of bed yet?"

She pushed back the covers, not wanting to make things any worse.

"Won't be long," she called back down the stairs as she padded along the sticky green landing carpet to the bathroom.

"Keep it down," grumbled Mick from the bedroom he shared with Viv. "We don't all want to know what you're doing."

Mercifully nobody had said anything about her being late back last night – and as yet Viv hadn't heard about Kelly losing her job. She hoped that by the time she next had to give Viv housekeeping money she may have found something else, although the optimistic feelings she'd had yesterday had drained out of her.

She washed quickly, pulled on a pink dress that Viv usually complained clashed with Kelly's auburn hair and hurried downstairs before she started shouting again.

"About bloody time," said Viv, "this tea must be well stewed by now."

Kelly poured herself a cup and spread margarine on a piece of toast that miraculously was only slightly 'caught' at one end. There was a new pot of strawberry jam in place of the usual marmalade and Kelly hunted hopefully for the lumps of fruit.

"Don't mess that jam about," said Viv, in the process of putting on her mascara. The words sounded odd because her mouth was half open as she twirled the mascara wand. "It was a present from an admirer," she said in a stage whisper, "but don't tell Mick."

Kelly grinned at the thought of Mick having a punch up with someone over a pot of jam.

"Don't know what you're laughing at young lady," said Viv. She looked at the clock and groaned. "Where does the bloody time go in the morning?"

She picked up her bag and headed towards the back door. "Get a loaf of bread on your way home will you," she said, turning back towards Kelly, "and peel the spuds for tea. I may be a bit late – there's a union meeting."

Kelly finished her toast and jam and put the sticky plate and knife in the sink on top of last night's dirty plates with their covering of solidified gravy. Mick was supposed to do the washing up but he only seemed to bother every two or three days, when there wasn't another clean plate or mug in the house.

She plaited her hair and after listening carefully at the bottom of the stairs to make sure Mick wasn't up and about, she hurried upstairs for the shocking pink cardigan embroidered with white daisies that went so well with the dress. The last thing she felt like this morning was an encounter with Mick's slab of lard body on the landing.

She left the house at her usual time, so as not to arouse suspicion, walking slowly down the road, wondering how she'd occupy her time until five o'clock. She'd thought of a few places in Tredannac Bay that she could enquire about jobs – the bakery, the small guest-house and the café, but the thought of working in any of them didn't exactly fill her with delight, even if they had a space for her. Her next step would be to take the bus to Launceston and try her luck there.

When she saw Jed's car waiting at the crossroads, she blinked and rubbed her eyes as if she'd seen a mirage. She hurried across the road to him, scared that he and the car would disappear in a puff of pantomime smoke by the time she got there.

Jed knew he should've taken himself out of temptation's way and headed back to London like Mirabelle wanted him to. He knew that if he came back here to Tredannac Bay - to Kelly - he'd be getting himself into something he may not be able to stop. He'd sat up most of the night in his luxurious room in the hotel at Penzance, writing furiously, carried away by his new idea, fuelled by thoughts of Kelly, feeling like a love-sick teenager.

He'd looked from his hotel window at the path of moonlight crossing the dark sea like a pathway and the white edges of the waves as they lapped the shore wishing that he could always have this creative freedom.

Mirabelle didn't understand there were times when he needed to just sit and think. She'd bustle in, scattering his pages of notes, piling them back up again in the wrong order and say, "Since you're not doing anything at the moment, sweetie, will you come and help Daddy move his desk, " or "I've been looking for a handsome man to take me out to lunch."

By the time the desk had been moved to Mitch's satisfaction, or they'd lingered over lunch in one of the wine bars, the ideas that Jed had been so keen to get working on had faded away like early morning mist.

Last night, somewhere between completing an outline of the first scene of the film and dozing for a few hours, Jed developed an overwhelming need to see the house on the cliff again. After a six o'clock breakfast of croissants and black cherry jam and two large cups of coffee - they didn't do a cooked breakfast until eight thirty - he headed for Tredannac Bay.

He kidded himself he'd go to the ruined house, write some notes, take some photos and then go back to Penzance and write the next scene before heading back to London. There was no reason that Kelly should even know he'd been there today.

The nearer he got to Tredannac Bay, the worse the muddled feeling in his head got, like a transistor radio that wasn't properly tuned. He parked the car and headed towards the cliff pathway. The unsettled feeling subsided with every step. He reached the ruined house and sat with his back against one of the crumbling walls, eyes closed, listening to the sound of the sea and the cries of the gulls.

The last time he'd come here with Kelly, he'd experienced a feeling like a flashback to another time – had felt a premonition of disaster and of being torn away from the woman he loved. Today he experienced a feeling of peace and knew what Kelly meant when she said it was like coming home – as if the house was waiting for him.

He took some sound recordings with his Dictaphone, made notes and did a few sketches, reluctant to walk away, wondering what sort of magnet had drawn him here and introduced him to his soul mate at a time when other events in his life made any sort of future for them so difficult.

He walked down from the cliffs, tasting salt on his lips, looking at how the early morning sky had that just-washed look of clean sheets, and got back in his car intending to head back to Penzance, collect his things and return to London.

Knowing he was acting stupidly, he started the ignition and headed for the crossroads where he'd dropped Kelly last night, feeling certain she'd be there.

"I never thought I'd see you again," she said, getting into the car.

Jed noticed her eyes were full of tears, making them look like liquid amber. He brushed the tears away with the tips of his fingers, noticing her full lips, feeling a longing to kiss them. He drew back from her. This mustn't go any further.

"Where to?" he said, starting the ignition.

"Anywhere away from here," she said. "Just so long as I'm back by five because Mum still doesn't know I've lost my job. I was hoping I'd find another one before she does."

"Penzance then," he said.

EIGHTEEN

Kelly sank back against the soft dark blue leather seat, hoping nobody had seen her get into the car. What if someone thought she was being abducted and took the registration number and called the police? She didn't want Jed to get into trouble because of her.

She'd tossed and turned all night thinking about the things he'd said to her, recalling every touch of his hand and the look in his eyes, the caring way he'd put his jacket round her last night when she was cold.

Her mind felt tired with going round in circles thinking of places where she could get work. If she was brave, maybe she could get a live-in job in Penzance or even London. Maybe Jed would help her. It was funny how her Gran had encouraged her to be brave and to take risks and that gradually, since she'd died, Kelly had got out of the habit. Going for the audition for the play at school had been the last brave thing she'd done. She knew what some of the girls thought of her – 'Smelly Kelly Smith from No Hope Street'.

When she had slept last night, she'd had a vivid dream about being in a theatre. She was standing in the wings, ready to go on stage. The heavy wine red velvet curtains were closed and she could hear the loud buzz of conversation from the audience. It was stiflingly hot and the air smelled of oranges and cloves. Kelly was tightly laced into a yellow silk dress that reminded her of buttercups. She was wearing a powdered wig and full stage make up, but something was wrong.

There were no other actors that she could see, just a metallic voice telling her she'd be on stage in two minutes.

"I haven't seen a script," she said. "I don't know what to say."

She awoke just as the curtains were gliding open, revealing a packed auditorium. She was alone on the stage, with no idea of the part she was playing with a sea of faces watching her, waiting for her opening lines.

She told Jed about the dream as they drove along country lanes and through villages. She could tell he was listening, even though he didn't take his eyes off the road.

"It's a classic uncertainty dream," he said, "because you know what it is you want to do, but you don't know how you're going to do it yet. Maybe it's telling you to be ready for an opportunity."

Kelly hoped Jed was hinting that he might be able to help her. She thought how great it would be to send Viv a postcard saying she'd eloped with Jed and wouldn't need a job in the biscuit factory or anywhere else.

Jed told Kelly about his plan to write a stage version of his film script. He didn't tell her it was because he'd written the first draft of the movie with a view to Mirabelle playing the starring role, but he wanted to write a stage version for Kelly.

"I'd like to experiment with a very simple set – none of these ornate painted backgrounds, just a few props to suggest where the action's taking place."

Kelly nodded. "When I did Romeo and Juliet the scenery painting took longer than the rehearsals. My teacher, Mrs Wilson, originally said she'd wanted to do the play with Shakespeare's words and a modern setting."

"Why didn't she?"

"The headmaster overruled it – and as she'd already disagreed with him because she wanted me to be Juliet and not Susan Baker, she thought she'd better give in over that one."

They arrived in Penzance and Jed parked the car in a space facing the sea. The tide was coming in, the crest of the waves shining turquoise in the morning sun as they turned over into bubbling white foam and raced up the beach. The rhythm was hypnotic.

Kelly sat watching, fiddling with a strand of hair – a

habit she had when she felt nervous.

"At least you don't bite your nails," said Jed, taking that hand in his. The auburn ringlet flopped down onto Kelly's shoulder again. Her hand settled in his like two pieces of a jigsaw fitting together. She looked up at him through her eyelashes, feeling the insistent beating of a pulse in her throat. He leaned across and kissed her gently on the lips. She relaxed back into the seat, feeling as if she was melting inside. He pulled away first, seeming almost angry with himself.

"I'm sure you'll want to see the shops," he said briskly.

"I'm happy being wherever you are," Kelly thought to herself. She waited for him to come round and let her out of the car as he'd done last night. She couldn't believe how special it felt. She wasn't really bothered about shopping, but if that's what he wanted to do, it was fine by her.

They began with coffee and chocolate shortbread in a little café called The Scarlet Ark hidden away in a courtyard. They sat in the tiny garden that was crammed with pink geraniums and purple petunias. A model of Noah's ark, painted scarlet, had been put there for children to play on.

"Just imagine what people must've thought of Noah all those years ago," said Jed. "He must've come across as real crazy – building a hulking great boat because he'd heard it was going to rain"

"And why didn't he get rid of things like flies and mosquitoes while he had the chance," went on Kelly, wishing with all her heart that she and Jed had a future together, like the family on the next table. A dark haired little girl with plump brown legs was climbing the shiny red wooden steps up to the deck, helped by her dad. Her mother was expecting again, her full belly straining against her blue dress. Kelly glanced at Jed, wondering if he could read her thoughts, but his look gave nothing away.

"You've got a point there," said Jed, taking a sip of his

coffee. "That could make a really good play or story – the creatures Noah could've left behind and how they made an alternative society.

Round the corner from The Scarlet Ark was a shop that sold expensive lingerie. Kelly stopped to look at the frothy cream lace bra and knickers in the window, thinking of the ones she was wearing that had gone chewing gum white from being washed so often. She squirmed with embarrassment wondering what Jed would think if he saw them.

"*He's not going to,*" she said to herself, feasting her eyes on the confections in the window. "*I'm not like my sister. I'm not.*"

"Go in and try some on – I dare you," said Jed.

Kelly smiled at him. "I couldn't – I'd feel awkward saying I couldn't afford them. That woman in there looks just like Miss Bates. I don't think she'd take kindly to having her time wasted."

"Who said she'd be wasting her time? Come on."

Jed pushed open the door, which set off a buzzer. The sales lady looked them both up and down as if they were about to commit a robbery.

Kelly gazed around at the dainty looking gilt chairs and the elegant displays of lingerie in every possible colour – rose pink, turquoise, chocolate brown and lilac. The shop even smelled expensive – a combination of vanilla and rose petals.

"My girlfriend would like to try on a set like you've got in the window," said Jed.

"And what size is madam?" asked the woman taking a tape measure out of her pocket.

"I'm not sure," said Kelly, not daring to catch Jed's eye.

She followed the woman into a small cubicle and took off her dress, trying to ignore the way she looked down her nose at Kelly's off-white bra and knickers.

"Madam is a 34C", she said icily. "Are there any other

colours you'd like to try?"

"Have you got anything in black?" asked Kelly.

The woman sniffed as if to say that showed what sort of girl Kelly was and went away to get them.

Half an hour later, Kelly and Jed left the shop. Kelly was carrying a black and gold carrier bag with the shop name 'Caprice' on it containing two sets – the cream and the black.

"I can't let you spend money on me like that," said Kelly. "Give me your address in London and I'll pay you back."

"There's no need," said Jed.

He still hadn't said anything about his life in London, other than he'd needed to get away from it to cure his writer's block. Kelly didn't like to ask in case the fragile bubble of magic suddenly burst.

"Now, what about lunch?" asked Jed, "where would madam like to go?" He did a good imitation of the sales lady in 'Caprice' with her vinegar bottle face that had changed to a sickly grin when Jed produced his wallet and paid cash for the lingerie.

Kelly took a deep breath. "I'd like to see your hotel room. Couldn't we have lunch there?"

Jed had pointed out the imposing building overlooking the sea when they first arrived. Kelly had noted the revolving doors and the marble tiles and polished wood of the reception area, the silver doors of the lifts that led to the different floors and the dramatic curve of the carpeted staircase. A liveried doorman stood outside, ready to welcome new guests.

A thought had been running through Kelly's mind since this morning when she first got in Jed's car. Several girls in her class at school had already lost their virginity. One girl called Carol Phillips who had a face like a cow's arse had bragged about how her boyfriend had paid for a hotel room in Launceston. They'd had an en suite bathroom with free samples of soap and shampoo and he'd bought her fish and chips afterwards.

Kelly bet that none of the girls she knew would've been

anywhere like this. She hadn't expected to have today with Jed – that alone was a gift. If he wouldn't accept her money, maybe this was a way of repaying him as well as creating a special bond between them for always.

The fear of pregnancy and of ending up like Miranda flashed through her mind. "*That won't happen to me,*" she told herself, "*Jed wouldn't let that happen. And anyway, I'm not like her.*"

"You sure about this?" asked Jed.

She nodded.

He raised her fingers to his lips and kissed them gently. "Come on then."

The doorman greeted them as they went in through the chrome and glass revolving doors. Jed called briefly at the reception desk.

"Are there any messages for me?"

The immaculately groomed woman shook her head. "No sir."

"I don't wish to be disturbed this afternoon."

"Very good, sir," she said.

They went up in the lift to the third floor. Kelly's feet felt as if they were sinking into the red and grey carpet as she walked along the wide corridor.

"You didn't tell me you'd got a suite," she gasped as Jed unlocked the door. The room reminded her of a stage set for something like Romeo and Juliet with its huge four-poster bed hung with cream and blue brocade curtains. She wondered what it would be like to spend the night in a bed like that, enclosed behind the thick curtains or looking out at the moonlit sea. Nell Gwyn would've slept in a bed like this when she was with the King. Thinking of her, Kelly felt less nervous as she gazed round the room taking in the blue and cream sofa and chairs and the window seat where Jed said he'd spent several hours writing last night.

"Look at that view!" Kelly was entranced by the variation in colour of the sea from deep indigo to pale turquoise.

Jed came up behind her, wrapping his arms round her as she stood gazing from the window. "I was watching the path the moon made across the sea last night. Does that sound daft?"

Kelly shook her head. "It was shining in my bedroom window last night. That's probably why I had that dream. Maybe I thought I was under a spotlight."

She leaned back against him, feeling the comforting warmth of his chest through his blue cotton shirt. He wasn't rushing her and she didn't know whether to feel glad or sorry.

"And what would madam like for lunch?" he murmured against her hair.

Kelly was tempted to say 'just you,' but she didn't want to sound like a tart.

"I don't know," she said. "What do you usually have?"

"How would you like ham and salad sandwiches?"

"I'm glad you didn't say smoked salmon," said Kelly with a giggle. "I had some at a wedding once."

"Can't stand it either," said Jed. "It's like eating bits of soggy flannel – not that I do that either," he added.

He moved away from Kelly and picked up the phone to call room service. "A plate of ham and salad sandwiches, a bowl of chips and a bottle of champagne please," he said.

"Champagne?" Kelly's eyes widened. This was way better than anything Carol Phillips had.

"We both deserve it," said Jed.

Kelly stroked the black and gold carrier bag from 'Caprice.' "I feel as if I've been spoiled enough for one day."

"Even though you had to be measured by the dragon?" asked Jed

"Yes."

Jed's face was close to hers and she reached up and kissed him on the cheek.

"Thank you. They're beautiful."

"So are you, Kelly." Jed's voice was husky as he kissed her gently on the lips.

There was a knock at the door. "Room service!" shouted a young lad as he wheeled in a silver trolley with their lunch on it – the bottle of champagne in a silver bucket full of ice cubes. "Anything else I can get you – sir, madam?"

"That's fine thank you," said Jed, giving him a tip.

He opened the champagne and poured a glass for Kelly. "I'd better go easy on this stuff myself – I've got to drive you back."

Kelly wished he hadn't mentioned Tredannac Bay. Today it had been easy to weave a fantasy that they could be together for always. Kelly knew it had to come to an end, but what was wrong with trying to make the magic last?

She sat with her legs curled up on the sofa, leaning against Jed as they shared the sandwiches and fat chips oozing salt and vinegar. Jed had also ordered strawberries and cream. The strawberries gleamed bright as rubies in a cut glass dish and there was enough clotted cream in a silver bowl to have fed the whole of Penzance.

"My Gran would've said we were eating for our futures," said Kelly, catching a stray piece of tomato with her tongue.

"What a brilliant expression."

"She was full of them."

Kelly took another sip of champagne, wondering what her Gran would think if she could see her now. She'd be sure to ask how this was going to further her career as an actress, but Kelly couldn't think about that at the moment.

"You still miss her, don't you?"

Kelly nodded, not trusting herself to speak.

"Remember what I'm telling you Kelly," Gran had said. "Whatever happens, stay focused on your dream. If you do then it's sure to happen."

Jed hadn't suggested taking her back to London with him and Kelly didn't know how to broach the subject without sounding pushy.

"You take the first bite." Jed was holding a large strawberry out to her covered in thick cream.

She took a bite. "Now what happens?"

"I take a bite. The one who ends up with the stalk makes a wish."

They finished the bowl of strawberries and most of the cream. Kelly had ended up with eight stalks and Jed with seven.

"You get the extra wish," said Jed.

Kelly giggled. "Must find the loo," she said, stifling a hiccup.

"The bathroom is through there," said Jed pointing to a door on the far side of the room.

Kelly's feet sank into the thick cream carpet. She'd discarded her sandals before lunch. It felt like walking through warm sand and she wiggled her bare toes luxuriously. She knew Jed was laughing at her but she didn't care.

She took the precious gold and black carrier bag with her. The champagne had made her light-headed and she felt as if she was in the middle of a dream and that in a few moments she'd wake up in her cold, damp bedroom.

The bathroom was every bit as exotic as the bedroom. It was tiled from floor to ceiling with cream tiles patterned with tiny blue flowers. There was a large, deep bath that Kelly longed to get into, a shower cubicle surrounded by shiningly clean glass and a washbasin and loo. The floor was cushioned lino scattered with pale blue mats and there were at least four fluffy cream towels.

Kelly went to the loo and then, stripping her clothes off, freshened herself up with some of the free samples of soap and body lotion, feeling like a film star as she rubbed the peach-scented cream into her body.

She tossed up which bra and pants to put on – the black or the cream lace and decided on the cream. Looking at herself in the long bathroom mirror, her auburn hair loose and falling to her waist, she smiled, hoping Jed would feel his money was well spent.

The look on his face when she walked back into the room told her everything she wanted to know.

She walked into the circle of his arms, noticing the thud of his heart and the warmth of his skin through his dark blue cotton shirt.

His lips closed on hers and this time the kiss wasn't interrupted by a knock on the door.

"You're very hard to resist," he whispered.

"Don't try," she said. "Kiss me again."

Kelly's stomach felt as if she'd gone down too fast in a lift. She swayed dizzily.

Jed lifted her into his arms and carried her to the bed where she lay with her hair fanned out around her. He locked the door before he came back to join her, kicking off his shoes and socks as he did so.

"Are you sure about this, Kelly? Is it all right for me to kiss you like this?

He was mapping out the territory of her body with tiny kisses, beginning on her closed eyelids and moving down to her throat, shoulders, breasts – she could feel his warm breath through the delicate lace of her bra – belly and lower...

She lay there feeling the sensations in her body, watching the colours dance inside her head – hot pink, orange and forest green.

She reached out, pulled his shirt from the waistband of his trousers and ran her fingers across his taut belly, heard him groan with pleasure. His fingers fumbled with the catch of her bra and soon her breasts were free, warmed by his kisses. She felt herself grow damp between her legs as he sucked her nipples, heard herself moan.

He kissed her gently, slid her pants gently down her legs. Kelly didn't open her eyes until she felt him parting her legs slightly. Her eyes snapped open in alarm.

"Shh," he whispered, "it's OK."

Then she felt his mouth against the inside of her thighs, moving upwards until it reached that secret place. His tongue probed gently, sending sparks of coloured light through her head. She arched her back and screamed her pleasure.

"I want you," she screamed. "Oh Jed I want you."

He'd drawn back from her. "Are you sure, Kelly? I mean – you're a virgin aren't you and that's something special. Not something you give away lightly to the first Tom, Dick or Harry."

She pulled him toward her, undoing the buttons on his shirt, unzipping his jeans and sliding them down over his hips, relishing the feel of his skin against hers.

His penis, released from his briefs, was stiff, the skin warm. Kelly leaned over and kissed it, feeling him shudder. She drew back, feeling maybe that wasn't what nice girls did and yet he'd ...

They kissed some more and he returned to that place between her legs. This time his tongue was more insistent, drawing longer screams from her, making her feel as if she was floating somewhere in rainbow coloured space.

"Wow," Jed kept saying.

She felt his hardness against her, felt him lifting her knee slightly to let him in, felt an agonising pain as he entered her and then they found their rhythm, climaxing together, Jed collapsing against her shoulder.

Afterwards they both slept, waking when the afternoon sun poured in through the window bathing them in a patch of light.

It was only as she awoke, Kelly realised that they'd made love without using a condom and that there was every chance she'd end up the same as Miranda, pushing a pram round Launceston, just like everyone had said she would.

Jed, waking up from what had been the best time he'd ever had with a woman, wondered how he could have taken leave of his senses like that. He'd felt from when he first woke this morning that today had a fairytale quality about it, but now reality was kicking in and with it the knowledge that he'd have to return to London and face Mirabelle.

He had the mad idea of suggesting to Kelly that they take off somewhere, just the two of them but he suspected she'd fallen for him because of the person she thought he was – someone with a nice car and money who could buy her the good things of life. She may not be so keen if she knew he was poorer than she was.

Jed's motto up till now was 'finish one relationship before you began another'. He'd gone against that and in doing so had treated both women badly. The least he could do was to return to London, finish things with Mirabelle and find a way to salvage his writing career. It was best to leave Kelly with a beautiful memory of today and let her go back to her life in Tredannac Bay. He had nothing to offer her and when he left her at the crossroads this time, there could be no going back.

NINETEEN

Kelly emerged from the bathroom having had the most wonderful bath she'd ever had in her life, complete with peach and vanilla bubbles. Jed was on the phone when she came back into the bedroom. She heard him say: "Yes, I promised I'd be back in time for the meeting and I will."

The voice on the other end of the phone was loud, American and female. A sense of reality kicked in like painkillers wearing off after an anaesthetic.

"Was that your wife?" Kelly felt sick, but she needed to know

"I'm not married," said Jed, putting his arms round her and holding her close. "It's just some unfinished business. Nothing I can explain right now, but it's the reason why I've got nothing to offer you at the moment. I've no job, no money and no fixed abode."

Kelly had laughed at this. How stupid did he think she was? "What about your flash car and all this?" She'd swept an arm theatrically round to encompass the magnificent room in which they'd so recently made love. "What did you pay for this with – Smarties?"

"Kelly, don't be like this. I'm being financed by a friend at the moment, just until the film script sells and I'm back on my feet."

"If she's American and in love with you then she won't take kindly to you playing around behind her back."

"Kelly, please believe me, I wasn't – am not – playing around. What we've got – had – comes once in a lifetime. Sometimes a day with someone can change your life, like you've changed mine."

They drove back in silence to Tredannac Bay.

"So that's it, is it?" said Kelly when they arrived at the crossroads. She knew she sounded bitter and shrewish, but she couldn't help it. "You've had your fun and now you're dumping me?"

"It's not like that." There were tears in Jed's eyes when he turned towards her. "I wish with all my heart that things were different. I love you Kelly and I want to be with you but for now, I have to go back to London and finish what I've started if I'm ever going to be able to offer you anything in this life."

Kelly walked slowly away from Jed's car, not stopping to wipe away the tears pouring down her face. She knew without turning round that he was sat there watching her and wished with all her heart he'd call her back. Finally, she heard the engine purr into life and the wheels turn, taking him away from her. She didn't turn round.

Despite the warmth of the day, Kelly shivered. Her feet felt as if she was wearing lead boots as she went down the side entry and in through the back door. With a sinking feeling she noticed Miranda's double pushchair. She wondered what had happened. Miranda only visited during the week if she had problems with her husband – which judging by the way she was leading off in the sitting room was probably what had happened. Kelly could hear the angry rise of Miranda's voice and the hard-done-by twang even before she quietly opened the back door.

She glanced with distaste at the double pushchair. It was made of cheap fabric and was caked in soggy biscuit and spilled orange squash that Miranda never bothered to clean off. The pushchair sat there as a grim warning as to what happened to girls who had sex outside marriage. Kelly closed her eyes for a moment, trying to hold onto the magic she'd so recently experienced with Jed.

Another voice in her head that sounded more like one of Viv's warning messages said: "That's typical of men. They have their fun and then they dump you and go back to their wives."

She went in through the back door, ignoring the raised voices in the sitting room, and crept up to her cold, damp bedroom that was so different from that palatial hotel room overlooking the sea. She felt stiff and sore and all she wanted to do was creep under her blankets, go to sleep and not wake up.

She wasn't destined to have any peace. She'd just stashed the carrier bag containing her precious new underwear in the back of her wardrobe when the door burst open and Viv stood framed in the doorway, her face a mask of anger.

"What the hell do you think you're playing at?"

"What d'you mean?" Kelly couldn't be bothered to fight with her mother.

"That Mrs Wilson was round here wanting to know why you'd not gone to apologise to Miss Bates and get your job back. Then that nosey cow along the end was quick to tell me you'd been seen in some posh bloke's car. What the hell are you playing at, Kelly? I thought you had more sense."

"Why do you always believe the worst?"

"Because I know what it's like. How could you be so stupid, Kelly? What if you're pregnant? Who do you think is going to look after the kid? That bloke, whoever he is, won't. He'll have got away scot-free like they always do."

"Don't call me stupid, because I'm not. Why don't you ever go on like this to Miranda? She's been in far more trouble than I have. She's never had a job…"

"Don't you start on me, just because your fancy man's run out on you," Miranda had come up the stairs when she heard her name mentioned, the two snotty nosed children following behind her. "I've told you before Kelly, the same shit comes out of your arse as anyone else. Don't try and make out you're better than me – especially now."

"I've done nothing wrong," said Kelly. "Just leave me alone."

"You're coming to the factory with me in the morning, young lady – after we've been to the doctors for one of those 'morning after' pills they've been talking about in the paper."

Kelly was about to argue back when there was a loud hammering on the front door.

"It's Nathan," said Miranda looking scared. "What do I do, Mum?"

"You tell him what you told me, you daft cow, that you won't go back unless he starts pulling his weight a bit more. Be nice about it. You want to go back to him don't you? Come on, I'll come back down with you. I bet you anything you like he'll be glad to see you and the kids."

Kelly was left alone. She lay fully dressed under the bedclothes listening to the rise and fall of voices downstairs as Miranda and her husband made up their differences. Eventually she slept. When she awoke in the early hours of the morning, the house was silent apart from the dripping tap in the bathroom and Mick snoring in the bedroom he shared with Viv.

Kelly went to the bathroom and washed herself with a damp flannel. She felt as if she could've done with another bath to wash away the bad feeling from yesterday afternoon. The last words she'd had with Jed spiralled round in her brain and she wished more than anything that she could take them back.

The thought formed in her head that maybe he hadn't left Cornwall yet. Maybe if she went to his hotel she'd have a chance to make up their quarrel and persuade him to take her to London.

She dressed quickly and packed as much as she could into the blue rucksack she'd taken on her last school trip to Exmoor, pausing when she heard Mick's heavy tread on the landing. She heard him peeing in the bathroom, stomp back along the landing and the creak of the bedsprings as he settled down again. She waited until she heard him snore again before she resumed her hasty packing. She was careful to remember her lucky black china cat, the amber necklace Mrs Wilson had given her on the night of the play and her new underwear in its black and gold carrier bag.

She put on the thick black jacket with its fake fur collar that she'd worn to school last winter, and went down the stairs, careful to avoid the third one from the bottom that creaked. She paused in the kitchen, realising that this might be the last time she saw it, taking in the cracked red plastic framed mirror where Viv did her make up every morning, the ancient toaster and the table with its covering of sticky crumbs.

Kelly would've liked a cup of tea. She'd had nothing to eat before she went to bed last night and her stomach growled with emptiness, competing with the dull ache she felt in her lower back and pelvis. She knew that if she started boiling the kettle and rooting in cupboards then Viv was bound to wake.

Kelly unlocked the back door and went out into the coolness of the early morning, closing the door behind her. She hadn't left a note.

She crept along the passageway, conscious of how her footsteps echoed. She hurried along to the crossroads, feeling as if she was being watched and that at any moment Viv or Mick might come after her.

She paused for breath when she reached it, half expecting Jed's car to be there waiting. A lorry approached and Kelly stepped out to thumb a lift. The driver stopped. "I thought you were a ghost. Where are you going love?"

"Penzance," said Kelly.

"Hop in then."

It was only when she'd got into the warmth of the cab and the driver set off that Kelly realised what a risk she was taking.

"Running away from home, are you?" he said after a long period of silence, leering at her with bloodshot dark eyes.

"No," said Kelly. "I'm going to meet my fiancé."

"Getting married are you?" said the driver, turning the large steering wheel with fat sausage fingers. "You look very young for that – very young."

123

"I'm nineteen," said Kelly, crossing her fingers behind her back, not sure if that made things worse or better. "And I'm going to live in London with him."

"Ooh, there's posh," said the driver, brushing a lock of greasy hair out of his eyes.

He slowed down and leered at her, reaching out a podgy hand and patting her knee. "So you'll be used to it, then?"

"What?" Kelly decided to play dumb, play for time and hope he stopped in Penzance like he said he was going to. According to the signposts, they were very close now.

"You know," he said. "Bury the beef bayonet, and all that."

They were on the approach road to Penzance. Kelly recognised some of the landmarks from when she'd come with Jed yesterday. She needed to get out of this lorry, but was struggling to find a reason to ask the driver to stop.

Help came in the form of an accident just ahead of them. Two cars had collided at a t-junction and the traffic was gridlocked.

"It's my lucky day," said the driver. "It looks like we'll be here for a while so maybe you can give Mr Stalky a bit of attention."

To Kelly's horror the man had his jeans unzipped and his throbbing penis was exposed. He took her hand and placed it on it, a sickly grin spreading over his sweaty face.

Kelly suppressed a shudder of revulsion, taking a tight hold of the pulsating object.

"That's right, baby," groaned the man, his eyes half closed now.

They sparked open when Kelly walloped him hard with a spanner that was lying within reach on the greasy dashboard. Before he had time to recover himself, she'd wrenched open the door, grabbed her rucksack and scrambled to the ground, landing in a heap as she did so.

She got to her feet, her left knee where she'd scraped it on the gravel oozing blood.

The passenger door of the truck was wrenched open.

"Come back and finish the job you little bitch," yelled the driver.

Kelly didn't look back. She hobbled past the queue of traffic lined up behind where the accident had taken place. The sound of police and ambulance sirens cut across all the other noises as she dodged down an alleyway between two shops and stood leaning against the wall, feeling sick and shaky.

She heard the sound of engines restarting and from her hiding place was relieved to see the truck move slowly past. She waited a few more minutes and then, following the signposts, she headed towards the seafront and the Grand Hotel. It was still only eight o'clock.

In the public toilets, she cleaned up the wound on her knee with some damp loo paper, washed her face and brushed and plaited her hair so that it fell in one thick copper braid down her back.

She paused nervously outside the hotel. The doorman let her in but the head to toe look that he gave her spoke volumes. The same woman as yesterday was on the reception desk. If she recognised Kelly, there was no sign of it as she checked the register carefully with long frosted pink fingernails.

"Mr Matthews checked out last night following an urgent call from London," she said in a cool, clipped voice. "I'm afraid he didn't leave any note or forwarding address."

"How would I get to London," asked Kelly. She half expected the woman to say that they were running a hotel not a travel agency.

"A coach leaves at ten thirty from the bus station," she said.

Kelly thanked her and walked back across the entrance hall, her sandals making a slapping sound on the marble floor.

She'd have plenty of time to draw some money from her Post Office account and buy a ticket. She didn't know what would happen when she got to London, but surely Chelsea couldn't be that big – and once she found Jed she knew everything would be all right.

TWENTY

My Mum told me about Kelly's disappearance the week after I'd moved to London. It shook the whole of Tredannac Bay at the time. At first nobody knew whether she'd been abducted or had just run away.

There'd been a family argument the day before and Kelly had lost her job at the museum. There was talk of a dark haired bloke with a posh car who'd been seen in the area over a couple of days. Given how nosy most people around Tredannac Bay area, it was amazing that nobody had taken the registration number.

I did remember seeing her with someone on the day Jamie and I first got together. My only thought at the time was 'trust her to end up with the best looking guy on the planet.'

When Mum wrote and told me the news I know I should've told the police when they appealed for information, but I was too full of resentful feelings about Kelly to do anything that may have helped her.

TWENTY-ONE

Kelly sat alone in the back of the taxi feeling bewildered by the volume of traffic and people. The taxi driver was black and his accent hard to understand.

"Where in Chelsea you want, lady?"

"I'm looking for a man called Jed Matthews – he's a writer."

"I not know him. Where he live?"

"I haven't got an address for him," said Kelly, watching the counter whirr round on the fare stage dial, realising that this part of the exercise wasn't going to be as easy as she'd hoped.

"I drop you by Town Hall," said the taxi driver. "Maybe you can ask someone else?"

Kelly noticed that he charged her less than he should've done as he wished her good luck and drove off along the street. She stood for a few minutes, feeling uncertain as to what to do next. She noticed a phone box and wondered if there was a directory. Amazingly there was, but one look confirmed that to call all the J Matthews listed would take more money than she'd got in her purse. The coach fare had cost more than she'd expected and she hadn't even got enough money left to pay for a hotel for the night.

She walked slowly along the darkening street, looking in the windows of cafes and restaurants, hoping to catch a glimpse of Jed, not knowing what she'd do if she did. What if he was with another woman? How embarrassing would that be?

She was desperate for the loo and equally desperate for a cup of tea. Eventually she came to a café that looked cheap and cheerful compared to the ones she'd first seen. The windows were steamy and edged with red gingham curtains and a jukebox was belting out the Rolling Stones hit '*Satisfaction.*' A young man with long straggly blond hair wearing black jeans and a faded Woodstock t-shirt was playing air guitar as he gyrated to the music.

He winked at Kelly as she pushed open the door.

"I'll come and serve you in just a sec – must have my daily fix of Mick Jagger."

The tables were red and grey Formica and there was red lino on the floor. An old lady in the corner dozed over her mug of tea. In the opposite corner two men played endless games of pontoon with a greasy pack of cards.

Kelly's stomach growled with hunger at the smell of frying sausage and onions on the griddle behind the chrome-plated counter.

"A mug of tea please," she said. Food would have to wait until she knew where she was spending the night.

"We're open all night," said the air-guitarist, as if he'd read her thoughts. "If you change your mind and want anything to eat."

Kelly sat in the corner sipping her tea, wondering what to do next. She looked at the old lady whose head was now slumped uncomfortably over the table, slack jaws drooling. Kelly wondered what the air-guitarist would do if she put her head down on the table and did the same. It was warm in the café, there was a loo in the corner, and it was tempting not to venture out into the dark hostile street.

She looked at her watch. It was still only just after ten o'clock. She wondered how long she could make her tea last, sipping slowly down to the cold dregs.

"You've got nowhere to go, 'ave yer?"

Kelly's eyes were drooping with tiredness but they snapped open when the young girl who'd just arrived came and stood by her.

The girl was waif-thin with short dark spiky hair and deep blue eyes edged with black mascara. She wore a short red satin dress and a black leather jacket that reminded Kelly of the night she'd gone to the restaurant with Jed and he'd put his jacket round her.

"How would you know?" she asked, aware that her soft Cornish burr marked her out as a stranger here.

"I know what I know," said the girl pulling a comic face. "Zoe's the name, survival's the game."

Kelly smiled and the smile turned into a yawn.

"You're knackered, I can see that much." 'Ave you eaten anything?"

Kelly shook her head.

"Two sausage sandwiches over 'ere, Ben," she shouted. "And make sure they're on the 'ouse. You owe me, remember?"

"What does he owe you for?" asked Kelly.

"Cleaning this place, that's what. The usual girl didn't turn up and so it looks like I've got meself another job. It doesn't pay much, but then so long as you manage to stitch a bit together, duck and dive, get by, what does it matter?"

She sat down opposite Kelly, rummaged in her small black handbag and produced a battered pack of cigarettes. She offered one to Kelly. "Smoke?"

Kelly shook her head.

"Lucky you - save a fortune – and you won't end up with a cat's bum mouth by the time you're forty."

Kelly thought of Viv and felt a stab of guilt that she hadn't left a note or contacted her to say where she was. Better to do that once she was settled, she thought. Once she'd found Jed.

"What's up? You've gone quiet. Who do you know with a cat's bum mouth?"

Kelly was saved having to answer by the arrival of the food. Ben had also brought two mugs of tea and a bottle of tomato ketchup, which Zoe promptly grabbed, peeling back her top slice of bread and pouring it on.

"This stuff's like the buses," she complained. "It either all comes out at once or you get nothing at all."

Kelly didn't answer. She was busy tucking into her

130

sandwich, burning her tongue on the hot fat oozing from the golden sausages.

Zoe sat watching her. "So what's your story Miss Country-mouse?"

She seemed friendly enough, but Kelly wasn't sure whether to trust her or not. Her instincts said she should, but then she'd felt the same about Jed and he'd left her.

"I'm looking for someone," she said. "A man called Jed Matthews. He's a writer and he lives in Chelsea."

"Is that what he told you?" asked Zoe. "And I bet he spoiled you rotten for a few days, made you fall in love with him, got into your knickers and then he buggered off quicker than you can say "I'm pregnant."

"You don't think I could be, do you?"

"What?"

"Pregnant."

"Didn't he use anything – you know – a condom?

"I don't think so," said Kelly.

"Then you need to see a doctor, double quick, you daft little cow."

Kelly's eyes filled with tears.

"'Ere, you're supposed to eat that sandwich, not wash it." Zoe took a big bite of hers and chewed it, a look of concentration on her face. "Don't worry, there's nothing we can't sort out between us – and who knows, we might even find your Mr Matthews."

"I know he was telling the truth when he said he lived in Chelsea. There was just some – problem – why he couldn't take me with him."

"Probably a problem like a wife or live in girlfriend," said Zoe, her face looking hard, "that's typical of blokes. The only one I'd trust is my cat Charlie."

Kelly finished the last of her sandwich and sat sipping her tea.

"So let's get this straight," said Zoe. "You've followed this Jed person all the way to London and now you've got nowhere to live and no job."

"I'd lost my job back home," said Kelly, "so that's no different."

"OK," said Zoe. "Here's what we do. You come home with me, and then tomorrow we go and visit the doctor so's he can give you summat, and then I'll take you to someone I know who'd very likely offer you a job – especially a looker like you. It's clean work, shall we say, but you just need to watch yourself a bit. Good money though."

She stood up, zipping her leather jacket, and turned to leave.

Kelly hesitated, wary of leaving the safety of the café.

Zoe came back, and pressed her hands flat on the table, leaning across so that her face was close to Kelly's. "Look love, what choice 'ave you got? Trust me or don't trust me, that's up to you, but I'm tryin' to make sure you don't have the hassle I had when I first got to London." She turned away towards the door again, looking back at Kelly over her shoulder. "But if you want to take your chance on getting fleeced or raped that's up to you."

Kelly got to her feet feeling stiff and sore from sitting so long and followed Zoe out into the neon-lit London night. She followed her along a maze of streets where down-and-outs slept under cardboard sheets in shop doorways. One or two had luxury accommodation over heating vents from basement restaurants. Most had only a moth-eaten blanket for warmth. Kelly shivered thinking that this could so easily be her – still could be if Zoe wasn't true to her word.

Kelly tried to force her tired brain to take notice of landmarks in case she needed to leave in a hurry, but she was too confused by the twists and turns, the noise and the traffic.

They turned into a narrow street edged with tall houses – the type that had once had servants' rooms in the attics and kitchens in the basement. Most of them were now divided into flats, the neglected outsides of the buildings with their faded white plaster reminding Kelly of Miss Havisham's wedding cake in 'Great Expectations.'

"Down 'ere," said Zoe, stopping outside one of the worst looking ones. Deep Purple blared from one of the upstairs rooms. A black lace dress was thrown from an open window and Kelly heard a girl scream. Then a blonde head appeared two floors up, glaring down at Zoe.

"You better leave that there you thieving cow until I come down for it." The girl sounded drunk. The window banged shut.

Zoe laughed. "She better be quick. That's how I got this one." She indicated the red satin dress she was wearing. "Lucy's got good taste I'll give her that. Let's go and get a cup of tea. I'll give her half an hour and then if she hasn't come down, I'm having it."

Kelly followed her down some wrought iron steps to a basement yard crowded with junk – an old mattress, a few burnt saucepans and a stuffed tawny owl in a glass case.

"That bloody brother of mine," said Zoe. "He was s'posed to get the rag man to come and take all this stuff. Next thing we'll be 'aving rats and then we'll have the Council on our case. The last thing I want is for this place to be declared unfit for human habitation or whatever they call it. It might be grotty but it's cheap."

She produced a key and opened the black painted front door. There was an overpowering smell of some sort of chemical.

Zoe sniffed. "Bloody Barry's been doing his camera stuff here again. I've told him not to. That stuff gets right to the back of my throat."

She led Kelly out to a small kitchen, the sink crammed with dirty dishes.

"And he's not done the washing up like he promised."

She switched on the electric kettle and rinsed a couple of mugs.

"'Ere, what's all the clatter? What're you moaning about now Zo?" demanded a gruff voice from the room beyond.

"Well if it ain't the creature from the black lagoon," said Zoe.

Kelly looked in alarm at the figure that had just appeared in the kitchen doorway. He was tall, thin and with hollow looking dark eyes. His brown hair was matted and in need of a wash. The black tracksuit he was wearing looked moth-eaten.

"I was working OK, so stop giving me a hard time. And I hadn't got anywhere else to go to develop my films. I thought you wanted me to get back on my feet?"

He stopped and stared at Kelly.

"Who've you brought back now - another of your waifs and strays? I thought you'd have more sense after the last time, Zoe. We can't afford to carry passengers."

"I'm not asking you to," said Kelly defiantly. "I didn't ask Zoe to bring me here. She asked me."

"Leave her alone, Barry," said Zoe. "Kelly's seeing about a job tomorrow, aren't you Kelly?"

"Best of luck if it's with old rough balls Gordon," grumbled Barry heading back to the darkened living room. "You'll need to watch yourself there, love."

"Take no notice of him," said Zoe. "Bedroom's this way. We'll have to share."

The bedroom was worse than Kelly's old room in Tredannac Bay – the walls black with mildew in places and the grey and pink flowered paper peeling. The bed was unmade and Kelly could see flakes of tobacco on the grubby powder blue sheets. The room smelled of cheap perfume and blocked drains.

There was a chipboard wardrobe with no door, pulled well away from the wall and a chest of drawers on which was a porcelain figurine of a woman in a pink crinoline and a photograph in a silver frame of a girl with short blonde hair and sad dark eyes.

They were the only decent items in the squalid room – apart from the clothes hanging in the wardrobe, which Zoe said were mainly thrown from the window upstairs when Lucy and her bloke had a row. She'd gone out and rescued the black lace dress while the tea was brewing.

"If I had a nicer place I could go on the game," said Zoe. "Only joking," she said when she saw the shocked look on Kelly's face. "Bathroom's through there – the lock doesn't work too well, so sing loudly if you're on the throne. We don't want Barry getting an eyeful."

Kelly's last thought when she fell asleep next to Zoe in the grey darkness that filtered through the metal bars on the basement window was that if she had enough money left, maybe she should catch the coach back to Penzance and admit defeat. Looking for Jed in Chelsea had sounded so simple a few hours ago. Now she was here in the bewildering chaos of London, it seemed like looking for a needle in a haystack.

TWENTY-TWO

Jed arrived back in London feeling exhausted. Every mile of the journey separating him from Kelly felt as if his guts were being wrenched from his body. It had taken all his willpower not to race back to Tredannac Bay and beg her to come away with him.

His ambition to succeed as a writer kept him driving towards London. He'd given up a good job and his relationship with his father to follow his dream. Much as he felt drawn to Kelly, without an income of some kind he had nothing to offer her. He thought bitterly that he had more to offer her when he had his bed-sit and the job at the supermarket than he did now that he was being financed by Mirabelle.

He told himself he'd finish the film script and repay Mirabelle everything he owed her. Only then would he be free to trace Kelly again. He bitterly regretted taking things as far as he had with her and raising her expectations – but there'd been a kind of madness that day. A madness that felt totally right.

At Exeter he'd stopped in a truckers' café for tea and toast and sat lost in his own thoughts in the hot steamy atmosphere. As the jukebox played '*Satisfaction*' for the tenth time, his mug of tea grew cold as he made frantic notes for a stage version of the film-script, imagining Kelly as the heroine in a yellow silk dress. It would be his tribute to her, even if they never met again.

Feeling heavy-hearted, he got back in the car and headed towards London. Mirabelle greeted him with enthusiasm, sweeping him into the sitting room to look at swatches of fabric in various shades of pink that the bridesmaids' dresses were to be made of. Jed listened unenthusiastically, thinking how Mirabelle's Texan accent grated on his nerves and why hadn't he noticed it before. He looked at her perfect American teeth and thought of Kelly's where one of the eye teeth was slightly crooked and how that gave character to her face. He thought of how

Kelly's eyes glowed liquid amber when she smiled and felt a burning longing to be back at the crossroads waiting for her.

"Say, honey, I got this special deal with *Time* magazine for our wedding. Isn't that great? They'll do an article and photographs covering the movie as well as the wedding and *Harpers & Queen* want to take photographs and do an article about how we met."

Jed wondered which was more important to Mirabelle – the wedding or the film or just being the centre of attention. He sat back against the sofa cushions with his eyes closed, thinking of Kelly and the ruined house on the cliffs that haunted his dreams.

He went to bed craving sleep but Mirabelle had other ideas. She slid across on top of him – an action that was so different from the way Kelly had behaved that Jed's erection rapidly died.

He felt her hands on him, trying to coax him back to life.

"C'mon sweetie," she whispered, "it seems so long since we were together."

"Sorry," said Jed, "I'm really tired."

Mirabelle snuggled against him in the stuffy darkness of their room. "I thought it was me that was supposed to say that kind of stuff – you know, 'sorry honey, I've got a headache' and all that." She sounded aggrieved.

"Sorry," said Jed, wondering why he was apologising. He felt like shit and if he couldn't be with Kelly all he wanted was to sleep alone.

He spent the next ten days working flat out to complete the film script and send it to the director Aaron McIntyre. All he could think of as he worked late into the night was of travelling back to Cornwall to find Kelly.

The script was greeted with enthusiasm and Jed was grateful that Mirabelle was occupied by arranging a celebratory lunch the following Friday. She was too tired at the end of each day of dealing with caterers, florists and dressmakers to initiate sex like she usually did.

Having completed the script, Jed's thoughts were now occupied with completing the play he was writing for Kelly. He swore to himself he'd get it performed somewhere, he didn't know how, so that one day she'd hear about it and understand how he felt about her.

Compared to the film-script that he'd had to force himself to write, this piece of work flowed from his pen as if someone was dictating the words. As soon as it got light on the Friday morning, Jed washed and dressed, collected the portable Olivetti typewriter he'd bought in a junk shop in Penzance and went out. The morning air was fresh and clear and for the first time in a couple of days he felt as if he had space inside his head. Once he'd escaped the house, all thoughts of Mirabelle's lunch were forgotten.

A few people were making their way to work, but the streets were quiet. Jed could smell a mixture of exhaust fumes, frying bacon and coffee. A girl in a pink crocheted hat and long patchwork skirt was busking near the Town Hall. Her guitar had psychedelic patterns all over it and she was singing that Joni Mitchell song that Kelly had said she liked – the one about clouds.

Jed stood watching her as she finished the song and then tossed a half crown into her guitar case. She looked up and smiled.

He turned away so she couldn't see how moved he'd been by the song.

"You need some breakfast," he told himself, pushing open the door of Trattoria Venezia, its walls hung with paintings of Venice canals, the crumbling buildings adorned with overflowing pots of geraniums and strings of washing. He'd noticed before that the café had a room at the back that looked the sort of place where he might find the peace and quiet that he

craved.

"Am I OK to work in here?" he asked the dark haired Italian man behind the counter.

"You pay for your breakfast and you can do what you like," he said with a smile. Carnival masks decorated the maroon velvet curtains behind the counter, reminding Jed of a theatre and he knew Kelly would love this place.

He ordered a sausage and egg sandwich and a pot of coffee. The sandwich came complete with tomatoes and mushrooms fried in olive oil and the coffee was frothy and flavoured with chicory. He set up his typewriter, re-reading what he'd written in his notebook earlier that morning, as he ate his breakfast.

He'd chosen a table in the corner – he'd never liked the feeling that someone could get round behind him. That was one thing he'd hated at school, the way that teachers walked up and down the rows of desks looking over your shoulder and pointing out what you'd done wrong.

Jed knew he should've left a note for Mirabelle – but he was indulging in a wonderful feeling of being released from something, being free to write what he wanted. This work was precious to him and he wanted to protect it, much as he wanted to preserve his memories of Kelly.

After breakfast and a second pot of coffee, he felt better and was surprised to find that it was nearly eleven o'clock. The pages had grown steadily from his typewriter and Marco, the Italian behind the counter, had watched him in amused fascination.

The tide of customers rose and fell – people in for breakfast or coffee on the way to work or collecting cakes and sandwiches.

"Then we have ze ladies in for coffee and zen the lunch," said Marco as he wielded a broom across the terracotta coloured floor tiles clearing crumbs and crumpled yellow napkins. "You have Italian typewriter," he said. "You will write good story – from ze heart." He clasped the broom to him as if he loved it.

"*Lunch!*" thought Jed, his heart sinking into his boots. He gathered his papers together and put them in his folder, placed the cover on his typewriter made his excuses and hurried out of the café.

The girl was still busking by the Town Hall, and had now been joined by a young man with dark curly hair and dusky brown skin, the lively music of his fiddle combined with her voice creating a totally different sound. The street was noisier too – traffic snarled to a standstill and horns blaring.

Jed wished he could go back into the café and just stay there until all that he'd wanted to say had poured out. Then he thought of today's lunch. Mirabelle had put a lot of time and energy into planning it and making sure every detail was perfect, the least he could do was be there. He'd wanted writing success for so long, had lost contact with his father and caused his mother heartache and now he was within an ace of throwing it all away because he'd fallen in love with a girl who may have forgotten him already.

"Where the hell have you been?" screamed Mirabelle when he got in through the door. "I've been worried sick."

A florist was carrying in a huge arrangement of pink roses and white lilies. The caterers were busy with champagne bottles. Jed could smell garlic bread and something hot and spicy simmering in the kitchen. He headed up to his study, putting the typewriter down by his desk, feeling like a plant wilting in the hot-house atmosphere. He put the folder containing his new work on the desk while he unlocked his filing cabinet.

Mirabelle followed him up the stairs, taking small angry steps because of her killer heels and the fishtail skirt of her shocking pink devore velvet dress. Her pink lipsticked mouth was set in a hard line.

"You didn't show up for the *Harpers & Queen* magazine interview and I didn't think you'd be here for lunch. I was thinking I'd have to say you were sick or something."

She stared at him as if seeing him for the first time. "What's got into you since you came back? You're not the same guy. What do you need to sneak around the streets with a typewriter for when you've got one right here? What's that you've been working on? "She ripped at the blue folder, her long pink nails tearing the edge of a page.

She stood, hands on her hips like an immaculate virago, while Jed peeled off his jeans and sweater and headed for the shower. She was still there when he got back a few minutes later. The scalding hot water had helped to clear his head and make him feel fresher. Standing in just his underpants, he went through his wardrobe looking for a shirt and trousers.

"So what're you being secretive about?" Mirabelle went on. "Why are you using a portable typewriter? Isn't your study good enough? What's all this stuff you've been writing? Why haven't you told me about it?"

Jed waited for her to run out of steam.

"It's not that there's anything wrong with my study here – I love it. What writer wouldn't? It's just – I can't work with you constantly looking over my shoulder, fiddling with my research notes and chattering on about wedding dresses and guest lists."

He paused, noticing the hurt look in her dark eyes. "Writing's about following pathways inside your head – can you understand that? I know it sounds weird. It's about being somewhere else – someone else even. I need space and I need quiet."

"But half the time you're not doing anything," she said. "You're just staring out of the window."

"I'm in the story," he said, "that's what happens when you write - and you keep dragging me out of it. It's like being woken up every time you get off to sleep."

There was a discreet knock on the door.

"Mirrie, Jed," said Mitch, "your guests have arrived. I had them shown into the sitting room for now and they've all got drinks.

Mirabelle flounced off, checking her reflection in the glass as she went, her pink velvet dress hugging her figure. Jed noticed the artificial smile she pasted onto her face as she headed towards the stairs.

"Ya know, son," said Mitch as they went slowly down the stairs, "ya need to wise up about women. I know what her dear Ma was like before our wedding. Near drove me crazy. Everything detail had to be just so, every scrap of ribbon perfect."

Jed didn't say anything.

"She'll be fine," Mitch went on. "Let her have her head – be the star of this movie of yours, have a fairytale wedding and then sure as oil's black, she'll settle down and become a perfect wife and mother just like her Ma.

During lunch, wine and champagne flowed freely. Aaron McIntyre, the film director was full of praise for the script that Jed had written.

"I'm setting up auditions in the Café Royal for early November," he said. "That should give us time to iron out any wrinkles in the script and plan the scenes and locations." He picked up a large chunk of garlic bread and bit into it, scattering crumbs across the white damask cloth.

"My Mirrie's still good for the heroine, isn't she," said Mitch, sounding as if he didn't doubt that the answer would be yes.

Aaron swallowed his mouthful of bread and reached for the dish of Coronation Chicken, putting a generous spoonful on his plate before answering the question. "You'll certainly get *a* part," he said, looking intently at Mirabelle, "but I've got a feeling this movie could be bigger than I first expected. Therefore we need to make it look more important – raise the stakes – get all the publicity we can. I love the double whammy of the wedding and the film premiere. That'll set you and Jed on the road to stardom."

Jed sat next to Mirabelle, saying little, picking at the plateful of food that she'd piled up for him, 'as if they were already wed' Mitch had joked. Jed remembered a famous writer once saying that Hollywood was like a fish-market in evening clothes. He was nowhere near Hollywood yet, but he had the feeling he didn't want to be.

When lunch was over, he excused himself, saying that he had a meeting with his publisher. Mirabelle shot him a questioning look but didn't say anything. He hurried upstairs and collected the green folder that contained the poems he hoped would form his second collection. He'd completed the last of the poems while he was in Cornwall and had called the collection 'Seascapes and Dreams' in memory of Kelly.

He felt relieved to be outside, even though the air was full of traffic fumes and the streets were crowded. He knew he'd behaved oddly since he got back, but saw it more as a coming to his senses. He wondered what would happen when he plucked up the courage to tell Mirabelle he didn't love her enough to marry her.

Over lunch he'd listened to the loud banter of Aaron McIntyre and his entourage. He'd picked his way through food he didn't want and had smiled politely and laughed in the right places. Behind the mask he'd created, he was fiercely planning what to do next. He wondered why he hadn't thought of trying to contact Kelly by phone. He knew there would be problems trying to find someone with the surname of Smith, but when he was writing this morning, he'd found the information sheet about the museum where Kelly was working when he first met her. Surely if he rang and soft-soaped the old bag who managed the place she might tell him where Kelly lived.

He found a phone box, fumbling in his pocket for the right coins. The line was faint, made worse by the traffic rumbling past.

"Can I help you?" The vinegary voice on the other end of the phone sounded as if that was the last thing she wanted to do.

"I just wondered if you could tell me how I might contact Kelly Smith. I have an ... an offer of work for her."

"She no longer works here."

"I know – and I know it's probably not ethical, but do you maybe have a home number for her?"

"No, I do not. Good day to you."

The phone was slammed down, the sound echoing across the miles.

Jed pushed his way out of the phone box. He went into Chelsea Library, rummaged through the telephone directories until he found the right one and sat in the corner scanning the list of names. He came up with a list of five Smiths in Tredannac Bay.

He found another phone box in a quieter street. There was no answer from two of the numbers and two didn't know anything about anyone called Kelly. The fifth call rang for some time before it was answered, the man's voice sounding gruff.

"If you're the police or someone checkin' up, for the last bleedin' time she ain't here. Her Mum's convinced she's buggered off to London after some bloke. Call back later and speak to Viv. Let a bloke get some sleep round here."

The phone was slammed down on Jed for the second time that day, leaving him holding the purring receiver feeling stunned by what he'd just heard.

If Kelly was in London, then where was she staying? How would he find her?

Jed walked on, his imagination spiralled into endless ugly scenarios – Kelly sleeping on the streets, being raped in a dark alley or propositioned by men. She could end up dead in the gutter and he wouldn't know. If she'd come to London, then he was certain it was because she was looking for him.

He delivered the folder of poems to his publisher in Kensington and carried on walking, not sure where he was going. A poster in a shop window caught his eye – an advertisement for a performance of a new play. Jed vaguely recognised the name of the playwright from a magazine he'd read. The play was being performed in The King's Head pub at Islington, described as being 'one of the most inspiring new venues in London.'

"It's modelled on the theatre revue bars in New York," said an American voice next to Jed. "The place doesn't look much at the moment but the guy that runs it'll soon change that."

Jed turned to see a scruffy looking man with curly brown hair and an infectious smile. His tweed jacket was patched at the elbows and his brown shoes were badly scuffed.

"Here are two tickets for tomorrow night," said the man, "on the house. Let me know what you think." He pushed the tickets into Jed's hand and was gone, swallowed up into the late afternoon crowd.

Jed stood looking at the tickets feeling a surge of excitement, sensing somehow that this might be where his future lay. He decided not to tell Mirabelle. He'd make some excuse and go alone.

TWENTY-THREE

One of my first assignments when I moved to London was to go with one of the senior reporters to a pub called The King's Head at Islington. It wasn't until afterwards that I found out it was Mike Jackson's own idea, not the editor's.

Mike was dark eyed and olive skinned and would've made a great male model. He was always showing off his latest clothes purchases from Carnaby Street and the Kings Road. He'd done a piece on Mr Kipper who'd displayed designer suits in dustbins. Mike had got himself in the photo somehow, looking a cross between a film star and a gigolo

I didn't think he'd look twice at me – a seventeen-year-old girl fresh from the country.

"I've got tickets for a play tonight," he said, lounging on my desk surrounding me in the overpowering smell of Old Spice after-shave. "Do you fancy coming with me? Dinner's included. Deal is – I buy the drinks, you write the piece about The King's Head. Pick you up at seven?"

I was about to say something about being too young to go in pubs, but then realised how square that would sound to someone like him. After all, this was London. People did things differently here.

I knew my aunt wouldn't be happy about me being out after ten, but if I told her it was an assignment for work she couldn't really complain. I put on my best dress – purple crushed velvet with bell sleeves – and took care with my make up, piling my hair on top of my head.

"Don't you go giving him the wrong idea," said my aunt as I tottered down the path in my high heels.

"This is work," I said, showing the shorthand notebook I had in my bag. "I need to look smart."

Several of the girls in the office had warned me about Mike – his reputation for wandering hands and for getting other people to do his work and then claiming the credit. I told myself they were probably jealous because he hadn't asked them to go out with him.

Mike's eyes lit up when he met me at the end of the street. "Who looks a dolly bird then?"

He hailed a taxi. "Expenses are there to be claimed," he said, putting a hot arm round my shoulders; his breath already smelled of beer.

I pushed down the feeling of uneasiness telling myself it was because this was a new situation. This was my first ride in a London taxi and I absorbed every detail of the leather seats, the glass door between us and the driver and the meter that whizzed round calculating the fare.

"We could be up to anything back here," said Mike, "he'd never know."

The thing I first noticed about The King's Head was the feeling of energy as soon as you walked in. It wasn't smart – quite the reverse. The wallpaper in the bar was peeling off the walls and the stairs that led to the Ladies were dusty and uncarpeted. A large hessian sack of rice stood on the bottom step.

A hot spicy smell from the kitchen collided with the smell of beer in the dimly lit corridor.

"Hope you guys like curry," said the man behind the bar with a mischievous grin. His clothes looked crumpled, as if he'd slept in them. "I don't want any bad reports in that paper of yours."

"Susan's writing the piece," said Mike introducing me. "So blame her." He took a large swallow of beer.

I sipped my glass of wine, trying to look sophisticated and not wince at the sour taste, and looked at Dan Crawford under my eyelashes, wondering how he'd mastered the knack of seeming to be everywhere at once – serving behind the bar, laying tables in the back room, checking on progress in the kitchen and going up to talk to the actors.

"When he gives us the tour in a minute," said Mike, his eyes looking glittery and dangerous, "you'll notice the place hasn't been touched since 1938. They were talking about knocking it down at one time."

"You guys ready for your tour?" Dan's grin was so infectious that I smiled back. Friends at school used to say I didn't smile enough, but with Dan Crawford you couldn't help it. He had brown curly hair that didn't look as if it was combed very often, and he wore crumpled trousers and shirt and a threadbare tweed jacket with leather patches on the elbows.

The stage area was painted matt black and there were a few rusty looking spotlights reminding me of the night we'd done Romeo and Juliet at school. Scenery was minimal and a few props littered the stage - a bowler hat, a chair and a vase of flowers on a small round table.

Behind the stage was a long narrow room with one disgusting looking toilet in what had once been a broom cupboard.

"Our dressing room," said Dan. "Providing there aren't too many actors." He paused. "If there are then some have to change in my flat – up there – and then they come down the fire escape across the roof and back into here."

"Does your wife mind about people being in your flat?"

"I'm between wives," he said, a look of regret or relief flashing across his face. "There never seemed to be time."

He'd guided us back to a round wooden table in the corner, squeezing through the people who'd already gathered while we'd been upstairs. Most of them looked intellectual or trendy or both and were talking about the play we were about to see.

A waitress with an elfin face and slim hips encased in tight black jeans put large plates of chicken curry and rice in front of us. There was a generous dollop of what looked like apricot jam on it.

I waited for Mike to pick up his fork and take the first mouthful, making a play of jotting down some notes in my book.

"You can't beat a good curry with a pint or two of beer," he said. "Do you like curry?"

I didn't like to say I'd never eaten it before. It wasn't something our family did. Claire, my friend at school, was always on about the curries they ate at home – but her Dad had served in India during the war and had learned to cook them there.

"You OK?" Mike touched my hand.

I picked up my fork. The first mouthful nearly blew my head off. I took a sip of wine and the burning feeling intensified. Eating rice with a fork wasn't easy either and there didn't seem to be any spoons about.

"Do they always put jam on it?" I asked.

Mike nearly choked on his beer. "Its mango chutney not jam," he said when he'd stopped spluttering.

"Oh," I said, feeling stupid.

"Don't drink until you've finished eating," he said, his eyes gleaming with amusement, "it doesn't burn quite so much." He went to the bar and fetched me some water. .

"You don't have to finish it," he said. "This isn't school dinners – and you won't offend me if you leave any. " He paused. "There'll be some ice cream round in a while"

I put my fork down and sat there trying hard not to feel like a schoolgirl.

Thankfully the waitress with the elfin face came and cleared the plates and I was soon cooling my hot mouth with the small portion of vanilla ice cream she brought me.

Mike went to the bar and brought back another pint of beer and more wine for me. While he was gone, I'd whipped out my notebook again and made a few more notes for my article.

"You're keen aren't you?" said Mike. "Come on, bring your drink, it won't be long before the play starts."

We followed the people filing into the next room. Mike found seats for us in a dark corner at the back. As soon as the lights dimmed, he put his arm round me. The play started – a *psychological thriller set during the Second World War - and his other hand got more adventurous, gently stroking my left breast. I pushed his hand away and at first he took the hint.*

The first half of the play featured several quick changes of costume, which was especially amazing, knowing what the conditions were like backstage. I thought of how lucky we'd been at school to have whole classrooms to change and get made up in.

I made a few brief notes while I was in the Ladies. It didn't seem appropriate to whip my notebook out while the play was in progress. When I got back, Mike had bought me another glass of wine, despite me saying I only wanted orange juice.

"I forgot," he said. "Sorry."

He didn't look sorry.

I sipped my wine. It was hot in the pub, my mouth was dry and I felt light-headed. This time when Mike put his arm round me and fondled my breasts, I didn't push him away. His lips closed on mine, blotting out my view of the actors on the makeshift stage. Nobody sitting near us seemed to notice what we were up to. That, for me, was the difference between London and Cornwall. What would've been instantly talked about in Tredannac Bay was completely ignored here.

The play ended to a standing ovation. Mike held my hand as we left the theatre. I visited the Ladies again, my notes this time a lot sketchier, mainly because Mike had spent the second half snogging my face off. He was waiting for me in the bar when I came out. Dan Crawford was talking to a tall dark haired man. I knew I'd seen him somewhere before, but for the life of me couldn't remember where.

"You ready?" Mike held me tight as we left the pub, which was just as well because my legs felt unsteady as we hit the cool night air, making me giggle.

"Hay foot, straw foot, that's it," he said, making me laugh even more.

I was still laughing when he pulled me into a dark

alleyway. It didn't take many minutes to realise that he wasn't messing about. I'd rather not describe what happened next, but let's say I felt used, cheap and like a sixpenny whore.

"Don't, Mike," I'd tried to say, feeling sick now from the wine I'd drunk.

"You're a bloody prick teaser," he said, "a silly little girl. It's no good leading me on like you have been all night and then saying no. Blokes can't stop just like that."

I stumbled out of the alleyway. Passers-by looked at me but didn't offer any assistance. Mike was close behind but I was too unsteady on my legs to run away. He acted all concerned now we were back in public view, hailed a taxi for me and told the driver where to drop me, pushed me in and dropped a ten shilling note in my lap.

I arrived back at my aunt's house with a splitting headache, my hair like a bird's nest and my shoes caked in mud. All I wanted was to get in a scorching hot bath and scrub every vestige of Mike away, but I knew that wouldn't be possible because Aunt Shirley only allowed baths on Saturday night and this was a Tuesday.

She was already in bed when I got home. I couldn't even run the hot tap because that would've set off the geyser in the bathroom. I bathed my face in cold water, relishing its icy sting and then scrubbed every inch of my body. I crumpled up the beautiful crushed velvet dress, knowing I'd never want to wear it again. Tomorrow, on my way to work, I'd dispose of it in the nearest litterbin.

I felt bruised and shaky and as soon as I lay down on my bed, the room started spinning round. I only just made it to the toilet before I vomited, the sound rousing Aunt Shirley. I looked up to see her framed in the doorway clad in pink winceyette nightdress and hairnet and curlers.

"It's probably that mucky stuff they gave you to eat," she said, her voice sounding muffled because she hadn't got her teeth

in.

I couldn't tell her the food had been the least of my problems.

"No work tomorrow if you're no better." She fetched me a glass of water and cleaned the loo with bleach. "Now off to bed with you."

I laid in bed my stomach churning, knowing that I'd have to go into work to complete the article. I could see how stupid I'd been. There was no way I should've drunk all that wine when I wasn't used to it. If I'd had any sense, I'd have taken notice of what the other girls had said about Mike and checked things out properly with the boss first.

I crawled into work half an hour late, pretending that I'd been to the dentist, in time to see Mike talking to Jane, the new office junior. She was about the same age as me with long blonde hair and Mike was looking at her as if she was the only woman in the world.

"If you're studying shorthand at college, you should take every opportunity to make use of it," he was saying to her. "Maybe you'd like to come out with me on Friday week and act as my secretary for the day."

His dark eyes were fixed on her china blue ones. Neither of them noticed me as I walked into the office. I wanted to hurry across and warn Jane not to go, remind her to think of fairytales and the undesirable characters in them. Mike was the wolf in sheep's clothing and she should stay away from him.

I sat at my desk, trying not to look at them, feeling sick and shaky as I typed up my notes from the night before. My shorthand book had absorbed the revolting smell of curry and I knew I'd never be able to eat it again without thinking of that night.

Something triggered a memory about the tall dark haired man talking to Dan Crawford just before we left the pub last night. I knew he looked familiar and now I remembered where I'd last *seen him. It was in the main street at Tredannac Bay on that hot summer day when I'd lost my virginity to Jamie. He was talking to Smelly Kelly outside the museum and I wondered why it was that whenever my life hit a low point Kelly was always there in the background.*

Thinking about her made me think of her sister Miranda and her two snotty-nosed children – and then with a sickening lurch as Mike walked past my desk in a wave of Old Spice aftershave, I thought 'what if I'm pregnant?' I'd got away with it last time with Jamie. Maybe this time I wouldn't be so lucky.

TWENTY-FOUR

The first thing Kelly did when she woke early the next morning was to grab her handbag to check whether she had enough money for her fare home.

With a 'lift going down too fast' sensation in her stomach, she discovered that her purse was empty. She scuffled through the contents of her untidy handbag hoping she'd find the money in a different section, but it was gone. Her frantic activity awakened Zoe and she sat up yawning and shivering, clutching the thin blankets around her for warmth.

"'What's all the noise about, Kelly?"

"My money's been stolen. I can't go home because my money's been nicked? Did you take it Zoe? 'Cos if you did I want it back."

"What do you take me for? I didn't take yer bleedin' money. I'm trying to help yer – not that you seem the least bit grateful."

"So I'm supposed to feel grateful for having my money nicked, am I?"

Someone from the flat above rapped on the ceiling. Kelly hadn't realised she was shouting.

Zoe got out of bed, shrugging herself into a long black cardigan that served as a dressing gown. "Have you checked yer bag properly?" She rubbed her eyes sleepily. "I could do without this first thing in the morning. Let's see if our Barry knows anything about it."

Kelly followed her into the darkened sitting room. A crumpled grey blanket lay on the brown tweed sofa on top of a torn blue silk cushion. An empty coffee mug stood on the floor next to the sofa next to an empty custard cream packet.

"That little shit, Barry," said Zoe pulling at the sofa to make sure he'd not left anything behind. He's cleared off with some of my stuff too. He's even taken my emergency bottle of vodka – and that black dress I picked up last night. Christ knows what he'll do with that. You're lucky he didn't run off with your rucksack. That's the last time I help him – ever. He needn't think he can come back here with a sob story and I'll take him in 'cos I won't."

"What about my money?" said Kelly, "how am I going to get home now?"

Zoe looked at Kelly with narrowed eyes. "What about the wonderful Mr Matthews or whatever his name is? Given up on him already have yer?"

Kelly slumped down on the sofa. "It just seemed stupid – an impossible task, like they have in fairytales - spinning straw into gold and all that stuff."

"Wouldn't know about that, love – never had anyone to read to me. One thing I do know is you must've felt strongly to do what you did so don't give up at the first hint of trouble or you'll never get anywhere in life."

"My Gran always said that," said Kelly.

"Come to that – if you're that set on goin' back to Cornwall or wherever it is, you could hitch a ride from someone - done it meself – here to Southend and back." She paused. "Thought the pier was a bit over-rated but the bloke was all right. He bought me coffee and a doughnut."

"I'll never hitch a lift again," said Kelly with a shudder, thinking of the journey to Penzance.

"What did he do – try to tickle your leg?"

"Worse than that – his... thing... was hanging out."

"You know what they say – if you see something you don't like the look of hit it with a big stick and then run like hell."

Kelly couldn't help smiling. "I did – hit it and run that is – and boy was he mad!"

"Spoiled his fun didn't you. Seriously, though Kelly, if you're gonna stay and make a go of things, then you need to toughen up a bit. There are guys out there who'll do worse than what that bloke did if you give them half a chance. You just need to get wise to their nasty little tricks and be ready for them. Now – cup of tea before we go round the doctor's. That's if bloody Barry hasn't nicked the tea leaves an all."

Later that morning, the doctor, who was Indian, did no more than ask Kelly a few questions before handing her a large white tablet.

"Please to be more careful in future," he said, pressing the buzzer for the next patient.

There was no fear of that, thought Kelly as she followed Zoe through a confusing mass of streets, noticing landmarks like Nelson's Column and the statue of Eros that she'd only seen in books before.

"Where are we going?" she asked Zoe.

"A magical mystery tour leading to your job interview," said Zoe. "Now remember what I said – this guy will try it on. Don't let him have his wicked way. Keep him guessing. One daft tart thought she'd get the job by letting him screw her. He just said 'thanks but no thanks' and there she was, out on the street with no job and a nasty reminder of him on the way."

"I don't like the sound of it," said Kelly.

"You're an actress ain't yer? Use yer acting skills. Give him the works – but don't give in, if you get what I mean."

In daylight 'The Black Tulip' didn't look very inspiring and neither did the surrounding area. Rubbish bins overflowed with fish and chip wrappers and the like and there were pools of vomit in the gutter. Kelly followed the path round the back of the building and rang the bell. A bouncer with a crew-cut and a neck like a prize bull let her in and she was almost suffocated by the smell of stale beer.

He led Kelly along a dingy passageway and tapped on a door that said 'T. Gordon - Manager.' A big man with a bald head and double chin sat with his feet up on the desk, a grubby looking phone clamped to his ear.

"What do you mean you can't do tonight?" he barked into the phone.

The desk was cluttered with crumpled letters and the remains of his egg sandwich smothered in brown sauce. The buttons on his white shirt looked as if they were struggling to contain his paunch. His grey jacket hung on a rusty hook by the desk. The air smelled of stale cigar smoke, whisky and old socks. From somewhere deep inside the building, Kelly could hear the throbbing of music. Her first instinct was to run away. Then she remembered that she had no idea where she was and thanks to Barry, she had no money. Zoe had been good enough to bring her here. The least she could do was try and get the job – whatever it was. She sat down with her hands clasped in her lap, trying to stop them shaking.

The man slammed the phone down and let out his breath in an exasperated gasp.

"Bloody women - can't rely on any of them."

He looked Kelly up and down. "What do you want?"

"I've come about the job," she said, trying to sound braver than she felt.

"What job? There ain't no job."

"I'll go then," said Kelly, not sure if she felt relieved or sorry.

She stood up, smoothing her dress down and turned to open the door. She didn't look round but she could sense his eyes on her and was reminded of the guy in the truck.

"Stop!" he said, just as she felt she'd got away. "I've changed my mind. Go with Giles and get your kit off and let's see what you can do"

He pressed an intercom buzzer.

"Giles – show her the changing rooms and put the stage lights on – and find some decent music."

The bouncer who'd let her in showed her to a grubby looking room that had a wide shelf running round it like a kitchen surround. The walls and ceilings were covered in mirrors and there was a mattress on the floor in one corner covered in blue and white ticking. There were hooks for hanging clothes on and a basket of what looked like stage props in another corner.

"The stage is through there," he said pointing to a tattered black curtain that Kelly could feel a howling draught coming through. "Be ready in five minutes."

Kelly stood in the middle of the room wondering what to do next. She heard a toilet flush and an old woman came into the room.

"Hello love," she said, smiling and showing stained teeth. "I was just 'aving a bit of a clean up and then I had to go, as they say. Are you here about the job? You look young to me – very young. Had much experience – you know..." she nodded towards the bed.

Kelly shook her head.

"I didn't think so. You don't look the type. Go back to your Mum, love, before she misses you. Don't get mixed up in any of this lot. They're all bastards."

"I can't," said Kelly. "Not until I've earned some money."

"Well take old Bertha's advice and hang on to your lines as long as you can. Don't give anything away till you get a ring on your finger."

"*Bit late now*,' thought Kelly.

"I haven't got all bloody day," boomed a voice through the curtain.

"Go on then love," said Bertha giving her a gentle push.

Kelly stood in the pink glare of the stage lights wondering what to do. The music started up, so loud that she could feel it through the soles of her feet.

"Don't just stand there like a stuffed dummy girl – let's see some action."

She could smell Trevor Gordon's cigar and see his white shirt gleaming in the darkened room. The room had a low ceiling painted black and was crowded with tables and chairs turned towards the stage. The word 'stage' kicked into Kelly's brain. She needed to earn some money since hers was gone. Zoe had said this was good money for old rope. It wasn't the sort of acting she'd imagined herself doing – she could tell by the way other men had slid into the shadows at the back of the room what was expected of her. Even though the neon light at the front of the building had been switched off, she could see the word 'Strippers.'

She tried to imagine what Nell Gwyn would do in this situation and decided she'd give a star performance. Kelly swayed to the music trying to think sexy. She knew without looking that Trevor Gordon was getting impatient. She blanked out the chairs in front of her and tried to imagine Jed's face that day in Penzance as she slowly unzipped her dress and eased it down from her shoulders. There was a large black swansdown fan that someone had left at the side of the stage. Kelly snatched that up as she tossed her dress to one side.

Instinct told her to take it slowly. Thankfully she was wearing the new underwear Jed had bought her – the black set.

Kelly was just teasing her way out of her bra, covering herself with the fan, making sure they got only a suggestion of naked flesh. She heard a muffled gasp and a 'bloody hell' from somewhere in the space beyond. A quick glance confirmed that she'd got Trevor's full attention – and it looked as if he was having trouble controlling what was inside his trousers.

"OK", he said, when Kelly was down to her knickers. "Come into my office now and we'll discuss the job."

"Now," he said, his voice soft and menacing

This was the bit Zoe had warned Kelly about. She'd told her about the girl who'd gone into the office in just her pants. Trevor Gordon had taken what he wanted and then said there was no job for her.

Kelly wriggled back into her bra and picked up her dress,

preparing to follow him along the corridor. She was just wondering how she'd get out of here without getting trapped in a situation she didn't want and thinking this was going to be harder than escaping from the truck driver, when there was a hammering on the front door.

"Get rid of them, whoever it is," said Trevor. "Tell them I'm busy."

He gestured to Kelly to hurry.

"Sorry, boss. It's the police."

"What the fuck do they want?" He looked at Kelly. "Clear out of here in case they start asking awkward questions about your age."

Kelly stepped into her dress and zipped it up, feeling disappointed that after all that she hadn't got the job but relieved to be getting out.

"You're hired," he said as she reached the light at the end of the corridor. Come back at seven thirty tomorrow. You can replace Penny."

Kelly turned slowly. Zoe had warned her not to seem too grateful if he offered her work. "How much?" she asked.

TWENTY-FIVE

"He must've liked you," said Zoe, stretching out on her bed and blowing smoke rings at the flaking ceiling. A glass of vodka and lime was on the stained bedside table next to her. "Like I said, though, watch yourself. You'll be OK if there are other girls around, but take care not to be on your own with him – and don't let him flatter you into accepting a dinner invitation."

Kelly thought of the restaurant she'd been to with Jed and what that had led to. Had he really thought no more of her than the fat man in the night club? How could she have thought he cared about her?

"So how come you've helped me like you have," she asked Zoe.

Zoe inhaled and blew out smoke in a single stream. She propped herself on one elbow and looked at Kelly. "I s'pose I don't like waste. When I saw you sitting in that café looking lost, you reminded me of my friend Amy. We met at Art College and always planned to travel the world flogging our paintings..." Zoe's eyes filled with tears. She sat up, grinding her cigarette end into the overflowing ashtray and took a mouthful of vodka.

"I didn't know you're an artist," said Kelly.

"Was," said Zoe. "My Dad died, Mum ran off with the lodger and money was tight. I was working all hours to keep things going – make sure Barry went to school and that there was food on the table. Amy encouraged me to keep going with my college course – and I was doing well, selling a bit here and there. Then she got herself involved with one of the lecturers. When she got pregnant he didn't want to know. I promised I'd look after her when her Mum kicked her out and I would've done, but she went to one of those back street women. She had an abortion and she died."

Kelly moved closer to Zoe as the tears flowed harder. Zoe shook her off.

"That's why I help every girl I come across who looks like she needs it," she said, scuffing away the tears with the back of her hand. "That's why I might seem wild, but there's no way on this earth that I'll let any bloke do to me what that bastard did to Amy. That's why I couldn't go back to that college – I'd have killed him if I had."

TWENTY-SIX

The October afternoon smelled of apples and early frost when Jed headed off to The King's Head and his meeting with Dan Crawford. His mind buzzed with images from the play and how it would look in that setting.

He smiled to himself, thinking that he'd done the right thing not to take Mirabelle with him last night. He'd spent ages concocting various excuses in his head and despising himself for doing so, but then she'd announced over lunch that she was meeting up with a friend and would be back late. She'd not told him where she was going and he didn't ask.

She'd departed, leaving behind a waft of Dior perfume and blowing him a kiss so as not to spoil her lipstick. Mitch was away for a few days and so Jed sighed with relief that he had no need to think of further excuses.

Dan greeted him enthusiastically when he arrived at The King's Head. His clothes – the same ones as he'd been wearing last night – looked as though he'd slept in them. Jed sat in the deserted bar while Dan made coffee. The smell of last night's curry lingered on the tide of beer fumes, mingling with the smell of fresh chilli con carne.

"Penny for them," said Dan coming back with the coffee.
"What?"
"Your thoughts of course!" he said.
"Not worth that much," said Jed, taking a sip of his coffee and returning Dan's friendly grin.
"What have you brought me?"

Jed handed over the play-script and watched nervously as Dan turned the first page. The first customers started to appear in the bar and a dark haired barmaid came out to serve them. The daylight faded and the streetlights came on and Jed sat still holding his empty coffee mug, not wanting to break the mood while Dan read the script, the expressions on his face changing like sunlight on water.

"It's great," he said when he reached the last page.

Jed let out his breath with a whoosh, not even aware he'd been holding it.

"You really liked it?"

"I said so didn't I? It maybe needs a bit of tidying up but nothing you can't fix by April. I've got a gap in the programme then. Do you have any actors in mind for the main parts – or would you need to audition?"

"I did have someone in mind for the main female part, but I don't know where she is at the moment, so we'd probably need to audition."

"I usually find getting rid of a woman is the hardest part," said Dan. "You must tell me what your secret is."

They discussed time schedules, dates and scenery requirements over more coffee. The smell of food – chilli con carne with rice – got stronger and Jed's stomach growled with hunger.

"I could fix you a plate of food," said Dan.

Jed glanced at his watch, realising he was late for his meeting with Mirabelle and her friends. Feeling like Cinderella leaving the ball, he made his excuses, picked up his manuscript and hurried away.

Mirabelle made a tremendous fuss of him when he reached the wine bar. She pulled him down into the space next to her and snuggled against him, her white angora cardigan leaving fluff on his dark jacket. Her friends crowded round to be introduced and Jed felt swamped by the cocktail of perfumes and the roll call of names.

What he really wanted to do was go away somewhere quiet and think about all that Dan Crawford had said, to relive the conversation in his mind and absorb the bubble of excitement that his play – a tribute to Kelly – was going to be performed next year.

More than anything, he knew he couldn't go on living a charade. The questions Mirabelle's friends were asking about the wedding and where they were planning to go on their honeymoon echoed round inside his head.

"Gee, you must be so excited with the movie and the wedding," said a friend of Mirabelle's with smooth blonde hair and gleaming white teeth.

Jed smiled politely, casting about for some way of changing the subject.

"Is this your first visit to London?" he asked.

"Gee, no," giggled the blonde. "I just love your red buses and the little shops in Oxford Street and Carnaby Street."

Jed sat nodding and smiling politely while she chattered on about the galleries she'd visited and the clothes she'd bought. Behind his polite mask, he was thinking of Kelly. He'd genuinely hoped that when he got back to London he'd settle back into his life here, but thoughts of Kelly and the ruined house on the cliff continued to taunt him when he was awake and disturb his dreams at night.

A few days after he'd returned from Cornwall, he'd gone for a walk in St James's Park. He'd sat on a bench to make some notes about his play and a man had sat down next to him and started talking about his travels in India. His voice was soft and musical and he was dressed in a baggy black track-suit that carried the smell of cinnamon.

"In India they believe you have many lifetimes," he said, as if reading Jed's thoughts. "And sometimes, if the gods are kind, you meet again with those you love, travelling the road until you learn life's lessons and can step off the wheel of fortune for a while."

He'd stared at Jed with strange silvery eyes as if looking through him.

Jed had wondered if the man was a little deranged. He looked around to see how busy the park was. When he looked back the man was gone as if he'd faded into thin air. Jed had pinched himself, wondering if he'd dreamt the whole experience.

"So whaddya think? Do I stand a chance?" Jed was jerked back to the present. The blonde woman with the immaculate teeth was looking at him as if he was a brick short of a load. She'd been chattering on about a 'narvel' she wanted to write when she had the time and had told him in minute detail about the convoluted plot that seemed to rely on a remarkable number of coincidences.

Jed made a few encouraging remarks and then sat, eyes glazed, paying more attention to the passers-by outside than he was to the hubbub of conversation going on around him. He didn't like Mirabelle's friends. They were the ones who'd been at his book signing and he suspected that what they knew about poetry would go on the back of a postage stamp. If they knew how poor he really was, they wouldn't be so keen to talk to him.

TWENTY-SEVEN

Kelly had the dream again - the one where she was standing in the wings dressed in a yellow silk dress and a powdered wig. The dress was tightly laced and the dark enclosed space smelled strongly of oranges and cloves. She could hear the buzz of conversation on the other side of the red velvet curtains and her stomach churned with stage fright. She was alone on the dusty stage. The curtain would go up in five minutes – she'd just heard the bell – and she had no idea what she had to say.

"Sounds like you need to go back to where you lost the plot," said Zoe as they sat eating toast and drinking tea the next morning. "Carry on as you have done since you got to London and prove you can survive without the help of any bloke. Look for any chances there might be to follow your dreams of becoming an actress. I'm willing to bet anything Jed wasn't his real name and that he was no more a writer than I'm the Archbishop of Canterbury."

Kelly ached with tiredness and last night's tears of frustration following another fruitless search for Jed had left her eyes feeling gritty and sore. She had a headache from the vodka she'd drunk and at first she'd refused Zoe's offer of breakfast, but Zoe had been adamant they were going to start the day the proper way.

"Look, Kelly, no bloke's worth moping in bed for. How about we go to Portobello Market? I got some great clothes there last time I went. Then when we come back I've got the urge to repaint this place – bright pink or lilac to go with them purple velvet cushions they threw out upstairs during their last row. Makes a bit more sense doing up the place now Barry's not here to mess it up."

Kelly shook her head. "I don't really feel in the mood for shopping, Zoe."

Zoe looked at her with mock severity, softened with an

arm round Kelly's shoulder. "You promised me no moping about, OK?"

"OK," said Kelly. "It's what you said about going back to where I lost the plot...I need to go and see Nell Gwyn."

Zoe looked puzzled. "She's dead ain't she?"

Kelly giggled. "Yes, a long time ago. I meant the church where she was buried. You see, her birthday's the same day as mine and I've always felt there's this connection."

"Like the one you had with Jed, you mean?"

"Make fun of me if you want, but that's where I'm going." Kelly put her plate and mug in the sink and picked up her coat and bag.

"Make sure the ghosties don't come after you-oo-oo," said Zoe making a spooky face at Kelly. "Where was she buried, anyway?"

"St Martin-in-the-Fields," said Kelly.

The day was misty, with people looming in and out of the fog, as Zoe said, a cheerful day to visit a church. As Kelly walked, huddled down into the warmth of the coat and boots she'd bought with her first week's pay, she thought about the stories Mrs Wilson had told them about Nell Gwyn and how she'd risen from being an orange seller to being an actress and mistress of a king.

'If Nell managed to do that, then surely I can make the transition from night-club dancer to actress,' thought Kelly. After all, most of her evenings were spent putting on an act for seedy looking men that she didn't fancy at all. As Trevor the manager said, the aim was to get them creaming the inside of their trousers and buying plenty of booze. Thankfully, since that first audition, Trevor hadn't tried it on again. A blonde girl called Katie with enormous boobs had started the same week and she was the current favourite.

Kelly had heard her in the changing room, showing off the silver watch that Trevor had given her.

"It proves he really loves me," she'd lisped.

"Don't prove nothing, love," said Bertha. "The watch is probably fake and if you're not careful you'll end up either pregnant or with a dose of the clap, knowing what our Trevor's like."

Kelly didn't want to think about the night-club with its stuffy atmosphere and the forest of hands reaching forward towards the dancers. She tried to do what Zoe said and focus on what she really wanted. The fog was thicker here nearer to the church and Kelly's coat and hair were beaded with moisture. She had the strangest feeling that past and present were merging together and that she could be in one of those suspense films where the heroine got sucked into another life.

She shivered as the tendrils of fog swirled and eddied around her. A face loomed out of the whiteness, the eyes bleak and dark in a pale face. Kelly choked back a scream and hurried away.

"Kelly, wait."

"Jamie," she said, taking in the dishevelled looking figure swaying in front of her "What are you doing here?"

TWENTY-EIGHT

Jamie rubbed his eyes as he made his way towards St Martin-in-the-Fields thinking that was the last time he'd get smashed on whisky – it was too painful the next morning. He felt queasy and every step he took made his head feel as if a gang of goblins were beating the inside of it with hammers.

He could've done with some aspirins and a mug of tea, but he'd only got a pound left. He'd walked out of the house he'd been dossing in because he'd woken up to the sound of another argument between Phil and Lisa and he guessed rightly that the trigger for it was probably Lisa coming downstairs in her red satin dressing gown and finding him asleep on their sofa with a bucket full of sick next to him and the remains of the chips he and Phil had eaten on the way home still on the coffee table.

Lisa had shot him a look of pure disgust as she went into the kitchen to make two mugs of coffee.

"Get this hell-hole cleared up and get out," she'd hissed. "Phil was doing OK till he took up with you. And you better not have messed up that sofa – it's the only decent piece of furniture we've got."

She'd stomped up the uncarpeted stairs, the heels of her red feathery mules click-clacking on the bare boards.

Jamie got off the sofa wishing the room would stop spinning. He gathered up the cold greasy chips and carried them out to the bin in the kitchen, dropping some as he went. He didn't feel steady enough to bend down and pick them up. He took the bucket to the outside toilet and emptied it.

He vaguely remembered Phil saying something about Lisa going out with her sister last night and that she wouldn't be back till later today so they'd have a chance to have a real lad's night out. Then Lisa had changed her mind and come back early which was typical of most women.

Jamie put on his jacket and picked up his rucksack,

shivering as he stepped out into the foggy morning. Moving on was becoming a familiar feature of his life. Phil's was the third place he'd stayed at since his Uncle and Aunt kicked him out at the end of last week. He'd also left the job in his Uncle's firm – or rather, the Manager he'd been working for had insisted on Jamie being sacked.

"Why couldn't you have acted as if you wanted the job – as if you were remotely interested?" Uncle Alan had asked wearily when Jamie had been sent to his office. "You've already been given more chances than most new members of staff would've been given."

"Probably because I wasn't interested," said Jamie, knowing he was being insolent and not caring.

"I don't want your mother being worried," said Uncle Alan. "I've phoned round a few friends of mine and I've got you an interview at an advertising agency at nine o'clock on Monday. Let's hope you find that a little more interesting."

Jamie stared sullenly at his shoelaces.

"Look, James," said Uncle Alan leaning back in his conker brown leather office chair, "life isn't all beer and skittles. You're grown up now. It's time you started acting like an adult and being responsible for yourself. Smarten yourself up and take a bit of pride in your appearance."

Jamie stared down at the spiral pattern on the navy blue carpet until he was dismissed.

He went down in the lift and walked out of the office block feeling relieved that he wouldn't have to go back there and sit poring over boring piles of paperwork any more.

He caught a glimpse of himself in the mirror, comparing the scruffy looking figure with the trailing shoelaces with the boy with the neat haircut and crisp white shirt of a few months ago.

He'd had to force himself to get up every morning in his Uncle and Aunt's bleach and starch scented house. He'd eaten soggy cornflakes for breakfast every morning because his Aunt insisted on putting the milk on ages before he came downstairs and most evenings had been spent watching boring stuff on the television and listening to the endless clicking of his Aunt's knitting needles. He longed for bedtime when he could escape to his room and have a drink from his secret stash of whisky. It helped him sleep and was his private rebellion against the way his Aunt and Uncle treated him like a child.

The journey to work on the tube had been the only bit that he'd enjoyed – the coal smell of the underground tunnels, the bustle of people and the comforting sway of the trains. He sometimes wished he could travel round all day like some of the tramps did on the Circle Line. He knew from the whispered comments in the office that nobody would really miss him if he did.

"Can't even get the tea order right," was the mildest of the comments.

He'd thought of leaving a note and hitching back to Cornwall, but what would he do back there apart from being branded a failure? He was determined not to go home until he'd made a success of something, even if it wasn't the path that his parents had chosen for him.

In the end it was Caspian, a friend of Phil's – the only person in the office that he got on with – that gave Jamie a new opportunity.

Jamie had brought his bass guitar with him from Cornwall, much to his Aunt's disgust, as she had a low opinion of pop stars.

"Useless long-haired layabouts," she called the Rolling Stones every time their photographs appeared in the paper.

Alone in his dull bedroom with its dark Victorian furniture, Jamie slung the guitar round his neck and pretended to play, bumping and grinding his hips to an imaginary rhythm, trying out the effect in the long wardrobe mirror. Whenever he imagined a crowd of girls screaming at him, it was always Kelly's face that stood out from the crowd.

The band he was offered a place in was called Slide Rule and Caspian had great hopes of their future success. He was pale and thin with dyed black hair that had aroused caustic comments from Jamie's Aunt when Caspian called at the house to drop off details of the next rehearsal and another song for Jamie to practise.

"Your Uncle and I are worried you might be getting into drugs and other unsavoury things," said his Aunt that evening as they sat in the dimly-lit dining room eating gristly stew and overcooked cabbage. "Remember that we are in loco parentis while you're in London."

Her reference to "unsavoury things" meant women – another reason for Jamie's frustration. He deeply regretted the misunderstanding between him and Kelly but didn't know what to do to put things right. He was grateful to Susan Baker for getting him off the hook with Rocky and his gang, but although she'd given him her address in London, he hadn't bothered to get in touch.

One of his reasons for joining the band was that it would make him more appealing to women – despite the fact that Caspian who did vocals and lead guitar had made it clear to Jamie at his audition that success was what they were focused on, not getting into girls' knickers.

"Look at how The Beatles did things in the early days," he said, his lean face earnest. "They concentrated on getting songs written and playing the best they could."

The other band members – Daz who had spiky ginger hair and played the drums and a busty blonde girl called Coral who did support vocals turned their eyes towards Caspian with rapt attention.

Rehearsals took place in the basement of Caspian's father's house in Kensington. There were two rooms - one of them soundproofed to keep the neighbours happy. The room they rehearsed in was so cold Jamie's breath showed white in the damp air.

"You promised you'd get us a fire," whined Coral, licking chocolate off her fingers during one of their rare breaks. "Look, I've got goose-bumps on my chest."

"You shouldn't wear such low-cut tops," said Caspian, staring at her cleavage appreciatively. "And just think how we'll value our success after a start like this."

Jamie soon tired of the endless rehearsals. It was as bad as being at the office – with Caspian breaking off in the middle of a song with comments like "that bit wasn't quite right" and "can we just run through that again." Coral, the vocalist grumbled every time Jamie played a bum note and he had an uneasy feeling of being on his last warning.

Back home in his bedroom, Jamie practised imitations of Caspian's expression – the tight-pulled mouth and the blowing out of his thin cheeks as he said "one more time – and let's get it right for once" with that look that seemed especially reserved for Jamie.

Despite how resentful Jamie felt, he'd only missed one rehearsal, and that wasn't his fault. On the Friday he'd lost his job he'd called into a bar on his way to Caspian's and one drink had led to another and before he knew where he was, he'd stumbled out into the dark unfamiliar street with only a few minutes to go until the start time.

Caspian's house was within view when he found his path blocked by two big men with crew-cuts who'd been in the pub playing darts.

"Give us a tune," said the one, reeling against Jamie.

Jamie could smell the alcohol on the man's breath and he was scared. It brought back memories of the experiences he'd had in Cornwall with Rocky and his gang.

"I think he's saying no," said the other man, "seems to me like he needs to be taught a lesson."

Jamie didn't see the man's fist coming towards him. He fell awkwardly to the ground, landing on his guitar with a loud crack. He closed his eyes as the blows rained down on him from fists and feet. Before the two men lumbered off, he felt a hand rummaging for his wallet.

When he opened his eyes again, the streets were silent and cold arrows of rain sliced into his shivering body. His guitar was wrecked but it had probably saved him from breaking a bone.

He went to Caspian's house, but although he knocked as hard as he could, nobody came to let him in. He stumbled home to find that his Aunt had locked the front door. He stood with his finger pressed on the bell, feeling sick and shaky. His shirt was ripped and covered with blood and his right eye felt stiff and swollen.

The door opened with a clashing of bolts to reveal his Aunt standing there in curlers and hairnet, blue candlewick dressing gown and slippers.

"What is the meaning of this outrage?" she demanded her thin nose quivering. "This behaviour really can't go on, James. Come in and explain yourself – I'm not providing a spectacle for the neighbours."

A net curtain opposite was already twitching.

"It wasn't my fault," Jamie said through swollen lips, "I got set on by two thugs."

"Coming out of some pub or other, I suppose?"

His Uncle came down, clearly bad-tempered from being woken up. "This is the last straw, James. I won't have your Aunt upset like this. First thing in the morning I'll be on the phone to your father and get him to come and fetch you. Now get yourself cleaned up and go to bed. I don't want to hear another peep from you till the morning."

His Uncle and Aunt went upstairs, leaving Jamie to stumble up after them. He found cotton wool and antiseptic in the bathroom and cleaned himself up as best he could, knowing that he'd be in further trouble for leaving the immaculate black and white tiled bathroom in a mess.

Afterwards, he lay in the dark trying to blot out what had happened, feeling as if he could do with a drink to steady his shattered nerves. The whisky bottle he kept at the back of his wardrobe was empty. The longing for a drink drove him downstairs to his Uncle's drinks cabinet. With shaking hands, he picked up the malt whisky, drinking it from the bottle until the trembling feeling subsided and he felt he could sleep. Even in sleep, however, the same scenes replayed in his mind ending with the inevitable scene with his father and being packed in the car like an unwanted parcel and driven back to Cornwall.

By five in the morning, he could stand it no longer. He got up, dressed and packed as much as he could carry in his rucksack. He left the wrecked clothing from the other night and his broken guitar on top of his unmade bed and crept down the stairs. Just as he was about to let himself out of the front door, he remembered his wallet had been stolen last night and he had no money.

He knew his Aunt kept her housekeeping money in a jar inside the bread bin. He went along the passageway to the kitchen, took what he could find, plus half a loaf of bread, some biscuits and a bottle of lemonade. They'd keep him going until he could find a place to stay.

He went out, closing the front door with a soft click, confident that Caspian would sort something out for him - after all he was a key member of the band wasn't he? There was a mattress in the other basement room that Coral and Daz used sometimes. Surely they'd give that up for him until he was back on his feet. Jamie was sure that when they all heard what had happened to him, they'd rally round and help. He'd find somewhere to rest in one of the museums for the day, at least it'd be warm there, and then make his way to Caspian's in good time for the rehearsal. He was sure Caspian would let him borrow a guitar until he got back on his feet.

Jamie arrived early for the rehearsal, but was shocked to find it was already in full swing and someone else – a skinny blonde girl – was in his place. In Jamie's opinion, girls had no business playing bass guitars.

He looked at Caspian. "This is a joke, right?"

"Wrong," said Caspian looking at him levelly. "This is Jodie and we're very glad to have her, especially as it looks as if her brother will help us with cutting a demo record."

So that was it.

"I'd have been here yesterday, but I got beaten up," said Jamie plaintively. "They broke my guitar."

"Deary me," said Caspian. "Play those last few bars again, Jodie. That was a really good idea of yours."

"Just wondered if you could help me out for a bit," said Jamie feeling increasingly uncomfortable.

"Look, Jamie, we gave you a chance. You blew it. Now split, OK? We need to get on. Got a gig for next week, remember. And you know what they say – you never get a second chance to make a first impression."

Jamie stumbled out into the orange glow of the streetlights, wondering what to do next. He knew the sensible thing would be to go back to his Uncle and Aunt's and admit how stupid he'd been and then wait for his father to drive up from Cornwall and collect him, but the thought of facing his mother's disappointment and the endless comparisons with his dead brother Danny kept him from taking that step.

He sat on a bench in St James's Park for a while, his clothes getting damp in the enveloping fog, feeling sorry for himself as he thought about the run of bad luck he'd encountered since leaving Cornwall.

A passing tramp, a plump red faced Father Christmas-like character smelling of meths, told him that the homeless could get help near St Martin-in-the-Fields.

"They baths me, gives me a bite of breakfast, looks at me feet and gives me whiskers a trim," he'd said jovially.

Jamie didn't need his whiskers trimmed or his feet looked at, but a bath and breakfast sounded great. Finding his way to St Martins proved to be more difficult. He was tired and hung-over and the swirling fog played nasty tricks on him. He felt as if he was lost in a dream he couldn't wake up from.

When he turned the corner and saw Kelly in front of him, he couldn't believe she was real. It was all he could do not to sob with relief when she suggested going for a cup of tea.

"What happened to your face?" she asked as they sat at a table for two in the corner of the café.

"I got beaten up and all my money got nicked," he said. "On my way to a rehearsal with my band," He'd thought she'd looked impressed by that. Encouraged, he'd told her about the unsympathetic response he got from his Aunt.

"How's the job going?" she asked.

He shook his head. "Bastards gave me the sack. It wasn't my fault. They kept picking on me. I couldn't do anything right."

Jamie warmed his hands on his steaming mug of tea. Kelly looked as if she was doing OK. Better than him anyway. She was wearing one of those afghan coats that were all the rage this year and mulberry coloured suede boots.

"Are you with that guy you came to London to find?" he asked. "My Mum told me you'd left Tredannac Bay."

Kelly shook her head, her face clouding over.

To cover his awkwardness at having upset her, Jamie started making up a story about taking a shortcut on the way to the rehearsal. He was warming to his theme – getting to the part where he, as an innocent passer-by, was set upon and his guitar got broken, thus ending his musical career – when the café door pinged and who should walk in but Coral, the singer in the band.

Jamie vaguely remembered she worked in an office during the day and concentrated on her singing career at night. She was wearing a short red dress over black tights and her high-heeled boots made a click-clack sound as she walked up to the counter.

"I've come for the coffees I ordered a few minutes ago," she said.

Jamie noticed the startled look on her face as she saw his reflection in the mirror at the back of the counter.

"Jamie!" she said. "I'm sorry about what happened – with the band and that." She was wearing her usual heavy black eye make up and her lips were the colour of black cherry jam. "I felt bad about Jodie taking your place without you having the chance to explain yourself, but Slide Rule is keen to get to the top, and like Caspian says, we can't afford to carry anyone with a drink problem. You'd have been out of it even if you hadn't been attacked coming out of that pub."

Jamie saw Kelly's face change as she listened to the exchange between him and Coral – not that he had a chance to get a word in edge-ways. He'd been planning to ask Kelly if he could doss on her sofa for a couple of nights, but knew without asking that the brief exchange with Coral had destroyed any chance of that happening.

"At least you've got a nice girlfriend," said Coral smiling at Kelly. "Good luck with everything Jamie."

"So what was all that about?" asked Kelly as Coral picked up the cardboard box full of take-away coffees and hurried towards the door. "I don't think you were quite telling me the truth, Jamie."

"She's not quite right in the head," said Jamie briskly. "She was always getting the wrong end of the stick."

"She seemed OK to me," said Kelly. "How much are you drinking Jamie? Is that why you lost your job and why your Aunt kicked you out? Can you get some help with the problem?"

"Why does everyone keep saying I've got a problem?"

stormed Jamie slamming down his empty mug. "Why does everyone keep getting at me?"

"Because it sounds like you have got a problem," said Kelly. "And you're the only one who can do anything about it."

She picked up her bag and hurried out before Jamie could stop her. The swirling fog surrounded her slender figure and then he was alone again. He slumped down in his chair and put his head in his hands. He sat there, not moving until the waitress came to take away the empty mugs. He sat until she came back to ask if there was anything else he wanted – they'd be starting to serve lunch in a few minutes.

The need for a drink drove him back out into the fog. As he walked, he mentally checked through the names of everyone he knew in London, and mentally crossed most of them off again as a source of help.

He walked with his fists rammed into the pockets of his jacket to try and stop them shaking. The only satisfaction he had was that by now his Uncle had probably been in touch with his father and would have to break the news that Jamie had disappeared.

TWENTY-NINE

Jamie was the last person I expected to find on my doorstep on a foggy October evening, just as I was on the brink of a major change in my life.

Mike had become deputy editor of 'The Echo' and the power had gone to his head. "Had any good curries lately?" he'd whisper if he saw me by the coffee machine.

Several pieces of my work ended up being published with his by-line. Once he even won an award for something that had been an idea I'd put forward. I did think about reporting him for harassment but knew that if I did so the whole story would have to come out. All I wanted to do was move on and get recognition for the work I was doing, but there was no way a creep like Mike was going to railroad me into making the wrong move. I took my time and waited for the right opportunity. I concentrated on building my reputation as a writer and moved from my Aunt's house into a small flat in Kilburn.

Then I won a competition that gave me the opportunity of working in Paris for six months. I jumped at the chance. We'd studied some Ernest Hemingway short stories at school and I'd been interested in what Mrs Wilson had said about the time he'd spent in Paris as a reporter for the 'Toronto Star.' Until then, I hadn't thought of writing as being something that would give opportunities for travel.

I remembered what he'd said about Paris being a 'moveable feast' and I couldn't wait to get there.

I was packing my suitcase when Jamie turned up looking dishevelled and so pleased to see me that I almost changed my mind.

"I called at your Aunt's house and she told me you'd moved. She wasn't going to give me your new address until I told her we'd been at school together."

I invited him in. We had a bottle of wine and I made a

huge Spanish omelette. While we ate I told him the edited highlights of my career to date. I left out the bits about me and Mike at The King's Head, but I did tell him about how he'd harassed me and stolen my work.

He'd sounded bitter as he'd said: "Yeah, there's always someone who'll shit on you given half a chance."

I wondered what had happened to make him like that, but launched into my story about how I'd managed to get revenge on Mike.

I found out that Mike and the editor's daughter, Sophie, were about to celebrate their engagement. Her parents were giving them the deposit for a house as an early wedding present and it looked as if smarmy Mike had landed on his feet yet again.

She changed her mind pretty quick when I phoned up pretending to be his live-in girlfriend wanting to know when he'd be home for dinner. Mike obviously had his suspicions as to who had made the call, but he couldn't prove anything.

Jamie and I shared the last of my bottle of brandy and then we went to bed together. The sex was much better this time than it had been during that first fumbled time in my bedroom at Tredannac Bay and I wondered where he'd got his experience from.

I was even thinking of delaying my trip for a few days – or wangling some way of taking Jamie with me when I heard him mumble <u>her</u> name again.

"Kelly."

He was hugging the pillow like he'd never let go.

That was when I knew I was going to Paris alone. And I was going to leave the past behind once and for all.

There was a full moon hanging like a silver coin in the velvet dark sky on the night I flew to Paris. I gazed at the pitted surface, making out the shape of the man in the moon with his bundle of twigs and decided it was time to shed my old identity.

I wouldn't be plain old Susan any more – I'd be Sabrina.

I'd read an article about how the right name could change your life. If you think about it, Cliff Richard definitely sounds better than Harry Webb and you wouldn't look at Maurice Micklewhite in the same way as Michael Caine.

Sabrina was the name of a river goddess – the Severn, which was our longest river. There was a mystical link between the moon and water.

So there on the plane I became Sabrina instead of Susan and wrote it confidently on the first page of my new notebook. I wrote three resolutions – that I would look forward, not back, that I would make every effort to become a published novelist and that I'd no longer waste any time on a loser like Jamie Collins.

I loved Paris and even now I still treasure that memory of the first morning. Despite my late arrival, I'd got up early and left the hotel before breakfast to walk the just-waking streets of Montmartre. I walked on cobbles slick with melting frost past tall houses with dark green painted shutters. I followed a plump woman in a fur coat walking a poodle in a jewelled collar past steamy cafes that smelled of coffee and Gauloises, feeling this was where I was meant to be.

Ernest Hemingway once said: "If you are lucky enough to have lived your life in Paris as a young man, then wherever you go for the rest of your life it stays with you, for Paris is a moveable feast." This was the city where I fell deeply in love, lost that love and had to make the hardest decision of my life.

THIRTY

Kelly had been on the point of offering Jamie a place to stay. Coral's timely arrival saved her from making a big mistake.

"Don't feel guilty about him," she told herself. "Concentrate on your own dreams now."

She thought she heard footsteps behind her and dodged into a newsagents shop, intending to buy some chocolate. The front cover of a glossy magazine caught her attention. She took a closer look and felt dizzy with shock. She held onto the wall, worried that she was going to faint.

The photograph was of Jed with his arms round a dark haired girl who looked up at him adoringly. The article on the centre page spread of the magazine spoke of wedding plans for Jed and his beautiful fiancée, Mirabelle Jordan, and a sensational new film in the making in which she hoped to be cast in the starring role.

"Are you buying that?" asked the shop assistant crossly. "Or are you just messing up the pages for someone else?"

Kelly bought the magazine and went back out into the fog, her heart hammering wildly in her throat. She made her way to the church of St Martin-in-the-Fields and sat in a pew reading the article, feeling shocked and sick. Jed had played a nasty trick on her, making her feel that he cared about her when all the time he'd been engaged to this Mirabelle. He'd used the ideas Kelly had given him to create this film script and had dumped her when she was no more use to him.

Well, Kelly would show him. The auditions for the film were to be held next Monday at the Café Royal and Mirabelle or whatever her name was had been tipped to get the star part.

"It will all be decided fairly," the director had said, "but Mirabelle Jordan is the hot favourite at the moment unless someone surprising turns up."

Kelly sat with her eyes closed, as a plan formed in her

mind. She'd give them a surprise all right. She could remember one of Mrs Wilson's stories about Nell Gwyn. Nell was trying to worm her way into Charles the Second's bed and she'd heard that another actress called Moll Davies was the current favourite. Nell had given Moll some cakes laced with jalap – something that caused a massive dose of the shits apparently, although Mrs Wilson had put it more politely – and had gone to the palace in Moll's place.

Kelly knew she'd probably get arrested if she tried to feed Mirabelle anything that was going to make her ill, but there were other ways of succeeding. A thin shaft of sunlight created rainbows as Kelly glanced upwards at the stone angels, seeking inspiration from Nell Gwyn.

THIRTY-ONE

As I said, I'd been completely oblivious to what was happening in London because I was having such a fabulous time in Paris

At first I'd wandered the streets, enchanted by landmarks like the Arc de Triomph and the Sacre Coeur. I'd visited every café frequented by Ernest Hemingway and sat with my notebook, watching people and listening, flooded with inspiration for stories and poems.

Mum and Dad, in the process of moving to Spain, were happy because they'd got something to brag about. 'Our daughter Jennifer with the degree in Medieval History, successful husband and 2.4 children and our younger daughter Susan currently working in Paris as a journalist' sounded impressive to them.

I never told them about Georges.

We met in early November near Notre Dame. I'd been covering an assignment for the paper at The Louvre and had paused on my way back to buy a crepe stuffed with ham and cheese, warming my cold hands on it as I walked.

He was a photographer, loitering for trade by the hostile grey waters of the Seine. There was something exotic about his tousled mass of dark hair and chocolate dark eyes, but it was his hands that I noticed most of all. They were artist's hands with long slim fingers – 'piano-player's hands' my Mum used to call them. The minute I saw them I felt a wave of lust. I wanted him to touch me.

"I take your photo," he said.

"Non," I replied, still eating the last of my crepe.

"Oui," he said. "I take no money. It is early present for ze Christmas."

I hesitated. Mum and Dad had always had something to say about the right way to meet men. In their world you had a formal introduction at a dinner party. Jennifer had met her husband at a Faculty party during the first year of her University course.

I smiled, thinking how they'd take a dim view of me being picked up by a photographer on a street corner - even if that street corner was in Paris.

"Oui," I said.

He took my photo against a background of exotic flowers in front of a small shop that smelled of lilies. He motioned me to wait and went in, coming out with a single red rose which he pinned to my black velvet coat.

He held my hand and his touch was every bit as electric as I'd expected. As we kissed for the first time outside Notre Dame, rain began to fall from a gunmetal sky.

"We must get warm," he whispered against my hair, leading me to a bar with green velvet seats that smelled of garlic and almonds in equal measure where I drank my first glass of calvados. I didn't bother to tell him that his touch had warmed me far more than the fiery apple brandy. I knew he felt the same.

My French was better than Georges' English, but his talent as a photographer was undisputed. He worked as a freelance covering news stories as well as trying his luck with tourists in all the local hotspots. A few days after we met, he tipped me off about a news story that was about to happen – the result of a crime of passion that happened near the Eiffel Tower. I sat in a café once frequented by Hemingway as I wrote the story, thinking of something he once said: "There is nothing to writing. All you do is sit down at a typewriter and bleed."

The editor made a huge fuss about the story, congratulating me profusely, and so did Georges. That was the night we became lovers. It began with dinner in a beautiful little restaurant in Montmartre. Then we walked the cobbled streets gazing at the stars in the velvet-dark sky and the white marble perfection of the Sacre Couer.

"I should go home," I said, feeling light-headed with wine

and lust, aware that the narrow streets we were walking down were dark and unfamiliar. Memories of that night with Mike at The King's Head surfaced and I felt a surge of panic when Georges stopped outside a tall building with faded blue shutters.

"Where are we?" My mouth was dry and my stomach churned.

"Mon apartement," his breath was warm against my cheek, his touch gentle – so different from that time with Mike that I relaxed against him.

"Is OK," he said kissing my lips gently.

We went in through the front door and into a small lift of the type I'd only previously seen in old French films. It stopped on the top floor where Georges unlocked an indigo blue door that led to his tiny apartment. It had a balcony just big enough for two metal chairs and a small table and I squeezed onto it, marvelling at the street theatre evolving below me.

A girl in a short red skirt and black beret was in a romantic clinch with a man outside the shuttered windows of the bakery opposite.

"Je t'adore," he was saying in between kisses.

"We do better than that," said Georges pulling me back into the room. I hadn't noticed his bed on the way in, but now I couldn't take my eyes off it. The frame was brass with big round knobs on the corners and it had a white bedspread patterned with pink roses and crisp linen sheets that smelled of lavender.

His lips tasted of wine and honey as he kissed me. The kiss deepened, creating dampness between my legs as it did so. I held him tighter, my stomach somersaulting as if I'd gone down too fast in a lift.

He caressed my breasts through the thin fabric of my blouse and I touched the warm skin of his back where his shirt had come un-tucked from his jeans.

My legs felt weak as he undid the waistband of my skirt and touched the hot skin just inside my knickers. I wanted him to go on, wanted more, but he didn't rush me, kept me on a slow burn.

I clung onto him, standing so close that I could feel the hardness of him against me. I gently unzipped his jeans and touched him feeling a thrill of satisfaction when I heard him moan. I undid his belt and the button on his jeans so that I could touch him as he was touching me, fingers of fire igniting the passion between us.

At last, when all our clothes were shrugged off like shed skins, he lifted me onto the bed and we made love all night, finally coming together as dawn broke over Montmartre in a patchwork of crimson, pink and gold.

We slept and awoke in each others arms as the sun streamed like liquid gold through the muslin curtains.

Georges got out of bed and made strong black coffee. Then, pulling on jeans and a sweater, he went down to the bakery and came back with warm croissants for our breakfast.

I never went back to my lodgings after that. Later that day, I moved my things into Georges' apartment and we were blissfully happy until the blustery April day he was knocked down by a car not far from where we first met. He died instantly.

A few days later I discovered I was pregnant.

THIRTY-TWO

Jed was furious. Mirabelle had agreed to script changes on his behalf - and had only thought to mention her telephone conversation with Aaron McIntyre the day before the auditions at the Café Royal.

Jed had received a note from Aaron saying that he'd found a great place to film the car chase.

"The guy is obviously over-working," said Jed as Mirabelle returned from yet another shopping trip loaded with an assortment of glittery carrier bags full of lingerie, shoes and make up. "There isn't a car chase in my script."

Mirabelle had the grace to blush. "Gee honey, I guess I should've told you. Aaron thought it needed spicing up a little, you know – a couple of fight scenes and a car chase. I thought you'd be OK with it especially as he'd got another script writer to do those bits. It's not important is it, sweetie? You'll still get your payment for the original script and be acknowledged as one of the writers on the credits."

"But it's not the way I intended the film to be," stormed Jed, knowing he was over-reacting. Changes like this happened all the time in publishing, let alone the bigger world of Hollywood.

He wished with all his heart that he could put the clock back and return to that last time when he'd held Kelly in his arms. If he could only find her again, this time he'd never let her go. The longing for her was eating away at his heart.

He'd finished editing *'The Yellow Silk Dress'* and Dan Crawford was enthusiastic about it, but Jed knew the part of the heroine would be difficult to fill because he'd written it for Kelly and nobody else could take her place. The auditions for the film at the Café Royal were happening tomorrow. Aaron McIntyre was certain they would attract mass-media attention. "I'm aiming to create us a block-buster," he said. "This movie's gonna make us all rich."

At one time Jed would've responded enthusiastically to this. Now all he could see was a bleak future if Kelly wasn't part of it.

THIRTY-THREE

It occurred to me by Tuesday lunchtime that the only way to find out the end of the story was to go back to Tredannac Bay and try to pick up the broken threads.

I had no connection with the place since Mum and Dad moved to Spain.

"Thank goodness we're not still living in Cornwall," said Mum when I broke the news of my pregnancy.

I'd hoped they'd be sympathetic – after all they doted on Jennifer's children – but it seemed that one born out of wedlock was a different matter.

"You can't have it here," said Mum as if I'd proposed keeping a dangerous animal. "You'll have to get rid of it."

"I knew it was a bad idea you living among those foreigners," said Dad, taking a large mouthful of brandy and staring moodily at the ultra-blue Spanish sea. "Give me the little creep's address and I'll make sure he pays for a termination or whatever you call it."

"Georges is dead," I said.

"Trust him to wriggle out of his responsibilities.

I thought of Georges' chocolate dark eyes so full of love and the gentle touch of his hands and I ached with loss.

I returned to London but had left it too late for a termination. I gave birth to my little girl on a cold December night. A crescent moon hung in the velvet dark sky surrounded by a scattering of stars and I remembered the first night I'd spent with Georges and how he would always be a special part of me wherever I went.

I named her Georgia and with a heavy heart gave her up for adoption. I'll never forget her tiny face and starfish hands or the way my last morning with her seemed to go in slow motion – bathing and feeding her and then dressing her for the last time in a white nightgown.

When the lady from the adoption agency arrived to collect her, I almost surrendered to a mad impulse to take Georgia and escape on the first bus that came along. Instead, I mutely handed her over and watched as she was carried out of my life.

Since that day I've never stopped thinking about her. I was told that a couple from Hertfordshire had adopted her and I hoped they loved her as much as Georges and I would have done. I wondered if she was married and a mother herself by now. Just lately there had been stories in the paper of birth parents being traced and happy reunions and I'd felt a surge of hopefulness that this could happen to me too.

I called my novel 'Georgia' after her. I'd written my life story so that she'd know who her father was and how much I'd loved him. I'd so far had no luck finding a publisher for it but I had no intention of giving up until I did.

Rod wasn't happy when I said I needed a couple of days off. "Why d'you need time off?" His mouth turned down at the corners and I knew his bloodshot eyes would be suspicious behind his dark glasses.

"To go and talk to some local people and get some more information."

Can't you find out what you need to know on the internet?"

"No, I can't. Do you want to know what happened to the girl who impersonated Mitzi Shapiro or not?"

I could tell by his face he'd forgotten the challenge he'd given me on Monday morning.

"I know where she is," I said, crossing my fingers behind my back and hoping my hunch was right.

I imagined his eyes lighting up like Jamie's used to when he spotted a drink.

"Two days," he said.

On the journey down to Cornwall I wished many times over that I hadn't made such a stupid comment. How bad was I going to feel on Thursday afternoon when I had to go back to Rod and admit I'd failed?

I won't fail I told myself. I'll not give that bastard any reason to look smug.

It's funny how memories are distorted by time. The road that led to the school seemed shorter than I remembered it when I used to walk that way with my friends. The village looked trendier, more upmarket.

The house I'd lived in with my Mum and Dad had been given a make-over. It was now painted marshmallow pink and the lead-paned windows that had been my Dad's pride and joy had been ripped out and replaced with big picture windows. The garden had been landscaped and decking added, taking away all its character and the rose bush I'd bought them one Christmas that they'd planted by the front door had disappeared.

I stood so long outside the house itemising all the changes that a lady cleaning the upstairs windows came out to ask if there was anything I wanted.

"I knew some people who lived here once," I said, turning away so she couldn't see how upset I was.

"It's never the same when you go back to a place," she said sympathetically. Her face was plump and kindly. "Was it anyone I might have known?"

"Probably not," I said, turning away from her.

I parked my car by the church and walked to the crossroads where Kelly was supposed to have been picked up by the mystery man from London, wondering how she'd felt and what had happened to her. I stood with my eyes closed listening to the sounds around me – traffic and birdsong, the whine of a lawnmower. I could smell roses and cut grass on the soft breeze and taste salt on my lips.

I decided to follow the road in each direction from the

crossroads and see what I gained from my search.

The drab collection of council houses where Kelly used to live had been transformed into neat-looking town houses with block-paved drives. I knocked on the door of the one that used to be Kelly's. There was a silver Mazda MX5 on the drive. The man who opened the door bore no resemblance to Kelly's Mum's boyfriend. He reminded me of Rod in some ways – but younger and minus the perpetual sunglasses.

"I'm not trying to sell you anything," I said.

He looked at me suspiciously. His shirt was gleaming white to match his teeth.

"Someone called Kelly Smith used to live here," I said. "Do you know where she is now?"

"Haven't a clue love," he said. His voice had traces of a London accent, "must be before my time."

He'd shut the door before I got to the end of the drive.

I tried the rest of the houses for good measure, but it seemed that the memory of Kelly had moved out with the old tenants.

I walked along the road to where the grandly named business park used to be. When I lived here, it was a collection of tin sheds like aircraft hangars that housed the biscuit factory where Kelly's Mum worked and a pickle factory. Most of the kids from school ended up in one of the two places if they weren't lucky enough to go to college or escape altogether like I did.

The biscuit factory was considered one up from the pickle factory because you didn't come home stinking of onions and vinegar and the free samples were worth having.

My heart sank as I walked up the tree-lined avenue towards the smart brick buildings. A black and white metal sign read 'Tredannac Bay Business Park.' The place was a hive of industry – completely unrecognisable from how it used to be but again there was no trace of the biscuit factory and nobody who remembered anything.

With a sinking heart, I made my way down the haunted lane towards the harbour. Even this seemed less scary than it used to. The overhanging trees had been cut back so that dappled light flowed in and there were tubs of pansies and signs advertising 'Britain in Bloom.'

The road down to the bay hadn't changed much. The Copper Kettle Café where Jamie and I had sat together was now The Fisherman's Net internet café. The walls were indigo and silver and it was quieter than The Copper Kettle used to be. Most of the people in there – young as well as old – were looking intently at computer screens. The tempting smells of frying bacon and hot toast wafted towards me and I suddenly realised how hungry I was. I pushed open the door and went in.

One end of the café had been made into a small art gallery and I took my coffee and bacon sandwich and went to study them. One painting in particular – a full moon over a ruined house caught my attention with its haunting magic. The artist was someone called Scarlet Matthews. Something about the name rang a bell. I sat drinking my coffee, trying to remember.

An elderly lady had got up from one of the computer terminals and was making her lop-sided way over to me.

"Mrs Wilson," I said, remembering my old English teacher, the person responsible for giving my part in the play to Kelly and fucking up my life.

"Kelly's done well for herself, hasn't she?" were the first words she said to me in nearly thirty years. .

Frustration fought with relief inside me that at last I'd found someone who knew something.

"I haven't done so badly myself," I said stiffly.

"I know" she said, "but then I never had any doubts about you being successful. Kelly always had more problems to overcome."

"I need your help," I said.

THIRTY-FOUR

"Bet they throw you out as soon as you walk in there," said Zoe as Kelly put the finishing touches to her outfit, "even if you do look like a Russian Princess or whatever you're pretending to be."

"They will let me in," said Kelly, her jaw set in a determined way as she added another coat of mascara to her already thick black eyelashes. "I wish this dress wasn't so tight though, I keep thinking I'm going to stop breathing any minute"

The yellow silk dress had come complete with a corset and Zoe had had great fun lacing her into it.

"You're bulging out in all the right places," she said, leering at Kelly's bosom.

"I just hope I don't need to get out of it in a hurry."

"I'm more worried about getting you out of it in time to take it back to the shop tomorrow"

"Tomorrow," said Kelly, her stomach feeling like lead at the thought. She wondered what would have happened by then. She knew the chances of her – an unknown actress and nightclub dancer – getting the part were practically zero, but she had to try, if only for the chance of getting back at Jed. She was sure he'd be there to support his wife-to-be.

"So why exactly are you going?" asked Zoe, as if she'd read her thoughts. "Are you doing all this because you desperately want to be in the film or are you hoping for a repeat performance with Mr Wonderful? I wish you the best of luck in that dress if it's the second option!"

Kelly sat in the limo she'd hired feeling sick. It was one thing to plan things to create maximum effect. It was another thing to do them. She remembered what Miss Wilson had said on the night she'd played Juliet.

"Don't pretend you're playing the part, Kelly. Be Juliet."

Kelly took a deep breath as the limo pulled up outside the Café Royal and the driver got out to open the door for her.

She was a Russian Princess. She'd eaten fresh mango and yogurt for breakfast before leaving the glittering onion domes of St Petersburg and she'd flown into Heathrow in her private jet.

She touched the necklace Mrs Wilson had given her for good luck when she'd played Juliet and swept into the Café Royal as if she was walking onto a stage.

"I am 'ere for ze auditions," she said to a uniformed man with a clipboard.

"What name is it?" he asked slowly, taking a good look at her cleavage.

Kelly scanned the list that the man was holding.

"I am Mitzi Shapiro," she said.

"Right, Miss Shapiro – please come this way."

He led her to a room lined with mirrors where a lot of elegantly dressed women were preening and primping. The air was thick with a cocktail of perfumes.

She recognised the lady Jed had been photographed with, sitting on a gilt chair in the corner. Her fingers were drumming impatiently on her gleaming white satin dress.

A set of double doors at the far end of the mirrored room led to the place where the auditions were being held. A secretary in a black skirt and jacket and red blouse emerged waving a clipboard.

"Attention please," she said clearly. "I'm sorry it's been a long wait for some of you, but if your name's on the list you will be seen. Coffee and tea will be served shortly. Could Augusta Wakefield please follow me?"

Dozens of pairs of eyes watched as a leggy blonde in dark green velvet followed the secretary into the inner sanctum. Three minutes later, she reappeared looking downcast.

"They clearly haven't got a blonde in mind for this part," she said in a breathy little-girl voice, "so I wonder why my agent sent me in the first place." Her searchlight gaze swept around the room. "I'll be surprised if they find the right person here today."

"Bitch," muttered another blonde girl as Augusta swept out of the room. "I can't stand a bad loser."

Kelly's tongue felt as if it was sticking to the roof of her mouth. The room was stiflingly hot and the corset she was wearing cut into her skin. She wished she'd thought to bring a bottle of lemonade, although that would've created the need for the loo and she wouldn't want to be stuck in there when her name was called.

"Hope they have a lunch break," said the girl sitting next to Kelly. She had short dark hair and reminded her of Zoe. "Nervous energy always makes me hungry."

There was a flurry of activity in the entrance hall. All the heads turned that way.

"The press have arrived." The collective whisper ran round the room and all the girls sat up straighter, some whipping out compact mirrors to check their make-up yet again.

The secretary came to the door again and called 'Mitzi Shapiro.'

Kelly followed her into the inner sanctum.

Three men sat in front of her amid a barrage of white light, reminding her of her audition at the nightclub. One of them was Jed.

For a long moment they stared at each other as if nobody else existed. He looked thinner than when Kelly had last seen him and there were dark shadows under his eyes.

One of the other men cleared his throat.

Kelly heard Bertha's voice in her head saying:

"All men are the same, love. They're all led by what their willies want to do."

She'd heard about auditions – about how nobody gave any instructions, they just waited to see what you'd do. She remembered Jed saying something about what it had been like when he'd pitched an idea to a publisher – that the man set a timer, gave him five minutes and then sent him out of the door.

Tearing her gaze away from Jed who looked as if he was having trouble staying in his seat, she focused on being Juliet, making up her own lines in places.

"We are star-crossed lovers destined to be together for all time," she said, her voice clear and throbbing with emotion. She looked at Jed as she said this, noticing how his blue eyes sparkled with unshed tears.

Someone with a camera took close up shots from different angles, then a buzzer sounded and Kelly's time was up. She swept out of the room in a rustle of silk and a wave of exotic rose-musk perfume, noticing the collective murmur of approval as she did so. She didn't look back.

THIRTY FIVE

When Kelly entered the room, Jed didn't know how he managed to stay in his seat. Relief flooded him, and all he wanted to do was crush her in his arms and not let go. Dressed as she was in figure-hugging buttercup yellow silk she exactly matched the image in his mind of the heroine of his play. Her amber necklace and the amber combs in her rippling mass of auburn curls matched the liquid beauty of her eyes.

He forced himself to sit still, afraid that she'd vanish like morning mist if he moved from his seat.

Like the born actress she was, she stood in the Cyclops glare of the spotlight waiting until she'd got the full attention of her audience.

Jed remembered the story she'd told him about her recurring dream about wearing a yellow silk dress and being on a stage with the curtain going up but with no script. Exactly the situation she was in now.

It had already been explained to the prospective movie stars that they had five minutes to make an impression. The timer was set when they walked in one door and when it went off, they departed through the other.

Up till now the expression on the faces of Aaron McIntyre, the director, and his sidekick Ben Stacey had been impassive. Jed could tell that, even before she'd opened her mouth, Kelly had their full attention.

When she spoke her first line about the star-crossed lovers Jed knew she was referring to the legend of the ruined house and the affinity they both felt for the place. Listening to her voice, Jed could almost hear the sound of the sea. The buzzer went. Her time was up and she'd disappeared through the other door in a rustle of silk, leaving behind an echo of her rose-musk perfume.

"Gee that was some dame," said Aaron mopping his

forehead. "I guess we'll need to see the rest of the candidates but I've got a gut feeling we've found our star. Put her on the list for the call-backs this afternoon," he said to the secretary when she bustled in with the next girl's details.

Jed made an excuse and left the room. He had to talk to Kelly.

He caught up with her outside the building where she was taking a breath of air. Taxis came and went, picking up unsuccessful candidates, some in tears, all immaculately dressed.

Kelly started like a deer about to flee when she caught sight of Jed, her eyes pools of liquid amber.

"Hey, don't cry," he said, "or you'll spoil your make-up."

"I never thought I'd see you again," she said. "I didn't know how to find you. I walked along every street in Chelsea."

"When I heard you'd come to London I was worried sick. I've spent hours looking at every young girl with hair like yours.

She stiffened as he came close to her.

"Who's the lady in white that was in the photo with you? Is she the 'unfinished business' you had in London? If so it doesn't look unfinished to me."

Jed felt as if his heart was being wrenched from him. He took hold of Kelly's hands.

"Kelly, please believe me, it's you that I want. I've tried every way I can to get in touch with you. I even phoned old vinegar-face at the museum and she told me you'd left. I called every Smith in Tredannac Bay and some bloke said you'd gone off to London. "

"So when's the wedding?"

"The only woman I'll ever marry is you, Kelly – but I won't do so until I've got something to offer you – and I won't have that until this movie is cast and under production."

"At that point the secretary came out. "Mr Matthews

where have you been? Mr McIntyre is waiting to discuss the callbacks."

"You'd better go," said Kelly, "Your fiancée will be wondering where you are."

Jed walked away, his feelings in turmoil.

THIRTY-SIX

The afternoon dragged on and Kelly started to get anxious about the time. The dress was supposed to be back at the clothes-hire shop by six and she'd only booked the limo one way because that was all she could afford. At this rate, she'd be like Cinderella creeping away from the ball after midnight dressed in rags.

Her head ached with tension and suppressed emotion. She wished with all her heart she'd told Jed she wanted him as much as he wanted her. She couldn't bear the thought that he'd gone away thinking she didn't care.

Her stomach growled with hunger but she didn't dare eat anything in case she spoiled her dress.

The lady in white – Mirabelle – was holding court to a gaggle of press photographers as if she was already the star.

Kelly had a sinking feeling that all this effort was going to turn out to have been for nothing. Mirabelle was certain to get the part and this whole thing was just a glorified publicity stunt.

Kelly was in the Ladies, struggling with her voluminous dress in the confined space when she overheard Mirabelle talking to someone.

"Who was the girl in yellow talking to your fiancé?" asked a woman with a cut-glass accent. "It seemed like they knew each other pretty well."

"Some little foreign tart who fancies her chances because he wrote the script - nobody important. I guess I'll have to get used to groupies when he gets real famous." There was no mistaking the note of contempt in her Texan drawl.

Kelly stayed where she was until she heard the heavy outer door close. She stood by the basins running her hands under cold water. Determination rose inside her like mercury in a thermometer. Even if she didn't get the part, she'd give Jed and that film director something to think about.

She'd only just got back into the waiting room when the

secretary in the black suit called her back into the auditions room.

"Only two minutes this time," she whispered. "Good luck."

Touching her amber necklace for luck, Kelly took a deep breath and pushed open the door.

The three men were sitting there as before as Kelly took her place under the spotlight. She noticed the look that passed between the director and his sidekick. Jed was staring at her with a look of such naked hunger on his face she was almost stopped in her tracks.

"I'll follow you to the ends of the earth," she began, noticing the flare of hope in Jed's eyes. "I've never wanted anyone more than I've wanted you..."

There was a commotion outside and the door burst open. A woman with short spiky black hair scattered with rubies burst into the room.

"What the fuck is going on," growled Aaron getting to his feet. "You're supposed to wait your turn, lady. Where's that damned secretary?"

"I am ze real Mitzi Shapiro" said the woman, her full breasts almost bursting out of her low-cut red satin dress. "Zis woman is an impostor. I demand to have ze screen test."

"You can demand all you want, lady," said one of the men, "but it's not gonna happen. You're too fucking late, we're just doing the call-backs, but I think we've already made our decision." He looked at Kelly. "You can go."

Kelly left the room, circling round the outraged figure of the real Mitzi.

"I demand justice," she was saying. "I demand you 'ave zis woman arrested for impersonation."

The press surged forward and the cameras whirled as Kelly entered the waiting room with Mitzi in hot pursuit.

"You will not get away with zis." Mitzi made a grab at

Kelly, her long red nails biting into the soft flesh of her upper arm.

Kelly pulled away from her, worried that the yellow silk dress would get damaged. She looked around for Jed but there was no sign of him.

Yelling like a banshee, and resisting all attempts to restrain her, the real Mitzi pulled at Kelly's hair, dislodging the amber combs that held it back from her face. Kelly heard one of the combs crunch under the heel of one of Mitzi's red stilettos. She began to wonder how she'd get out of this situation when a man in a grey suit flashing an identity card pushed his way through the crowd of reporters.

"You'd better come with me," he said, steering Kelly towards a small room, pushing her gently into it and closing the door.

Mitzi hammered on it for several minutes calling out: "Serves you right, bitch. Ze police have you now."

"Are you a policeman?" asked Kelly licking her lips nervously. She looked around the small room wondering if she was about to be arrested for stealing someone's identity.

"I'm a private detective," he said. "I've been asked to trace you on behalf of a Mrs Jane Wilson. She has information she needs to give you relating to your late grandmother."

"What sort of information? I didn't know she even knew my Gran?"

"All I know is she's asking that you return to Tredannac Bay urgently. She's in Penzance Hospital about to undergo surgery."

He produced a crumpled letter from the inside pocket of his grey jacket and Kelly instantly recognised Mrs Wilson's handwriting.

"What do I have to do?" she said.

A taxi was waiting outside the Café Royal. Kelly got in

and asked the driver to take her back to Zoe's flat.

"I thought I was waiting for a guy," said the driver laying aside his newspaper and starting the engine.

"He changed his mind," said Kelly.

She closed her eyes with relief as the taxi sped along the busy streets. It was only at that point she realised she'd lost her precious amber necklace.

THIRTY-SEVEN

By the time Jed fought through the crush of reporters and cameramen, Kelly had gone. The air in the waiting room was a stifling cocktail of perfumes and a whirling kaleidoscope of colours as the girls who'd hung about in hopes of a second audition prepared to leave.

"I guess you know what my decision's gonna be," Aaron had said. "I sure hope Mirabelle won't be too disappointed. We'll give her the part of the maid so at least she'll get most of what she wanted."

Jed's heart soared knowing how pleased Kelly would be with the news. "Shall I call them back in?"

"Sure," said Aaron, "and see if that secretary can fix us some coffee. I reckon we could all use one."

As he edged his way past a trio of girls who'd somehow already heard that a decision had been made and were hovering in hopes that they'd be among the lucky ones, Jed noticed the glitter of amber under a glass table. It was Kelly's necklace – the one she'd worn to the audition that she'd once told him was one of her most precious possession.

Jed picked it up feeling like the prince with the glass slipper.

"Where did the girl in the yellow silk dress go?" he asked the doorman.

"If you mean the one that had the fight with the virago in red, I think she's gone, sir."

"Gone? She can't have. We need her here."

"All I know is she had words with a guy in a grey suit and then she went out of here like her knickers were on fire, if you'll excuse the expression, sir."

Mirabelle glided up to Jed, taking his arm in a gesture of possession. Her mouth curled upwards in a pussy-cat smile. "Has Aaron decided yet?" she asked, looking as if the part was already hers. "Where did that necklace come from?"

Aaron came out of the audition room looking as if he was about to melt. "Have you found her, Jed?"

"The doorman says she's had some urgent news and she's gone." Jed's voice cracked with emotion.

"Who's gone?" asked Mirabelle.

"That's typical," said Aaron, "I find the best actress of all time – and she does a disappearing act."

"I know where to find her," said Jed, with more confidence than he felt. "Give me twenty four hours and I'll bring her back."

"What are you all talking about?" Mirabelle looked annoyed. "When do we start filming?"

"We need to find Kelly first," said Aaron. "I'm making no firm announcement until then. Jed – you've got twenty four hours."

"Where are you going," said Mirabelle as Jed headed towards the main doors.

"I'm sorry to break it to you this way," said Jed, "but I'm in love with Kelly. I didn't realise how much until I saw her again today."

"So you're dumping me – after all I've done for you?"

"Mirabelle – I'll never regret having met you and you've helped me more than you'll ever know. When the movie's finished I'll pay back all the money I owe you. The keys to my car are on the desk in my study. One day you'll find the right man and you'll be thankful you didn't go ahead with our wedding."

He wasn't sure if it was his imagination, but Mirabelle didn't look quite as upset as he'd expected her to.

"I'm kinda relieved you've been the one to be honest," said Mirabelle dragging Jed into a quiet corner. "I didn't know how to tell you I was going a bit cool on the idea of the wedding. I found I was thinking about marrying you and then daydreaming about Gareth"

"Gareth?"

"He's Ben Stacey's brother and he's an oilman like my Pa."

Mirabelle wrapped her arms round Jed's neck and kissed him gently on the cheek. "Good luck sweetie. I hope you find her. And you can keep the car – it'll help you get there quicker – wherever you're going."

Jed hurried outside to talk to the taxi drivers to see if he could find the one who'd taken Kelly.

THIRTY-EIGHT

"What happened to you, you look like a road accident," said Zoe when Kelly tumbled into the flat. "Did you get the part?"

Zoe was lounging on the sofa eating cold baked beans out of a tin and reading a fashion article in 'Cosmopolitan.'

"I don't think so," said Kelly. ""I'm fairly sure it was just a publicity stunt and they'd already made up their minds. Oh Zoe, Jed was there – in the audition room. You can imagine how I felt when I walked in and saw him sitting there. It was like we were the only two people in the room. And he looked like he felt the same, in spite of his lady friend being there. Then he came and found me and I fucked things up by getting stroppy with him."

"I thought you'd get thrown out of there within ten minutes," said Zoe throwing the empty tin towards the bin and missing. How did you manage to trick the doorman?"

"It was dead easy. He was holding a sort of list and I looked down it and picked one of the names that hadn't been ticked off and he said 'Follow me, Miss Shapiro.' So I did."

"So didn't the real Miss Shapiro turn up?"

"It was fine until she did," said Kelly, struggling with the complicated fastenings of the dress. "Help me with these corsets will you? I got as far as the call back and then this woman in red burst into the room saying she was the real Mitzi Shapiro and threatening to call the police. She was really mad, grabbing at me and pulling my hair and there were all these TV crews taking photos and I didn't realise till I was in the taxi coming back here that I've lost my amber necklace – the one I was given when I played Juliet. Bet the cow's nicked it."

"So how did you get out of that one?"

"Some bloke in a suit pulled me out of the way – said he was a private detective who'd been looking for me. He got me out of the way of the mad bitch, but the only problem was that by the time I finished talking to him, I couldn't find Jed. I never got the chance to tell him where I lived."

"Did the detective bloke have a grey suit and thinning hair?" asked Zoe. "He called here – someone at the nightclub gave him our address. It sounded important so I told him you were at the Café Royal. Took the wind out of his sails I can tell you. What was it all about? He wouldn't tell me anything."

"It's my old English teacher, Mrs Wilson," said Kelly. "Apparently, she and my Gran were friends. She's in hospital waiting for an operation and wants to talk to me about something. It must be important if she's put a private detective on me."

THIRTY-NINE

Jed felt like the Prince going in search of Cinderella. He found a taxi driver outside the Café Royal who said he'd only just come back from taking Kelly home.

"She was a real looker – all dressed in yellow," he said.

"Can you take me to where you dropped her off?" asked Jed.

He got out of the taxi and looked at the dilapidated row of houses, some with boarded up windows, wondering which one was Kelly's. He heard loud music – Black Sabbath – coming from an upstairs room and the sounds of an argument. Jed headed towards the source of the noise, looking for some trace of Kelly.

The houses would've been respectable in Victorian times, probably boasting at least one servant. Now they looked little better than squats. Jed raced up the stone steps towards an imposing front door that had once been black. To one side of it was a row of door bells with smudged names next to them, none of them Kelly's. He pressed them all and stood waiting for a reply.

None came. He hammered on the door until his fists were raw. A few minutes later it swung open.

"What's all the bloody row?" said a large man with a shaved head wearing only a pair of jeans. "I bin working all night."

"I'm looking for my girlfriend," said Jed.

"Bloody careless to have lost her in the first place," said the man, about to shut the door in Jed's face.

"She's got long auburn hair and I need to find her urgently."

"Basement," he growled as the door slammed shut.

Jed squeezed through the rusted wrought iron gate and went down a short flight of concrete steps, finding himself in a rubbish-strewn yard. It didn't look as if the basement flat was occupied but when he knocked on the door a girl with short dark spiky hair answered it. There was a hostile look in her sapphire blue eyes.

"I'm looking for Kelly," he said.

"She's gone."

Jed slumped against the door post. "Gone where?" For the second time in a few minutes a door was about to slam in his face.

"I need to find her urgently."

The girl's eyes narrowed. "Who are you?"

When Jed arrived at the crossroads where he and Kelly had parted after that magical day in Penzance, it was as if the months apart had never happened. He told himself it was because he'd not slept for over twenty four hours but from the moment he parked his car by the church and took the familiar path down to the harbour and up onto the cliffs, it felt as if he was being guided by an unseen force.

Down by the harbour the early morning sun glittered on the sea like a mirror and there was the smell of seaweed and boat oil. Up on the cliffs, the temperature dropped as a sea mist rolled in blanketing the headland and the ruined cottage ahead of him, reminding Jed of his recurring dream.

The mist swirled and eddied around him and it felt unnaturally cold. Apart from the sound of the sea, all was eerily silent. Ahead of him, he could see the ruined house, the lichened grey stones reminding him of broken teeth.

"Kelly," he yelled. "Where are you?"

A shaft of sunlight cleared a patch of fog and he saw her in front of him. She was wearing jeans and a pink sweater and her beautiful hair was loose and rippling over her shoulders.

"Jed," she said, "oh Jed!" She ran down the narrow path into his waiting arms.

FORTY

When Kelly had arrived at the hospital it was well past visiting time and most of the patients had already been settled down for the night, although the corridors were far from quiet. A porter clattered along with a trolley and further down the ward a patient was calling for 'Ronald' over and over again.

Mrs Wilson was in the second side room that Kelly came to. She was propped up on pillows and reading '*A Tale of Two Cities*' – the Charles Dickens novel she'd always said was her favourite.

"Kelly," she said, relief flooding her voice. "I couldn't believe it when I saw you on the TV today. You certainly gave them a run for their money!"

"Why did you send a private detective after me?"

"I promised your grandmother I'd keep this letter from her in trust for you until you were older. Now feels like the right time – just in case…"

The words 'in case I don't survive' hung in the antiseptic laden air.

"You'll be fine," said Kelly, her voice faltering.

They heard footsteps in the corridor and the ward sister entered the room. "Visiting time finished three hours ago. Mrs Wilson needs her rest."

Jane Wilson pushed a thick cream envelope into Kelly's hands before putting her book down and allowing herself to be tucked in. "You certainly looked the part at the Café Royal," she said, "and that director seems keen to find you."

"He probably wants to prosecute me for messing up his auditions," said Kelly.

"Ivy would've been proud of you."

Kelly read the contents of the letter sitting in the hospital foyer with a cup of machine coffee. She was stunned to discover that her Gran had left her money for when she was older to finance her career as an actress. The letter explained the reasons why Mrs Wilson had been made executor and not Viv.

'*I wanted someone who was going to believe in you as much as I do, Kelly,*' read the spidery handwriting on the yellowing notepaper. "*The money won't be available to you until you're twenty-one. I know what your mother is like with money! I hope it will help you make your dreams come true.*"

Kelly had no idea how long she'd sat there in a state of disbelief.

One of the nurses from Mrs Wilson's ward who'd just finished her shift had given her a lift as far as the crossroads in Tredannac Bay. "You're the girl on the telly, aren't you," she said, her round face full of excitement. She insisted on having Kelly's autograph before she got out of the car and had driven away, no doubt ready to regale her friends with tales of having met a celebrity.

Kelly stood in the grey light of dawn feeling light-headed with shock. The events of the last twenty four hours were like a waking dream and she needed to try and make sense of things. Turning her back on her old home, she walked down the haunted lane towards the harbour. The main street was deserted and Kelly was amazed at how small the place seemed – and how safe – compared to London.

She walked past the Museum of Local Life, reliving the day when Jed had first stepped into her life. She was so deep in her thoughts she didn't notice a shadowy figure step out of an alleyway and block her path.

Mick looked the worst for drink, his face red and belligerent.

Kelly shrank from his touch as he grabbed her arm.

"So you're back are yer?" he said, leering into her face. His eyes were bloodshot and his breath smelled like a brewery. "That fancy man of yours had enough of yer 'as he? Come and tell old Mick about it – be nice to me and I'll see things are OK with yer Mum." He squeezed Kelly's arm as if testing bread for freshness, his podgy fingers straying towards her left breast.

Revulsion rose in Kelly.

"Get your hands off me," she yelled, pushing him away and running down the street.

"That's no way to treat yer step dad you ungrateful little cow," he shouted.

Kelly heard his lumbering footsteps behind her but she didn't look back. She reached the harbour and hid inside one of the fishermen's huts that they used for storing nets. It reeked of stale fish but she didn't care. Through a gap in the door she watched Mick stand for a few minutes looking this way and that before turning and stumbling back up the main street.

Kelly pushed open the door, taking big breaths of clean air and made her way up the cliff path. She hadn't intended to come here – in fact she hadn't really thought what to do next. Yesterday Jed had been so close she could touch him. Today he was gone from her life again.

A sea mist had fallen like a grey blanket as Kelly walked slowly towards the ruined house. Her eyes felt heavy. She wasn't sure if she was Morwenna or Kelly. When she heard Jed's voice calling her, muted by the blanket of mist it was as if it was part of her fevered imagination. Then the mist cleared briefly, she'd seen him and run forward into his open arms.

FORTY-ONE

Jed and Kelly phoned Aaron from Cornwall.

"I sure am glad to hear from you guys," the Texan said. "I was beginning to think this movie was jinxed."

"I didn't think I'd got the part," said Kelly. "I thought you wanted to get in touch so you could prosecute me for messing up the auditions."

"Messing them up? Gee honey – you did a great job creating all that publicity for us. The papers are full of it – the Cinderella girl in yellow silk who gatecrashes the auditions and then disappears, having stolen the starring role and Mirabelle Jordan's fiancé. They're making out that the movie is going to be fuelled by animosity and jealousy. The way things are going, we're gonna break box office records."

"But Mirabelle was OK about it – better than I expected." Jed was more upset about the fact that more changes had been made to the script by the other writer, so that it barely resembled his original work. Even his original title had been changed to 'Dragonflies.'

"Sure Mirrie's OK. To tell you the truth, it was love at first sight when she clapped eyes on Gareth. You could feel the energy vibrations – just like you and Kelly at the auditions. Let the reporters have their fun – think of the pay cheque."

Over coffee and bacon sandwiches in The Copper Kettle, holding hands across the table as if they'd never let go of each other, Kelly told Jed about the letter.

"Gran's professional name was Ivy Clarke and according to the newspaper reports about her performances, she could've been really famous."

"What happened?"

"She met my grandfather. Apparently he used to watch every single play she acted in. It must've cost him a fortune. He showered her with flowers and presents and cards saying how wonderful she was, wearing away her resistance until she agreed to go out with him."

"Then what happened?"

"She got pregnant with my mother."

Kelly took a sip of coffee before she went on. "He agreed to marry her and give the baby a name – provided she gave up acting. She did so because she loved her baby – and she passed her dream on to me. She's very specific about the money she's left me."

Kelly pulled the crumpled envelope out of her bag, took out the letter and smoothed it on her lap. "*This money represents my life savings. It is all for you, Kelly. It is NOT to be used for general living expenses. Keep it for the time when you have a difficult decision to make – believe me every life has one! Use the money to ensure your success as an actress. Don't allow anyone to stop you achieving your dream.*"

"The amber necklace was from her too – she'd given it to Mrs Wilson for safe-keeping. I feel so bad that I lost it at the auditions when the real Mitzi set about me."

Jed let go of her hand and rummaged in his pocket. "I knew there was a reason I followed you down to Cornwall." He handed her the necklace.

Kelly yelled with delight and flung her arms round him, upsetting the dregs of her coffee and causing three elderly ladies sitting by the window to mutter about the disrespectful behaviour of young people.

That afternoon they visited Kelly's mother.

"Don't mention the reason I came back," Kelly whispered to Jed as they waited on the doorstep.

"So you've come back, have you?" Viv glared at Kelly. She didn't acknowledge Jed or invite them in.

The same smells of burnt toast and stale chip fat drifted

from the kitchen. It was as if Kelly had only been away a few hours.

"Well – you're out of luck if you want your old room back. Miranda's in there with the kids."

"I don't want my room back," said Kelly. "I've just come to tell you I've got the star part in a film."

"I've heard about films like that," said Viv glaring at Jed. "Well don't come crying to me when he leaves you in the lurch."

FORTY-TWO

Before I travelled down to Cornwall I tracked down a copy of 'Dragonflies.' One of the technicians put it on video for me so I could watch it at home and I studied it frame by frame.

As I watched Kelly's breath-taking performance, I was reminded of the night she'd played Juliet and the standing ovation she'd received at the end. I remembered being stuck in the stiflingly hot prompt box wishing I'd got that sort of recognition.

In the weeks before 'Romeo & Juliet' my friends had spent whole lessons sending 'hate vibes' in Kelly's direction, hoping she'd be ill on the night so that I'd end up playing the part after all. My friend Mary had even made up some sort of magic spell involving deadly nightshade, a cat's whisker and a bird's feather.

As I've already said, it wasn't the part I'd wanted, it was the chance to be close to Jamie Collins. I'd secretly dreaded getting to school and being told that Kelly was ill and I had to play Juliet.

It was the first time I'd thought about Jamie for a long time and I made a note on my story-board to find out what had happened to him.

When I looked at the video of 'Dragonflies' I could see why people were captivated by Kelly. She had true star quality like Elizabeth Taylor or Bette Davis. Mirabelle Jordan, who played Kelly's maid in the film, although stunningly beautiful was wooden by comparison.

Mirabelle had never made another film but she'd carved out a successful career for herself as a celebrity chef – America's answer to Delia Smith. She'd written several recipe books and was currently in New York working on her next TV series – "Mirrie's Magic Menus."

I spent ages on a transatlantic call to her.

"I try to make it easy for people to cook great food and to treat each meal like a celebration," she said. "It's so important for a family to eat together, don't you agree Sabrina?"

I mumbled a reply. Eating together as a family had only ever happened on Sundays when I was a child. Mum always did a huge roast dinner and the table was laid with a white cloth, the best cutlery and wine glasses. During the week, Dad was nearly always working late – Jennifer and I had usually had our tea and been sent to bed by the time he came home.

Georges and I had been too passionate to think much about food. We'd fed each other croissants and pain au chocolat in bed after languid mornings of love-making and we'd eaten bowls of cassoulet with French bread and drank rough red wine in tiny bistros.

I felt a lump in my throat as Mirabelle went on talking, thinking of all I'd lost when Georges had died – the children we could've raised together- a family sitting round the table together sharing a meal. .

Mirabelle didn't appear to notice my lack of response. She chattered on about her husband, Gareth, and her four beautiful children – two boys and two girls.

"I'm so glad to have daughters," she said, unaware of how much her words wounded me.

"How did you feel when you didn't get the star part in 'Dragonflies'? I asked, trying to find a chink in her armour. "Were you sorry your relationship with Jed Matthews ended?"

"Jed was a great guy," she said. "If he hadn't written the original idea for the movie, then I wouldn't have met Gareth and he truly is my soul mate."

I detected no trace of bitterness in her response as I returned to my storyboard.

As I juggled the bits of information and pictures that were starting to form the outline of a story, I thought of Jamie, wondering what had happened to him.

The last time I'd seen him was just before I left for Paris, when he'd arrived on my doorstep on a foggy October night like a stray cat waiting to be let in. I'd been flattered that he'd read some of my articles – it was more than my Mum and Dad had done. Whenever I met up with my parents, Dad always went on about didn't I wish I'd made different choices because I'd have a really good job by now. I didn't bother to mention my writing to them and the modest success I'd had with magazine short stories because I knew they wouldn't understand.

Jamie had also been full of self-pity about what had gone wrong with his life but he had at least read some of my work. I was beginning to have a change of heart about him and then he ruined things again by murmuring Kelly's name into the pillow and not mine.

"Go home, Jamie" I'd told him. "Give up the booze and go back to Cornwall. You'll be dead in five years if you don't."

I have no idea if he took my advice.

FORTY-THREE

Niall Kennedy the letting agent found them a small flat not far from Jed's old bed-sit.

"I'm surprised to see you again, Mr Matthews," he said when they arrived at his office. Violet the Yorkshire terrier bristled and yapped on her red satin cushion until Niall picked her up and cuddled her on his lap. "I thought you were settled in Chelsea. I've nothing as grand as that on my books."

"It didn't work out," said Jed, "and we'd prefer cheap rather than classy."

The pay cheque he'd received for his part of the scriptwriting, less the amount he'd insisted on paying Mirabelle back, wouldn't last forever. On the strength of his current successes, he'd been offered some teaching at a local college, standing in for a lecturer who'd been taken ill.

"I don't know a thing about teaching," he said to Kelly as they lay in each other's arms in their new flat. "It feels like taking money under false pretences."

"You know more than you think," said Kelly. "Pretend you're an actor who's just been given the part of a teacher. Think what that means – how you feel when you get up in the morning – what you know about your subject. Just think what a difference you could make to someone's life."

Jed hadn't thought of it like that, but he thought of those teachers at his school who'd been memorable and inspirational and tried to colour his teaching with some of their qualities. However, although he welcomed the income it gave him and he got loads of ideas from the youngsters he was teaching, he longed to get back to his own writing.

The flat was so small it was difficult to find space to work. They joked that if one of them wanted to undress in the bedroom the other one had to go into the kitchen.

There was a small living room crammed with a stained

grey sofa and a scrubbed pine dining table and four unmatched wooden chairs. The bedroom was only big enough for a double bed and a rail to hang their clothes on. There was a tiny bathroom dominated by a huge bath with clawed feet and a kitchen that was more like a cupboard that housed a Baby Belling cooker and a greasy looking sink.

Kelly had covered the damp-mottled cream walls with posters she'd found in a junk shop – Van Gogh's 'Sunflowers', Seurat's 'Eiffel Tower' and Renoir's 'Les Parapluies.' She'd draped a rose pink throw over the sofa and placed a pink and green Chinese rug in front of the gas fire.

The filming of 'Dragonflies' had taken place in various locations – a stately home in Northumberland, the docks in London and a small fishing harbour in Wales. Jed had remained in London while some of the filming took place. There were three reasons for this – he was busy completing arrangements for the opening night of 'The Yellow Silk Dress' and secondly, he was frustrated at the way the second script writer had managed to totally misunderstand and destroy Jed's original idea. It no longer felt like the original script that he'd written. Thirdly, the press were having a field day, looking for any signs of discord between the actors.

"Will you be sorry when the filming ends, Kelly?" asked Zoe one night when she called round for supper.

They'd eaten spicy goulash and crusty bread washed down with glasses of cheap red wine. Kelly had begged the recipe from the chef at the King's Head.

"It's nothing like stage acting," she said, "and it certainly isn't glamorous. Like yesterday – I was standing around at the docks for over three hours and we did fifteen takes of the same scene. I suppose one thing is, you do get a chance to get it right – whereas you only get one chance on the stage – but I know which I prefer."

Zoe was still busy with her collection of jobs, ranging

from house cleaning to night-club dancing. Encouraged by Kelly, she was starting to do some artwork again, experimenting with multi-media techniques to create textured pictures in vibrant colours – sunsets in a riot of crimson, gold, rose and apricot and night-time landscapes in charcoal, silver, indigo and white with the moon shown in all its phases from crescent to full.

Over dinner, she'd shown them some of her old sketch books and Jed had been enthusiastic about her pictures of mystical landscapes and seascapes.

"They'd fit with some of my poems," he said. "Would you like me to show some of these to my publishers when I complete my next collection?"

"If you think they're good enough, I'd be honoured," said Zoe blushing to the roots of her short spiky hair. "I'd better put some practise in just in case they're interested."

As she left that night, she whispered to Kelly: "I always said I wouldn't ever sleep with a bloke again after what happened to my friend Amy, but seeing you with Jed I feel different."

FORTY-FOUR

Jed had kept in regular contact with his mother since he'd taken the (in his father's opinion) suicidal step of putting all his effort behind his writing. They'd always met up in neutral places like Debenham's café or Fortnum & Mason – places his mother usually went when she was out shopping so that she didn't have to lie to her husband about where she was going. Jed had never told her anything about where he was living or about Mirabelle.

Kelly went with Jed when he met his mother for tea in Debenham's cafeteria.

Jed cringed inwardly as Gloria poured the tea and smiled at Kelly. "I always hoped he'd find a nice girl and settle down," she said. "Forget all these funny ideas about writing."

"I'm afraid we're both bitten by the same bug, Mrs Matthews. I couldn't imagine a life without acting any more than Jed could imagine one without writing. It would be like deciding not to breathe or eat."

Gloria patted Kelly's hand. "You'll think differently once you've got a couple of children to look after."

"Doesn't she know anything about the film script – and the play? She should have a front row seat for that," Kelly asked Jed as they walked home.

"She wouldn't go anywhere without the old man – and all he can see is I've given up a good job to bum around."

Jed and Kelly couldn't spend too long worrying about the disinterest of his parents because the opening night of 'The Yellow Silk Dress' at The King's Head was approaching fast.

Kelly felt sick with nerves – at least she assumed that was the reason. It was after all some time since she'd performed in front of a live audience. She put her feelings of exhaustion down to their recent move to London and trying to make the flat habitable. She knew she should've seen a doctor, but they'd not as yet registered with one and in any case there hadn't been time.

The changing room at The King's Head was as cramped and dingy as when Jed had first seen it. The atmosphere was stifling because there was no window and the smell of chicken curry rising from the kitchen was overpowering.

Kelly's yellow silk dress was uncomfortably tight and she felt sweaty and giddy. The other members of the cast were laughing and joking amongst themselves and didn't appear to notice her discomfort. She leaned her head against the oval mirror on the wall, trying to find a cool spot to ease her aching head.

"Everything OK," Jed asked, looking every bit as nervous as Kelly felt.

"I just wish it wasn't so hot in here," she said.

Then, with five minutes to go until curtain-up, she fainted.

FORTY-FIVE

"I can't believe you turned him down," said Zoe when Kelly arrived on her doorstep the next day, "all those months mooning about the flat because you couldn't find him and then the guy proposes to you and you say no."

Kelly snuffled into a damp tissue. "You didn't see his face when I first told him I was pregnant. I was so worried the doctor was going to blurt it out, even though I'd told him not to. Jed's face went sort of white and he didn't say anything. Then a nurse came to take my blood pressure and he had to leave. He didn't come back for ages and when he did he got down on one knee by my trolley in the middle of the A & E department and said: "Kelly, will you marry me?"

"And what is your problem exactly?" Zoe made Kelly a mug of strong tea and then sat curled up on the other end of the sofa. "Wasn't that what you always wanted him to say?"

"Oh Zoe, can't you see? I – me and the baby – we'd be holding him back. He's already upset because his novel got rejected by several publishers and then the teaching at the college finishes at Easter. Money's tight because the film company haven't paid me yet. He's talking about going back to the supermarket and his Mum's been all fluttery and asking if he wants his old job with his Dad back.

I'm worried he'll take something he doesn't want in order to support me and the baby. That's why I turned him down – because I love Jed and I want him to be free to follow his dream."

"Does he know you're here?" asked Zoe.

Kelly shook her head. "The hospital said I could go, they couldn't find anything wrong with me. They asked if I wanted them to call Jed but I said no, I'd get a taxi."

Jed had spent a sleepless night at the flat worrying about Kelly, aware of the cold space beside him in the bed, wondering why she'd turned down his proposal of marriage.

"Go home, Jed," she'd said. "You'll think differently in the morning."

He'd spent the whole night thinking how empty life would be without her. He couldn't deny he was shocked when she told him about the baby – but then it wasn't the sort of news you got every day of the week. He knew that no matter how many awards he won for his writing, it would mean nothing if he didn't have the woman he loved beside him.

Jed finally fell into a fitful doze just before dawn, waking only when the postman rattled the letter box as he delivered the mail. He got out of bed, splashed his face with cold water, and without bothering to shave, pulled on a pair of jeans and a sweatshirt and headed for the hospital.

"Miss Smith left in a taxi a couple of hours ago," he was told.

Jed groaned. He'd planned to talk to Kelly and beg her to marry him - now it looked as if she'd made her feelings clear and run out on him again.

An hour later, Jed arrived outside Zoe's front door. He beat on the door, aware of hushed voices inside and a scurrying sound like mice before the bolts were slid back and the door opened.

"I think you'd better come in," said Zoe.

Kelly was huddled on the sofa, red-eyed from recent crying, but to Jed she'd never looked more beautiful.

"Kelly," he said, taking her cold hands in his, "if you won't marry me then I don't know what I'll do."

Kelly burst into a fresh flood of tears. "I want to marry you more than anything else in the world – but I can't – not now. You'll end up resenting me – us. We'll hold you back. I'll only bring you bad luck."

"Kelly," Jed's voice cracked with emotion. "This baby's

mine too – and your acting is just as important as my writing. I've spent all night thinking about this. We'll be a family – you, me and the baby. Families help each other, support each other's dreams – or at least they should do. Please say you'll marry me."

FORTY-SIX

Jamie didn't take Susan's advice and return home. Every time he thought about it, he felt sick, imagining the look of disappointment on his mother's face and the endless references to Danny and what a good son he'd been.

After he left Susan's flat, he drifted from one dead end job to another, living in a selection of squalid bed-sits and squats, spending most of the money that came into his possession on drink. He had a few brief relationships with girls he met, but they were in as sorry a state as he was and none of them lasted beyond a few weeks.

When things were going badly, he took to begging, hating the shifty looks on people's faces as they tossed a few coins into his cap – no doubt feeling relieved they weren't in the same situation.

It was at the end of a winter's day when he'd sat shivering outside Green Park Underground that he met someone who was to change his life. Jamie was feeling light-headed from sitting so long and lack of food. He'd been mentally trying to tot up the collection of coins to see if there was enough for a hot drink and a slice of toast – it'd have to be a take-away as most cafes didn't want the likes of him sitting inside – when he noticed a guy in a red and blue clown's costume watching him. He had a painted smile below a bright pink wig but it was the look in his eyes that Jamie noticed.

He wondered, fleetingly, if the clown was about to try and steal his meagre takings. Something of the sort had happened to Jamie before, and he'd gone hungry for another day. He palmed the coins and put them in his pocket.

"What are you doing this evening?" asked the clown. His voice was gentle and cultured – the sort that did those intellectual programmes on the telly.

"I thought I'd go up west and have dinner at the Savoy

and then go to a show," said Jamie wishing the clown would go away and stop asking daft questions.

"Fancy going somewhere warm where there's plenty of food?" asked the clown.

"If you hadn't noticed, I'm not exactly flush with money at the moment," said Jamie.

"You don't have to be – although a few pennies for the collection are always welcome."

"Collection? Collection for what?" None of it made any sense to Jamie.

"I call my ministry the Clown of God Project. I spend all day touring the streets and rounding up anyone who looks like they're wasting their talents and try to give them a second chance. Are you up for it?"

It was the best offer Jamie had had all day. He got to his feet and joined the motley collection of people following the clown. After a long walk on frost-glittered pavements, they reached a red-brick building with a red and blue painted sign outside.

The clown led them through two sets of double doors into a room that was so full of colour it was like being surrounded by a flock of parrots.

"Our arts project," said the clown, indicating the vibrant paintings.

Of even more interest to Jamie was the fragrant smell of meat and onions cooking.

"Cottage pie will be ready in about ten minutes," said a helper in a dark green apron.

Jamie's stomach growled with hunger.

"What's the catch?" asked a girl with short spiky blonde hair and a spider tattooed on the back of her left hand.

"Let's ask that question after we've eaten the pie," said Jamie.

They took their seats round long refectory tables and a

bell sounded. The clown, whose name was Jude, (with pink wig removed and make up cleansed) led them in a short prayer and talked for a few minutes about what they, the rescued souls, could do for the centre.

"I'm no use to anybody," said Jamie sadly as he ate his portion of cottage pie.

The other rescued souls were all, like Jamie, youngsters who had taken a wrong turning. The staff at the centre were full of stories of others who had gone before them who'd ended up seeing the light and been helped towards a better life.

"My parents split up when I was fifteen and I ended up on the game," said the girl with copper-bright hair who did some of the cooking. "The least I can do to repay Jude and the rest of the staff for their help in getting me back to college is to give a bit of my time here and help with the cooking and washing up."

Jude had pinned a long list of jobs that needed doing on the message board in the main room, ranging from designing a poster to advertise the centre to fixing the leaky tap in the kitchen.

"Jude's a whiz at getting people to donate anything from paint to tea bags," the girl went on. "You wouldn't think he nearly died five years ago."

"What happened to him?"

"He was on drugs – and then somewhere between Victoria and Paddington on the Circle Line he had a religious conversion."

Jamie didn't believe in religious conversions but the cottage pie had been good and he decided to stay in the centre a bit longer and design a poster for them. It was better than being outside on such a cold night.

"You're a good artist," said Jude. "Is that what you trained as?"

"No."

"Why not"

Jamie found himself telling the whole story like a confession. Afterwards, he felt as if he'd shed a great burden.

"Go home," said Jude, "and start again. Don't waste your talents."

Jamie didn't go home, but he tried over the next few months to reform himself. Several times he met up with old friends and went off the rails again. It was on one of these occasions when he'd drunk himself into a stupor and had ended up in the gutter – he couldn't remember how – and had woken up just as a black dog was about to cock his leg on him that he remembered what Susan and Jude had said and decided it was time to get out of London.

He hitched back to Cornwall, arriving in Tredannac Bay on a glorious July Thursday. Having arrived, he felt too nervous to go and knock on his parents' door. He walked down to the harbour breathing in the familiar smells of boat oil, salt and seaweed, realising how much he'd missed the sound of the sea.

A girl with short dark spiky hair was sketching the boats marooned at low tide. She was wearing jeans and a black velvet top and her face was a study in concentration as she held her picture at arm's length.

"That looks good," said Jamie.

The girl turned eyes that looked like fragments of a summer sky on him.

"My friend Kelly has been nagging me to go back to Art College," she said.

Jamie felt weird – as if the ground was tilting under him. "Your friend Kelly hasn't got long auburn hair has she?"

FORTY-SEVEN

"You'd think your Mum was the film star the way she's carrying on," said Zoe as she helped Kelly zip up the back of her ivory lace wedding dress.

"We've been getting on a lot better since she split up with Mick," said Kelly fastening her amber necklace and slipping on her ivory satin shoes.

"What happened?"

"She always used to think I was leading him on – but then after I'd left she caught him red-handed – or red willied – with the barmaid at The Three Tuns. He tried to say they were washing glasses!"

The two girls collapsed in a fit of giggles and Viv, coming up the stairs to Kelly's old room wanted to know what the noise was about. She was dressed in navy and shocking pink and the picture hat she wore wouldn't have looked out of place at Ascot.

"Your flowers have arrived," she said.

Kelly had chosen deep red roses to complement the pale gold of the bridesmaids dresses worn by Zoe and Kelly's niece Lisa.

"I shouldn't laugh," said Kelly, "this dress is already tight. It's a good job the wedding's no later or it wouldn't fit at all."

"Have you any idea what you're going to call the baby?"

"No contest – it's Amber for a girl or Ambrose if it's a boy."

"Don't know how I'm going to keep a straight face when the vicar says 'Do you Joshua Edward David take this woman' and all the rest of it. I don't see him as a Joshua at all."

"Neither did Jed from the age of about six. It's funny – even his Mum calls him Jed now instead of Joshie."

They made their way slowly down the stairs.

"I thought you said your Mum's house always smelled of burnt toast," whispered Zoe.

"Shh, she'll hear you."

Viv was in her element, bossing Lisa and Miranda and making sure the cars were arranged outside the house in a way that gave the neighbours the best view. The first thing Kelly noticed when she and Zoe arrived yesterday was that the house had had a make-over since Mick had gone. It now smelled of peach and vanilla air freshener and the Estee Lauder perfume Viv had bought especially for the wedding. Simon, her boss at the biscuit factory was attending as her escort and Viv had a gleam in her eye when she greeted him.

"Bet there's been something going on between them for ages," said Kelly. "She used to do enough over-time."

"I've heard it called some things," said Zoe, "but never that."

There had been some discussion as to who was going to give Kelly away.

"It doesn't have to be a male member of the family," the vicar had told them, so Viv, relishing the limelight was giving Kelly away.

The little Saxon church at Tredannac Bay looked beautiful. The wooden pew ends, the archway into the church and the wrought iron holders by the altar had all been decorated with dark red and gold roses, carnations and freesias, their scent mingling with the cocktail of perfumes as the guests assembled.

The organist played a medley of tunes, the notes rising and falling like birdsong.

Kelly felt nervous as she stepped into the porch. The smell of old stone, musty hymn books and memories surrounded her. Then she looked along the moss-green carpet that led to the altar and saw Jed standing there waiting for her. A shaft of sunlight lit up the stained glass window behind the altar and shone on him like a stage spotlight. The organist struck up the wedding march, there was a rustle of interest as all heads turned to look at her. She took a deep breath, tucked her arm through Viv's and stepped forward.

There were two surprises on Jed and Kelly's wedding day. Gloria Matthews had attended the ceremony dressed in a lilac two-piece that Jed hadn't seen before.

She'd warned Jed not to expect his father to attend. "He says he won't hear of me travelling by train," she said, "so he's going to drive me down to Cornwall but he says there's no way he'll attend the wedding."

Kelly and Jed walked out into the July sunshine and the crush of people taking photographs. They spotted Eric Matthews, smartly dressed in a charcoal grey suit, hovering by some lichened gravestones. Kelly had melted the ice by gliding across to him in her beautiful ivory lace dress and holding out her hands. Much to everyone's surprise, Eric took them and allowed himself to be drawn into the family group being photographed.

"The awkward old so and so told me he wasn't coming anywhere near the church," whispered Gloria to Jed as they sipped a glass of bubbly at the reception. "To look at him now, you'd think the wedding was his idea in the first place."

The reception was held in the upstairs room of The Anchor – the pub near the harbour where Jed had taken Kelly for lunch when she'd been working at the Museum of Local Life. It was a very simple affair – with most of the food being done by Zoe.

"Look on it as my wedding present to you both," she said.

She'd rounded up a local band looking for their first gig who agreed to provide music for the price of a few drinks and some top level publicity.

The light faded and the first stars appeared and then the full moon rose, forming a pathway of light across the dark sea.

"May this be only one of the happiest days of your lives,"

Viv said in her 'father of the bride' speech.

"From the way she and Simon are looking at each other, she'll be making an announcement of her own soon," whispered Jed as he drew Kelly into the first dance.

The other surprise of the day was Jamie who arrived immaculately dressed at the reception, hovering in the doorway until he caught sight of Zoe.

"You decided to come then?" she said as she hurried over to him. "How did you get on when you went home?"

"Mum cried. Dad ranted and raved and called me a stupid boy, but it was better than I expected."

"So what's next?" Zoe drew him onto the dance floor.

His smile lit up his sea green eyes. "I'm doing what I should've done in the first place. I'm going back to Art College. Mum and Dad took some convincing but I think they can see things my way."

"When are you heading back to London?" Kelly asked Zoe later that evening.

Zoe flushed. "I thought I'd hang around for a while. There's some great inspiration for artwork here and I've been thinking about what you said about going back to Art College."

Kelly followed the direction of Zoe's gaze and smiled to herself.

She hoped things would work out for Zoe and Jamie and that they'd be as happy as she and Jed were.

FORTY-EIGHT

The Anchor pub down by the harbour where Jed had first taken Kelly for lunch and where Mrs Wilson told me they'd had their wedding reception had been transformed since I last saw it.

A red, black and gold sign proclaimed 'The Tredannac Bay Arts Centre.'

I pushed open the heavy wooden doors and found myself in a light and airy café with views of the sea on three sides of it. My senses were teased by the tantalising smells of chocolate, vanilla and cinnamon.

Signposts pointed to other places – The Ivy Clarke Theatre, The Nell Gwyn Studio Theatre, The Amber Workshop, The Scarlet Gallery. I felt a stab of envy as I read the information panels on the café wall. They were like a family photo album – just like the story-board I'd spent the last few days compiling.

There were photos of Jed and Kelly on their wedding day, their two daughters Amber and Scarlet and the development of the building I was now standing in from bankrupt pub to gleaming Arts Centre. "I want creative local children to have more choice than I did when I left school," Kelly was quoted as saying.

"Kelly and Jed bought the old pub when it went bankrupt a year after their wedding," said the girl behind the coffee bar. "They financed it with the money Kelly got for starring in 'Dragonflies' and the legacy her grandmother left her. It was a struggle for them, though, doing the place up a bit at a time. The first play was performed in what used to be the downstairs bar with the old pumps still in there and wooden barrels to sit on."

I looked at Kelly's children – Amber who had Jed's dark hair and Kelly's amber eyes and Scarlet with Kelly's pre-Raphaelite hair and Jed's blue eyes – and thought sadly of my own lost Georgia.

Scarlet was an artist and in front of me was a stunning example of her work – a monochrome painting of a lighthouse in a storm – all bruise-dark clouds and wind-whipped salt spray, the only touch of brightness a tiny dot of red from the place where the light radiated.

I wished I'd had the sense to have started my research here. It would've saved me hours of work. The girl behind the coffee bar was really helpful and I thought there was something familiar about her dark hair and sea green eyes.

"My Dad's called Jamie Collins and he runs art workshops here," *she said.*

"Not the Jamie Collins?"

She smiled. "Is there more than one? Christ I hope not."

"I was at school with him."

"What's your name?"

"Sabrina – but he may remember me as Susan."

Feeling overcome by a tide of memories, I finished my coffee and went to explore the rest of the building, pausing when I reached the space that led to the two theatres. The door of the Ivy Clarke Theatre opened and a girl in a Victorian-style yellow dress emerged from the gloom beyond. Apart from the fact that she had a rippling mane of dark hair, she was the image of Kelly on the night of the play. Then Kelly appeared, dressed in jeans and black sweatshirt. Apart from a few lines around her eyes, she didn't look any older than when I'd last seen her.

She looked wary. "I'd heard you were checking up on us."

I wondered if she remembered the night of the play and Mrs Wilson telling me that, as a journalist, sometimes you had to write in a positive way about people you didn't like.

I took a deep breath. "It's been a fascinating assignment. I missed a lot of the events first time round because I was working in Paris."

She shot me a look that said it was typical of me to try to sound superior.

Amber whispered something to her mother and

disappeared back into the theatre.

"I missed all the stuff with the Café Royal and the film because I fell in love while I was in Paris." Emotion tore at my throat. "He died."

Kelly's amber eyes melted with sympathy. "Let's have a coffee."

We went back to the café and sat at a table by the window. The first fishing boats were leaving on the evening tide.

Kelly stirred brown sugar into her coffee. "Tell me about him," she said.

"I'm here to talk about you, not me."

"You need to tell someone," she said.

Coffee gave way to glasses of red wine as I told Kelly, once my arch-rival, about my romance with Georges, the birth of Georgia and my hopes that my novel would eventually bring her back to me.

"She'll come back to you. The tide of life brings everything back eventually." She looked up and smiled as the café door opened and a dark haired man walked in. I recognised Jed from the photographs on the wall. His hair was flecked with silver emphasising the intense blue of his eyes.

"I might have known I'd find you chatting to someone," he said.

"This is my friend Sabrina," said Kelly. "She's a brilliant writer. We were at school together."

"Pleased to meet you," he said. "I'd be interested to hear about your work."

The energy between him and Kelly was like sunshine or warm honey.

"I'd like to hear about yours too," I said. "It's all I need to complete my piece for the television company."

I stayed to watch that night's performance of 'The Yellow Silk Dress' that was being performed to celebrate Kelly and Jed's wedding anniversary. I sat on a red velvet seat in the orange and spice scented darkness of the auditorium feeling a glow of satisfaction that my work on this assignment was nearly done.

Later that night, sitting in my hotel bedroom, I switched on my laptop to find two emails – one from Rod saying that 'The Yellow Silk Dress' story was generating interest on both sides of the Atlantic. 'Providing you've done your part well, the programme is likely to pick up at least two awards,' he'd written. 'Well done.'

The second email was from the publisher who had shown an interest in the synopsis of 'Georgia' asking me to submit the complete manuscript. There was no guarantee that they'd buy it, but I felt a sunburst of hope swell inside me.

A crescent moon hung in the sky like a smile as I put the last of my storyboard together and began to type up my notes.